W9-BGF-485

Whitney, Phyllis A.

AF
Whi

Black Amber

| DATE DUE | | | |
|---|---|---|---|
| | | | |
| | | | |
| | | | |
| | | | |
| | | | |
| | | | |
| | | | |
| | | | |
| | | | |
| | | | |
| | | | |
| | | | |

11/13

# Black Amber

**Center Point
Large Print**

Also by Phyllis A. Whitney and available from
Center Point Large Print:

*The Quicksilver Pool*
*The Trembling Hills*
*Thunder Heights*
*Seven Tears for Apollo*

**This Large Print Book carries the
Seal of Approval of N.A.V.H.**

# *Black Amber*

# PHYLLIS A. WHITNEY

CENTER POINT LARGE PRINT
THORNDIKE, MAINE

This Center Point Large Print edition
is published in the year 2012 by arrangement with
McIntosh and Otis, Inc.

The text of this Large Print edition is unabridged.
In other aspects, this book may vary
from the original edition.
Printed in the United States of America
on permanent paper.
Set in 16-point Times New Roman type.

ISBN: 978-1-61173-431-7

Library of Congress Cataloging-in-Publication Data

Whitney, Phyllis A., 1903–2008.
Black amber / Phyllis A. Whitney. — Large print ed.
p. cm. — (Center Point large print edition)
ISBN 978-1-61173-431-7 (lib. bdg. : alk. paper)
1. Sisters—Death—Fiction. 2. Authors—Fiction.
 3. Publishers and publishing—Fiction. 4. Istanbul (Turkey)—Fiction.
 5. Large type books. I. Title.
PS3545.H8363B43 2012
813′.54—dc23
                                            2012005016

BELOW HIGH BALCONIES that formed a veneer for the huge American hotel, the newer part of the city dropped steeply away to the shores of the Bosporus. A mosque at the water's edge, its whiteness diluted by gray March rain, pointed minarets into the sky—an indication of Istanbul. Otherwise the view was blandly modern and bore little resemblance to the Turkey of Tracy's lively imagination.

She stood on her private balcony, looking down through driving rain at the city she had been trying to reach. Now, all in one breath, she found herself both eager for the encounter and a little fearful over what it might hold for her. Where once her coming might have been a simple, joyful thing, now there were too many troubling questions in her mind. Whether she wished it or not, they removed her from the casual objectivity of the tourist, and brought with them an involvement she could not avoid.

An involvement, in fact, that she had deliberately chosen. She had moved quickly to seize the opportunity that had brought her here and she must not be turned back by the first obstacle.

With a quick, impatient gesture she pulled off the blue suede beret she had bought for this trip and let wind from the strait ruffle her shining fringe of brown bangs. That the wind carried with it a splash of rain, she did not mind. She raised her face to the cold drops as if they might quench her angry reaction to the letter she held in her hand. Clearly a cool head would be needed if she was to deal with the man who had written it. She was curious about him and not at all certain how many of the tales she had heard about him were true, but she did not mean to be summarily dismissed by his letter.

She had waited three months to get here. Waited because there was no way for her to come at once. Now that she was here—arrived at the airport this very afternoon—she was to be sent home ignominiously and without a hearing. The sheet of notepaper crackled sharply as she straightened it and read for the third time the strongly formed masculine handwriting.

DEAR MISS HUBBARD:

The arrangement I agreed to with Mr. Hornwright of *Views* was to the effect that Miss Janet Baker would be sent here to assist me in preparing the manuscript of my book for publication. Her years in the Middle East, her well-established background and knowledge of Turkish mosaics, have made her a suitable person for this work.

Now I have a cable informing me that she will not be free for another six months and that a temporary assistant is being sent in her place: "A young woman who has been doing excellent work for us during the past years."

I can only assure you that this substitution is not acceptable to me. I prefer to wait for Miss Baker. While there is nothing of personal criticism implied on my part, I can only suggest that you take the next plane back to New York.

Sincerely yours,
MILES RADBURN


Tracy folded the stiff sheet of paper. One part of her mind whispered that it would be easy enough to accept this edict. Surely no one in the home office could blame her for a defeat which was so clearly not of her own making. If she went straight home she could turn her back on all she might find disturbing about Istanbul— simply go home and forget the plea and the warning that had come to her, forget the persistent questions that presented themselves to her mind. Let the past keep its unhappy secrets, since she could not now affect the course of destiny.

Yet even as she considered the cajoling voice, she knew that if she turned and ran she would never forgive herself later. Again she folded the paper, creasing it emphatically. She would not permit the letter to anger her. She would keep an open mind about Miles Radburn. She could not know what was true about him and what was not until she had met him herself. His reaction to her coming was, of course, not unexpected. And in all fairness, it might even be justified.

Mr. Hornwright had been thoroughly upset when he came home from Turkey. Miles Radburn's book on the history of Turkish tiles and mosaics would be an expensive art number for the book publishing venture on which *Views* was recently embarked. The tremendous resources that had made the magazine one of the foremost in the country were behind the venture, and the name of Miles Radburn would bring prestige to the list. While it was true that Radburn, after a conspicuous rise to success in his younger years, had done little painting in his late thirties, nevertheless his portraits were in museums and art galleries around the country, and there was still a distinction to his name that spelled good publicity for *Views*. Unfortunately, artists were seldom skilled organizers. Mr. Hornwright, on his visit to Istanbul, had been appalled by the welter in which a possibly important book was buried.

Radburn had reluctantly agreed to accept assistance if he could have the help of Miss Baker, whose work he knew. Mr. Hornwright, procrastinating and treading water, had promised to see what could be managed. In her work as a researcher trainee, Tracy was in a position to hear the rumors going around. Mr. Hornwright had known very well that Miss Baker was otherwise occupied, and he knew as well that Miles Radburn was not ready for her at this point. What Radburn needed was not an expert on Turkish mosaics, but someone efficient enough to straighten out the general confusion in which he seemed to be working.

Once she knew what was in the wind, Tracy had not hesitated. She had gone to see Mr. Hornwright, plunging at once to the heart of the matter. She had pointed out that she was more expendable than almost anyone else in the department. Yet she felt herself equipped to do the job he wanted done. By good chance she had already completed two or three minor assignments for Mr. Hornwright, and he at least knew of her existence.

He smiled at her eagerness, not without sympathy. "How old are you, Miss Hubbard?"

"I'll be twenty-three this month," she told him with dignity.

"Hmm. Still young enough not to know the impossible when you see it. An advantage, perhaps. Though it's quite likely Radburn will decide to send you home the moment he lays eyes on you. What will you do then?"

"If I can get there, I'll stay," Tracy promised resolutely. Because nothing had ever come to her

9

easily, there was an intensity about her that could be persuasive when she threw herself into something she really wanted.

Mr. Hornwright must have sensed this, for he considered her thoughtfully. "At least you're anxious to go. But if I send you, we'll have to move fast. We need to get you out there before he has time to oppose the plan. In fact, we won't let him know you're coming till you're on your way."

"I can leave as soon as you like," she said. "I already have an up-to-date passport." She did not add that it was unused and only a few months old.

There was still hesitation on Mr. Hornwright's part. "I don't know . . . Radburn won't like the switch. His mother was an American and he's lived here a good part of his life, but all the stubborn British half of him will rise up in protest. He has a remarkable trick of putting himself on the far side of a stone wall—with the other fellow out in the cold."

"If I can get there, I'll stay," Tracy repeated. She could be stubborn too. There were times when she thought that was the only reliable quality she possessed—a perverse stubbornness. She would reserve judgment about Miles Radburn, and she would not let him frighten her. She would hook her thumbs into her belt, dig in her toes—and stay.

"Good," said Mr. Hornwright. "I like that kind

of dogged spirit. But don't come crying to me if you run into that wall. If you go out there, you can't afford to fail. You might lose us the book altogether. A contract isn't enough to assure that he'll come up with the finished product. He's dragging his heels and you can ride herd on him, for one thing. You understand?"

"I understand," said Tracy.

"Then get started," Mr. Hornwright told her. She flew to the door, but he stopped her as she went through. "One more thing. If you know anything about Radburn's work, go easy on the painting angle. He's touchy about not working. He hasn't painted since a year or so before the death of his wife. You know, of course, about his recent tragedy?"

"I know," Tracy said. "I'll be careful," and she went down the corridor as if a stormy wind blew at her heels, whirling her along like a leaf.

The same wind whirled her breathlessly through two or three crowded days of preparation and briefing. It had whirled her into quick shopping for necessities and the suffering of shots. It had, at length, hurled her at headlong rate over ocean and continent, and set her down on this high, windy balcony, where she stood with Miles Radburn's dismissal in her hands—his decree that she was to turn around at once and go straight home before she had so much as caught her breath upon arrival.

She left the balcony and retreated to her room. On the bed table the telephone sat silent, waiting. She went instead to the full-length mirror on the bathroom door and regarded herself critically. What would Miles Radburn see if she presented herself to him?

There were five feet, one inch of girl in the mirror. A girl with glossy, well-brushed brown hair worn in a smooth twist at the back of her head. Only the bang fringe went loose and unpinned. Her mouth was too big and her nose doubtful. Her eyes, beneath thick lashes, were warm-gray, not cold-gray, and their expression always betrayed any intensity of inner feeling, of eagerness and excitement, or sometimes indignation that she might be experiencing. The charcoal-gray wool dress she wore was severe of line and simple of cut, and Tracy cocked one dark eyebrow in mocking amusement as she considered it. She had made that dress herself, as she made most of her own clothes. She was good at this sort of thing—very good. Some of the smart women at *Views* had even asked where she shopped.

Someday, she thought, staring at her image rebelliously, she was going to break that plain neckline with loops of wildly colored beads. She was going to run amok with bright scarves and jewelry and furbelows to her heart's content and be as thoroughly fussy and feminine as she pleased. Today just two ornaments broke the overall severity—a stitched leather belt with a gold buckle, and a simple pin near the neckline. The pin curved gracefully in the shape of a golden feather and she touched it now for reassurance before she once more hooked her thumbs into her belt. The pin was an old friend.

At least she recognized her slightly defiant, toes-in stance and smiled because it went with the gesture of thumbs hooked into the leather belt. She knew what it meant. The stubbornness and determination she could count on were there. She had dug in her toes. She was staying.

Having accepted the fact, the next step was to get herself to where Miles Radburn was. She went to the telephone and lifted the receiver. The switchboard operator spoke English. Tracy gave her the name of Mrs. Sylvana Erim, and spelled out a town full of *y*'s and *k*'s that she could not pronounce. The Erim name seemed to mean something and before long a distant ringing began.

"A widow," Mr. Hornwright had told her. "A Frenchwoman in spite of her Italian first name, who married a Turk and still makes her home in Turkey. Quite wealthy and socially prominent. Radburn and his wife first met her on their honeymoon in Turkey some years ago. Apparently she has furnished a haven for him while he works on this book. He's staying at her villa in a suburb across the Bosporus. If anything goes wrong, talk to Mrs. Erim. She's a civilized woman in the European sense. Very charming. And she gets things done. Remarkably unexcitable for a Frenchwoman."

A voice came on the wire, the words Turkish.

"I wish to speak to Mrs. Erim," Tracy said.

There was a silence that lasted so long Tracy began to think she had been cut off. Then a feminine voice spoke in her ear. A not unfriendly voice, pronouncing English with a French accent.

"This is Sylvana Erim."

Tracy identified herself.

"Ah, yes—you have been sent from the American publisher to assist with Mr. Radburn's book?"

"That's right," Tracy said. "I would like to see Mr. Radburn as soon as it can be arranged."

"But I have understood that a letter has been sent to your hotel," the cultured voice went on.

"I have the letter," Tracy admitted. "It tells me to go home. But I don't want to leave without at least speaking with Mr. Radburn."

There was a thoughtful pause and then a regretful, slightly amused sound. "But of course you wish to see him after coming such a distance. Sometimes he is like a bear—that one. Let us see what we can do. I will consider for a moment."

Again there was silence while Mrs. Erim considered and Tracy relaxed a little. She had a feeling that if this woman chose to help, her way would be smoothed.

The wait was not long. "As it happens, you have come at an opportune moment," Mrs. Erim continued. "My sister-in-law, Nursel—Miss Erim—is in the city this afternoon. I know where to reach her. I will ask her to pick you up at your hotel in an hour and drive you here to the *yali.* Bring a suitcase—you must stay for the night."

Mrs. Erim waited for no thanks, waited hardly for agreement, before ringing off. One had the impression of calm force and authority at work. Mr. Hornwright had been correct.

Tracy put down the telephone and proceeded to tear Miles Radburn's letter into very small scraps and drop them into the wastebasket. The small violent movement did her good. He was *not* going to send her home. There was more at stake than Mr. Hornwright had any knowledge of. In fact, if he had guessed her own concern in this, he might not have let her come. She could only hope that no one else would guess it either. In an odd way she would be incognito here, while using her own name. It was better to have no one suspect her real secret. She could find out more this way, with no one on guard against her.

What a long way Turkey seemed from the Midwestern town where she had grown up.

Though not as far as New York had been a few years ago when she had taken matters into her own hands, opposing the wishes of her parents. What warnings of disaster had rung in her ears! But she had found a job in New York. Then another job. There had been sadness over her mother's death, but not deep sorrow. She had lost all real touch with her mother long before. An estrangement with her father had continued and could not be helped.

Two years ago she had found this most fascinating of all places to work—*Views.* She had always wanted a finger in the creation of magazines and books. So far, it was a very small finger, but if she made good at this assignment with Miles Radburn, there was no end to the possibilities. Even more important, if she succeeded, she would be able to prove that Tracy Hubbard was someone in her own right, after all. Prove it to her father, to the world—and most of all to herself.

But she did not want to dredge up the past now. Not when she had just reached Istanbul. First she must see Mrs. Erim. One deliberate step at a time would keep her here.

She returned to the balcony and stood for a while looking down at the city that bore slight resemblance to the Istanbul she had read about. She had seen only a little more of it on the drive from the airport through the old city. Once within crumbling Roman walls, rain had obscured its outlines. She had been aware of the tight, cobbled streets of the old Stamboul section, slippery with mud; of erratic traffic in the narrow ways, and crowds of pedestrians, rainy-day-shabby, not unlike such crowds in any city anywhere. Of course Istanbul was not Turkey, any more than New York was America, she reminded herself. It was an entity in its own right, and not easily to be learned in all its complexities.

The hour was difficult to pass. She powdered her nose and repaired her lipstick. One step at a time was all she needed to manage.

Then the phone rang, announcing that Nursel Erim awaited her in the lobby. Tracy threw her gray coat about her shoulders, picked up her suitcase and handbag, and walked the miles of soft-carpeted corridor to the elevator bank.

Downstairs near the revolving doors of the entrance, the woman waited for her. She was young—perhaps only a year or two older than Tracy, and she had the great dark eyes, the beauty of feature that belonged to a Turkish background of wealth and family. She was dressed as faultlessly, as smartly as Paris or New York at their best, and while she wore no hat, her black hair was fashionably coiffed. A fur-trimmed coat hung open over her black dress. Around her throat several strands of pearls

17

gleamed against the black, and one knew their luster was real. Standing beside all this elaborate elegance, Tracy felt herself painfully simple and unadorned.

The vision came toward her with one graceful hand outstretched. "You are Miss—Miss Tracy Hubbard?" She faltered slightly over the name. "I am Nursel Erim. If you will come with me, please. As usual I am parked against the law." Tracy gained the impression that small lawbreakings did not in the least disturb Miss Erim.

Outside they hurried through the rain to a small sleek car that was already blocking passage on the drive. The doorman shook his head despairingly, but he held an umbrella over them as Miss Erim opened the door. She laughed as she gestured Tracy into the front seat and went around to get in beside her.

"In his heart," she said as she turned the car out of the hotel driveway, "no Turkish man believes that a Turkish woman should drive an automobile. Mustapha Kemal rid us of the veil, but human nature takes more than half a century to change."

They drove through rain-swept streets, downhill toward the waterfront, where they lined up for the car ferry. Nursel Erim, busy with a need for careful driving in late afternoon traffic, said little until they were on board the boat. Then they left the car and went upstairs to a dry, warm cabin for the short crossing from Europe to Asia. Here she became the courteous hostess, pointing out what little could be seen of the gray vista. Yet, for all her effort, there seemed a constraint upon her, as though she were not yet sure exactly how Tracy fitted into the scheme of things.

"This is the place where the Bosporus begins its course between the Sea of Marmara and the Black Sea." Miss Erim indicated roiling gray waters. "If you look closely in that direction, you can see Seraglio Point and the walls of the old palace showing through the mist. The site of ancient Byzantium was up there."

Tracy stood in the door of the cabin and gazed with interest upon the Marmara and the dividing protrusion of the famous point of land they were leaving behind as the boat moved toward the opposite shore. Crumbling stone walls ran down to the water, while in the mists far above rose palace roofs and windows.

"Of course visitors are always interested in the Seraglio and its stories," Miss Erim said. "It was just off that point that ladies of the harem who happened to be in disfavor were put into sacks and dropped into the Bosporus."

Tracy glanced at the girl beside her. Nursel Erim was regarding her with a somewhat sly amusement, as though she had told the story with deliberate intent to shock an American visitor and now awaited her reaction.

19

"At least it's a custom—you've discontinued," Tracy said dryly.

The Turkish girl shrugged. "The Bosporus has always invited tragedy."

"Do you live very far from Istanbul?" Tracy had no desire to think about Bosporus waters at this moment.

"Not too far. Our yali is in Anatolia, the area which makes up the Asian side of the strait. It is a very old house which has been in the family for more than a hundred years. You know the word *yali*? It means a villa on the water. There were many such villas on the Bosporus occupied by wealthy pashas in the old days."

"You live there with your sister-in-law?" Tracy wanted to bring the talk around to Miles Radburn, but she dared not plunge too hurriedly.

"My brother Murat and I live in the yali. Sylvana—Mrs. Erim, the wife of our older brother who is dead—has built a kiosk for herself, a land house, on the hill above. Thus we keep separate households, though my brother has his laboratory on the lower floor of the kiosk, where he can work in undisturbed quiet. He is a doctor but he does not practice medicine. He is well known for his contributions to medical research," she added proudly.

"Where does Miles Radburn stay?" Tracy ventured.

"Mr. Radburn's rooms are in the yali also,"

Nursel Erim said. There was the faintest change of tone in her voice as she spoke the name, but Tracy could not tell what it portended. The girl was on guard in some way and far from openly friendly.

By now the boat had slipped past Leander's Light—a squat white tower that rose near the entrance to the Bosporus. Oddly named, since Leander had drowned in the Hellespont, at the other end of the Sea of Marmara. As the boat swung wide with the swift current and nosed into shore at the town of Üsküdar, several small mosques with their attendant minarets were visible through the rain and the aspect looked more like the Turkey of Tracy's imagining.

They left the boat and the car followed a road that ran north along low hills above the water. Small villages clustered along the way, with snatches of open country between, and now her companion drove faster as if she were impatient to end the journey. There was a half hour more of winding road before they stopped beside a grilled iron gate set into a stone wall. It was opened for them by a gateman who flashed white teeth in a smile beneath his thick black mustache. From the gate a private road dipped steeply toward the water, then straightened around a curve, ending before the door of a square, three-storied wooden house. The house had weathered to a soft silvery gray and its veranda rows were

21

broken by a repetition of curved Turkish arches.

They left the car for a servant to put away, and Nursel Erim ushered Tracy into a long marble-floored passageway. A little maid bobbed into view, dressed surprisingly in a bright red skirt and darker red sweater, a red kerchief, flowered in white, covering her head.

Miss Erim spoke to her in Turkish and the girl answered, ducking her head shyly as she spoke.

"Halide says your room is ready," Miss Erim explained, turning toward the stairs. "Come, please—I will take you up. We do not live down here. The kitchens and storage rooms are here, and some quarters for the servants."

The stairs ran upward against the wall in a single graceful curve, a wrought-iron railing of fanciful design winding beside them as they climbed. Overhead, two stories above, an old-fashioned chandelier shed a pale glow upon dim stairs.

As they reached the second floor, a man suddenly confronted them. He wore a black, somewhat shabby European suit with a dark gray sweater and white collar showing beneath the jacket. His olive-skinned face was notable for its flourishing black mustache and eyes that were darkly vital and observant. No welcoming smile broke the somber quality of his expression, but Tracy felt that she was being weighed and assessed.

"This is Ahmet Effendi, our *kahya*—that is to say, our house man, who is in charge of all the details of our lives. If you wish anything, Ahmet Effendi will procure it for you."

There was a note of fondness in her voice and she spoke to him respectfully in Turkish before they went on. To Tracy she explained further as they mounted the second flight of stairs.

"My brother and I have our apartments on the second floor. Mine is over the water, his at the back. I have suggested to Mrs. Erim that we give you our third-floor room, since it is a pleasant one—and empty at present."

Again Tracy caught the odd, sidelong glance, as though the Turkish girl awaited some reaction.

The stairs ended in a large bare salon, drafty and gloomy, serving perhaps more as a vast hall than as a room in itself. A tall blue porcelain stove which sent out a glow of warmth soon lost in the wide reaches stood against a wall. A few stiff chairs were drawn up about a round table covered with red velvet that dripped silken bobbles toward the floor. At either end of the salon were closed doors, and along the side opposite the stairs French doors opened upon an arched veranda.

"In the old days," Tracy's guide explained, "the haremlik, the women's quarters, was up here. The selamlik was in the more convenient rooms on the floor below—where the men stayed. Of course women had the run of the house, except when male visitors outside the family appeared. Then they retired to their rooms up here."

She turned toward the end of the house that overlooked the water, pausing before a vast wooden door with an ornamental brass doorknob. This knob was apparently a stationary handle. The latch was near the floor and Nursel Erim operated it with a quick flick of her toe.

She saw Tracy's interest and smiled. "We are very old-fashioned here, as you will soon find. Please enter. We hope you will be comfortable."

The room was huge, with a high, distant ceiling. A little to Tracy's surprise, its furnishings were of a light-grained modern wood. A thickly piled gold carpet occupied a good part of the floor and there was an exquisite dressing table equipped with folding mirrors and a stool padded in gold satin. Doors opened on three sides of the room— one to the salon, one apparently to an adjoining room, and double doors upon the arched veranda that seemed to run all about the house.

Miss Erim opened the door to the next room and gestured. "This was Mr. Radburn's study at one time. Now it is unused. He has now moved away from the water. It is rather cold on this side of the house in the winter months, though I do not mind. I never tire of the Bosporus. And soon spring will be here. In the meantime there is an electric heater, if you wish, and I see that Halide has already brought coals from one of the stoves to burn in the *mangal*."

She indicated a large brass brazier rather like an open lotus flower, in which glowing red coals sent out a surprising amount of warmth. When she had closed the door to the adjoining bedroom and locked it, she turned about.

"This was Anabel's room. His wife, you know."

Tracy stood very still in the middle of the gold carpet, waiting for a sudden chill to go away. The Turkish girl was watching her, waiting. For what, Tracy was not sure. Perhaps for some remark about the recent and tragic death of Anabel Radburn. She knew that this was a moment for caution. There was nothing the people in this house could know about Tracy Hubbard. She must speak naturally, pass over the moment quickly.

"You knew his wife well?" she asked, and hoped that she sounded casual.

Nursel Erim bowed her smartly coiffed black head in sorrowful admission. "But of course. I knew her very well," she said, and was silent, suddenly remote.

She went next to the French doors that opened upon the veranda and set one of them ajar. There was still gray daylight outside, and the sound of rain falling on water. The Bosporus sped its winding course immediately below the jutting of the balcony, but Tracy did not step outside to enjoy the view. She shivered slightly at the draft and clung to the relative warmth of the room. As Miss Erim closed the door, a white cat darted suddenly through it and jumped upon the bed. There it sat erect, watching them out of huge, unblinking green eyes. Tracy liked cats and she made a move toward this one, but Miss Erim stopped her.

"Please! It is not a friendly cat. It is what we call here an Ankara cat—or, as you might say, Angora. But this one does not like people."

"Tell me its name," Tracy said and moved quietly toward the bed.

"It is named Bunny," Nursel Erim said, smiling slightly. "A strange name for a cat, is it not? It is one Mrs. Radburn chose. She found the cat when she first visited here, and she made it her pet. Turkey is full of stray cats, and I think she wanted to adopt them all. But Miles—Mr. Radburn—would let her have only this one. Sylvana is not fond of cats."

Tracy fumbled with the buttons of her coat and did not look at either the cat or Nursel Erim. If she kept her hands busy, perhaps the cold sickness would go away. She had not dreamed how hard this was going to be, or what an assault there might be upon her emotions at every turn. *Bunny!* Of all things, Bunny!

Miss Erim looked at her with alert concern. "I

26

will leave you now. You must be weary from your long flight. Please rest—and I will return in half an hour to bring you to Mrs. Erim."

"Yes," said Tracy in a small voice. "That will be fine. Thank you very much." She did, indeed, feel the need for rest.

She waited until her hostess had gone, then flung off her coat and lay cautiously down on one side of the great bed. The cat did not move. It neither scratched her nor leaped away in fright. It simply scrutinized her with that reserved and critical gaze. Nothing about it lived up to the frivolity of its name.

*Bunny,* Tracy thought, and felt suddenly helpless and alone. The coming meeting with Miles Radburn loomed as a frightening prospect, and all her cool reserving of judgment seemed an exercise in futility. Why shouldn't she believe the worst she had heard about him? Why shouldn't she be afraid?

She lay staring at the distant ceiling where an all-over design of diamond shapes had been decoratively outlined in strips of dark wood. Only the ceiling and the arched windows of the veranda beyond spoke of old Turkey. This was a modern room, a feminine room, perhaps furnished to please the woman who had once occupied it.

She looked at the cat again. "Bunny?" she said tentatively.

The cat did not seem to recognize her name. At least not in Tracy's intonation, but she raised her pink nose slightly and twitched her whiskers as if she drew in some impression by means of these antennae. Coming to a decision, she sprang gracefully from the bed and removed herself to a cushioned chair across the room, rejecting untoward advances from a stranger.

The room seemed to draw about Tracy, weighing in upon her with a sense of ominous oppression. Slow warm tears gathered at the corners of her eyes and spilled back into hard Turkish pillows. At the realization that she was giving way to gloom and self-pity, she rose and went in search of the bathroom Nursel Erim had indicated earlier.

Here there was plentiful tile and a huge old-fashioned European tub with massive fixtures. Behind it stood an iron stove, with a pipe running out through the wall. Apparently one bathed in hot water only by appointment with the stove. Sure enough, when she turned the basin faucets the water ran icy cold.

Nevertheless, it refreshed her as she bathed her face, and she reminded herself that she was tired. Tomorrow she would feel more courageous and ready to face Miles Radburn. She could only hope that the ordeal of meeting him might be postponed until she had a night's rest behind her. She glanced at her watch, wondering what time it was in New York. But only Turkish time mattered from now on, and she returned to her room and shrugged the thought aside, surrendering still another link with home and all that was safely familiar.

When Nursel Erim came for her, Tracy was ready. Her eyes were dry, her emotions under control. She did not speak to the white cat in parting.

# 2

"MRS. ERIM will see you now," Nursel said.

Again they traversed the big drafty salon. This time her guide went to one of the side doors and opened it to step out upon the veranda. Rain blew through the arches and the garden below was already dark and shadowy as daylight died. Hurrying, they rounded the house to the rear veranda where a passageway, covered with a roof and enclosed by glass windows, made its way over the private roadway that ended at the door of the yali, thus forming a bridge from the third floor of one house to the ground floor of the house higher on the hill. The kiosk, the land house, was very large, with trees growing all about.

"My brother's laboratory is down here," Nursel Erim explained, as they entered a marble corridor. "My sister-in-law's rooms are on the floors above. Our older brother built this house for her and gave it to her so that she holds it in her own name. Fortunately, he stipulated that Murat, his younger brother, be allowed this space for his laboratory."

A faintly resentful note was evident in the Turkish girl's voice. Apparently feelings were not completely amicable on the part of the younger Erims toward their sister-in-law. Tracy stored away the fact to be considered at another time, as all such facts about this household must be stored and considered.

Again curving Turkish stairs with wrought-iron railings took them upward. Again there was a central salon, apparently unused in the cold months. A sound of vehement voices speaking in Turkish came from a room at the rear of the house.

Tracy's companion knocked and then opened the door as a voice called to them to come in. The room had upon Tracy an impact of light and perfumed air, bustle and sound that was overwhelming. As she stepped into its brilliantly lighted expanse she saw that there were a number of men in the room, all talking at once. And there was one silent woman.

It was a huge room, high-ceilinged, but brightly lighted against the dusk by means of a crystal chandelier and several imported table lamps. Turkish divans ran about the walls, heaped high with colorful silken cushions. All about were little tables, inlaid with mother-of-pearl, or set with mosaic designs in tile or fine wood. The carpets were richly Oriental and several had been piled one upon another to give layers of luxury and warmth. Upon these carpets knelt several shabbily dressed men, their garments patched and repatched, as nondescript and baggy as Ahmet's had seemed, displaying their wares as if before a throne. Sitting on a cushioned divan, slightly raised by a platform that enabled her to survey the room, sat Sylvana Erim.

She wore a dark red, embroidered robe of wool that flowed over the curves of her figure. Beneath its floor-length hem showed comfortable Turkish slippers with red pompons on the toes. It was her face, however, that drew and held the eyes of the observer once they had rested there. She was, Tracy suspected, the sort of woman who came to full bloom in her early forties and was now at the peak of her years. Her fair hair was golden in the brilliant light, without any hint of gray, and she wore it waved softly back from a smooth wide forehead. Her eyes were startlingly blue and very deep and lustrous beneath heavy lids. An aura of calm assurance seemed to lie upon her in the midst of confusion. She sat relaxed, without moving, while bedlam reigned at her feet. The kneeling men called her attention to scarves

31

spread out here, a bevy of embroidered handbags there, brass trays beyond, all being energetically praised by their owners. Yet Sylvana Erim regarded all this in calm silence.

She saw Tracy and beckoned with a hand that moved without suddenness. "Ah—Miss Hubbard? Good afternoon. Please sit here beside me. I am sorry to receive you in the midst of my little bazaar. But it will soon be over. Ahmet Effendi— if you please—"

At once the mustachioed houseman stepped from behind the kneeling villagers and stood listening without servility as Mrs. Erim spoke to him in Turkish.

Since it seemed to be expected of her, Tracy seated herself on a lower divan next to the mistress of the house. Nursel Erim smiled with vague uncertainty at Tracy, and went away.

"If you will excuse me," Mrs. Erim said, "I will finish this small business."

Quietly Sylvana Erim singled out this article or that, rejected another, praising and blaming with equal calm. The men at her feet rolled up their goods, piled their brass and copper trays together, picked up their silver filigree jewelry, and took everything away that was not wanted.

When they had gone, Mrs. Erim reached for an elaborately shaped glass bottle from a nearby table and offered it to Tracy. "Cologne for your hands," she said. "Our pleasant Turkish custom."

The odor added further scent to the already perfumed air as Tracy sprinkled it upon her hands. It was fragrant and elusive.

"You like this?" Mrs. Erim asked. "It is attar of roses, but with an addition or two of my own. Myself I have distilled the essence from which it is made. A small amusement in which I take pleasure."

Tracy murmured her appreciation, finding herself somewhat in awe of this impressive woman. Mrs. Erim picked up a silken scarf that lay among the articles the men had left behind and shook out its bright yellow folds with a faint moue of distaste.

"A pretty thing, but the material and weave are of poor quality. I try very hard to restore our weaving of materials to the fine quality of the past. But we have lost some of our art and we have a long way to go. In articles of brass and copper we excel. For these I can always find a market abroad. But the weaving of silks has not yet reached a standard to be well received in America."

"Then you're not buying these things for yourself?" Tracy asked.

Mrs. Erim made a deprecating gesture. "No, no—these are made by people of the villages where I am trying to encourage more craft work for export. They know I wish to help them and that I can find buyers abroad for some of their work. This saves me the cost of sharing with an Istanbul dealer. It is not a business with me, but a small contribution to my adopted country. However, I have not invited you here to discuss inconsequential efforts. *Bien*—here is our tea. We may refresh ourselves as we talk."

Ahmet came in bearing a brass tray on which was set a small samovar and two glasses resting on delicate china saucers. There was a dish of lemon slices and a plate of tiny cakes. Unsmiling, almost sullen in his manner, Ahmet took a small teapot from the rack atop the samovar and held it beneath the spigot. When the water, already heated by the tube of charcoal inside, had steamed onto the tea leaves in the pot, he set it back upon its rack to keep warm while it steeped. He brought a small plate and napkin for Tracy, and then Mrs. Erim waved him away. Though he obeyed her gesture, he glowered as if he had a wish to stay, and Mrs. Erim sighed as the door closed after him.

"Ahmet Effendi's disposition does not improve with age. But what is one to do? He was a servitor in my husband's family and is very loyal to us. He is difficult at times, but he knows our ways and is devoted to all who bear the Erim name. Now you must tell me about yourself, Miss Hubbard, and about why you are here."

Tracy explained as best she could, while Mrs. Erim poured the steeped tea into small glasses

34

and passed the plate of cakes. As Tracy concluded, she nodded thoughtfully.

"It was not, I fear, a sensible plan on the part of your Mr. Hornwright. You will forgive me if I say that you are young and inexperienced for this work. Your use to Mr. Radburn can only be negligible. Is this not true?"

"I don't expect to be of much use to him in actual work on the book," Tracy admitted frankly. "Mr. Hornwright thought I might go through the material he has collected and find out exactly what remains to be done. Perhaps to sort and file will be the best service that can be offered Mr. Radburn at the moment."

Mrs. Erim's soft laugh had a ring of sympathy. "Files and order are, I fear, foreign to Mr. Radburn's nature. He will not welcome one who comes to tamper with his books and papers and sketches of mosaics."

"Perhaps tamper isn't the word I'd use, but I am here to sort through this material." Tracy's brows drew together in a frown of resistance. She must not permit herself to be swayed from her purpose.

The blond woman on the divan studied her frankly for a moment. "What you suggest is futile. The task would never end. But perhaps this is something you must see for yourself. It is possible that I can arrange for you to remain here for a week, at least."

"I'll need more than that for the job," Tracy said firmly.

Mrs. Erim's calm remained unruffled. "*Perhaps* I can arrange for you to remain a week," she repeated. "In that time the truth of the matter should be obvious to you. You will be able to report the hopelessness of this task to Mr. Hornwright. It will not be your failure, or the failure of anyone he might send, but simply the fact that Mr. Radburn does not wish to complete this book. When I invited him to come here to work, I had hoped that he would make this important contribution. But I am a realist, Miss Hubbard. I no longer have confidence that this is true."

Such a belief was not Mr. Hornwright's, Tracy knew, and she had no intention of accepting it herself.

"When may I see him?" she asked bluntly. "Does he know that I'm here?"

"Not yet. He is away and we do not expect him home until tomorrow. Perhaps then I can prepare the way a little. He has gone to the Istanbul side to visit a small mosque where the tilework is especially beautiful. Always he goes off on such trips. Always he collects more and more information, makes more and more sketches of mosaics. There is no end to this, though it is not necessary to represent the tilework of all Turkey in his book. A sampling from the various periods of history would seem sufficient. Your editor made this clear when he visited us. But tell me, my dear—why did Mr. Hornwright choose you in particular to come on this errand?"

Tracy answered carefully. "Mr. Hornwright thought I'd be useful at the moment. That is, if I can persuade Mr. Radburn to accept me."

"I like those who are open with me," Mrs. Erim went on. "It is possible that I may be able to smooth your way so that you may remain, as I say, for a week. I can promise no more. But that is something, is it not?"

Tracy could only nod. She did not know whether this woman was on her side or not, and she wondered about her claim that Miles Radburn did not want to finish his book.

"Tell me, Miss Hubbard," Mrs. Erim inquired, "do you know Mr. Radburn's paintings?"

"Yes, of course," Tracy said. "I've seen them many times in exhibits at home." She must be open, yes. But not too open. She was on uneasy ground here and she did not wholly trust this woman's calm and candid air. "Mr. Hornwright says he doesn't paint any more," she added.

The deeply blue eyes clouded for a moment, then were once more serene. "That is true. A sad and wasteful thing. But perhaps it will pass as all things pass with the healing of years. I too have lost those dear to me."

Tracy stirred her glass of tea with a tiny silver

spoon and said nothing. Mrs. Erim had partaken of none of the sweet cakes, but she sipped the lemon-flavored brew and allowed silence to envelop the room. Only a spattering of rain against glass broke the quiet. Sylvana Erim, while she gave the impression of potential vitality held in check, did not waste her energies. Because of her ability to be still without being placid, she cast an atmosphere of tranquillity about her. Yet Tracy found herself increasingly on guard. She wondered what would happen if this well-controlled woman were angered, or severely crossed. She would not, Tracy thought, like to be the one to oppose her.

Mrs. Erim replaced her glass and saucer on the tray and moved slightly against her cushions. "Tell me—you are comfortable in the room you have been given in the yali?"

"It is a lovely room," Tracy said, her eyes lowered. "Thank you for inviting me to stay here."

"The water sounds will not disturb you or keep you awake?"

"I'm sure they won't," Tracy said.

"Good! Myself—I cannot endure the mooing of horns, the whistling of passing boats, the voices that carry across water. That is why I persuaded my husband to build me this house in the woods, where I can be quiet, undisturbed. Let us hope you will sleep well tonight. And do not worry about tomorrow. I myself will have a small talk with Mr. Radburn."

"You're very kind," Tracy said.

The interview had come to an end. She murmured that she would go to her room to unpack a few things, and took leave of her hostess. Mrs. Erim did not accompany her to the door, but somehow the houseman, Ahmet, was there, ready to open it as she went out. Silently he led the way back through the covered passage to the yali and saw her to her room. When she thanked him, he bowed his head and went away, moving rather like a shadow in his dark, ill-fitting suit, quickly lost in the gloom of the big salon. It was rather a shame, Tracy thought, as she went into her room, that Ahmet was too late for the days of the Ottoman Turks. He would have looked well in a turban and flowing robes.

After her visit with Mrs. Erim, she felt slightly more encouraged about remaining at least for a week. She could not fathom the woman, or understand why she had aligned herself on the side of a stranger who had little that was practical to offer. But the fact that she appeared to have done so was a step in the right direction. Granted one week, it would be necessary to find a way to stretch it to two.

Tracy opened her suitcase and began to hang up a few things in the cavernous wardrobe of dark walnut that was the single out-of-harmony

39

note in the modern bedroom. The white cat had not stirred from its chair. As she moved about, it opened sleepy eyes to stare at her briefly, then seemed to dismiss her as a person of no consequence, and went back to sleep.

Before Tracy had finished unpacking, Halide came, lending a bright splash of color in her red clothes.

"*Hanimefendi*," she said, and added one of her few English words, "please?" as she indicated that she would take Tracy's things away to be pressed. She admired each article of clothing before she flung it over her arm and was interested in everything.

When the girl had gone with the few things Tracy had to give her, she opened veranda doors and went outside. The rain had lessened to a drizzle and in the dusk lights were coming on, climbing the hills of the European shore across the Bosporus, and marking the outline of a passing freighter. The strait was narrow and winding in this section, more like a river than an arm of the sea. Now that the last traces of daylight were vanishing over Thrace on the European side, the Bosporus looked like black marble, with light breaking its surface in oily swirls.

Without warning, as she stared at the water, pain swept through her—the aching of a wound too new to heal, and the hurt as well of an old, disquieting memory. Below the balcony dark water swept softly past, treacherously deep and strong in its currents. All through Turkish history these very waters had reflected the wickedness of Constantinople—a city that raised spires to God and cast loathsome secrets into the water that flowed at its feet.

She withdrew her eyes from the hypnotic play of the moving surface and turned her attention to a lighted area below the jutting balcony. It was stone-flagged, with stone steps running down to the water. Beside these steps stood Ahmet, with a boat hook in his hands. As she watched, Tracy heard the sound of a motor-driven craft turning from the main channel to come toward the yali. She could see the boat clearly as it neared the lighted landing. It was a caique with a high curved prow, decorated in a design of bright colors. Above the center portion of the boat an oblong of white canopy with gaily scalloped edges sheltered seats from the rain. A boatman stood in the stern, steering his craft toward the landing. Beneath the canopy sat a passenger, only his legs visible.

With well-practiced skill, Ahmet reached out with his hook, the caique was made secure with a tossed rope, and the passenger beneath the canopy stepped lightly from boat to landing. For an instant Tracy's fingers tightened on the damp railing of the balcony. Then she stepped back into shadow where she could stand unseen. As he crossed the paved area he glanced up at the house and light fell upon his face. It was a somber, rather craggy face with a dark, well-shaped head, the sides touched with early gray. Tracy had seen his photograph more than once and she had looked it up again before she left New York. The man was Miles Radburn. Did this unexpected return mean that she must face him tonight? At dinner, perhaps? Earlier she had been keyed to this confrontation, but now she shrank from the finality it might bring. Tonight she wasn't ready. Mrs. Erim had dissipated the need for immediate courage, and she was no longer braced for the ordeal of meeting him. Had that perhaps been the woman's intent, with her tranquil manner that seemed to dismiss the very thought of struggle as needless waste?

When Radburn had disappeared into the house below, Tracy returned to her room and closed the doors upon chilly dampness and the dark smell of the water. She could not settle down now, but paced the great expanse of gold rug, while the white cat opened its eyes and stared at her without expression. The room was growing colder in spite of the glow of coals in the mangal, and she turned on the electric heater and sat within the range of its radiance.

A knock on the door sent her flying to answer, anxious to know how soon the meeting would be upon her.

Nursel Erim came into the room, moving gracefully on her high heels, a touch of exotic perfume floating about her.

"I am sorry to disturb you," she said. "Mrs. Erim sends me to ask if you will mind having dinner in your room tonight. Then it will not be necessary to tell Mr. Radburn of your presence at once. A quiet talk this evening will prepare him for your appearance tomorrow morning. You do not mind?"

Tracy did not mind, and said so in relief.

The Turkish girl lingered, apparently unwilling to leave at once.

"You have all you wish?" she asked. Though she glanced about the room, her words had an absent sound as though they were an excuse for her lingering, rather than the reason for it. When she spoke it was almost as if to herself, as if Tracy's presence here were incidental and of no consequence.

"I have not entered this room for several weeks. Always the room saddens me. It is as if something of Mrs. Radburn remains. I feel angry when I come here. Angry because this very carpet, which my friend chose herself from a shop in Istanbul, should remain while she is gone."

Tracy heard her in silence. The girl stepped to the shuttered doors and peered out into the rain. "Always she loved the water. Sometimes we ran

43

off together and made boat trips so we might laugh and be foolish, with no stern looks to tell us we were not children. But there is no laughter left in this room. It is too close to the water she loved, water that betrayed her."

"She drowned, didn't she?" Tracy asked in a low, tight voice.

"Yes." Nursel nodded. "Out there within full view of the yali. Had anyone known, had anyone been at the windows to see, perhaps it might not have happened. It was on a gray evening such as this. Perhaps that is why it seems that this room is haunted by her presence whenever it rains."

Tracy must have made some small sound, for Nursel returned from her dreaming to look at her curiously.

"This disturbs you? I am sorry. These matters are of no concern to you. There is no presence of Anabel Radburn in this room for someone who never knew her. You must rest now. Later Ahmet will bring you a tray. This is convenient for you? You do not mind?"

"I don't mind," Tracy said. "Thank you."

"Then I will leave you here." Nursel cast a last glance around the room and her eyes lighted upon the cat. "You do not mind if the cat remains? If you prefer, I will take it away."

"Let her stay," Tracy said.

She waited until Nursel had gone. Then she went to the balcony doors and pulled cords that swung thick draperies of gold damask across them. She did not want to look out at the water now. Not when the night was so cold, so depressingly gray. The cat sat up and watched her with a certain wariness in its eyes and she went to stand before the cushioned chair.

"First of all," said Tracy softly, "we will have to change your name. I should probably cry every time I spoke it. You would do much better with something that sounds more Turkish. Of course no Turk would give an animal the name of a friend. But since I don't know anyone named Yasemin, perhaps that will do. How would you like to be called Yasemin?"

The white cat mewed delicately, though whether in acceptance or repudiation Tracy could not tell. She moved toward it without suddenness and picked it up firmly in both hands. Then she sat down in the chair within the beam of the electric heater and placed it in her lap. Yasemin neither spat nor scratched, but neither did she settle down to purr. She merely tolerated, without acceptance. Tracy stroked the soft fur and found comfort in the warmth of the small living creature in her lap.

Perhaps she and the cat both dozed a little, for when Ahmet knocked on her door, Tracy started up and found that an hour had passed. At her sudden movement, Yasemin leaped away and went to hide beneath the bed, as if she knew

Ahmet Effendi of old and had no liking for him.

The man set the tray upon a table, removed silver warming covers, and prepared her food with the expert movements of one long experienced. Apparently Ahmet could do everything. She tried to speak to him as she watched, but he merely shook his head at her words, indicating that he did not understand English. When he had gone, showing her first the bell she might ring when she was finished, she called Yasemin from beneath the bed, prepared a few tidbits for the cat, and then sat down before the tray.

It was good food, attractively arranged. A small steak, whipped potatoes, buttered beans of a variety she did not recognize. Apparently Mrs. Erim's household ate well, as the French knew how to eat. The short nap had refreshed her, Tracy found, and both she and Yasemin finished their dinner with good appetite.

When Halide had taken the tray away and brought more coals for the mangal, Tracy let Yasemin out into the house, where she vanished at once in the direction of the stairs. In the bathroom hot water had been prepared and Tracy took a steaming bath in the big European tub.

Returning to her room, hurrying, lest by some misfortune she meet Miles Radburn in the hall, Tracy meant to go at once to bed. But again the water drew her irresistibly. She slipped a coat over her nightgown, turned off the lights in the room, and parted the heavy draperies to step out upon the veranda. The landing area stood empty and quiet, water lapping gently against the steps. The rain had stopped, and in the stillness she could hear distant voices from a village on the nearby shore. A well-lighted ship went past, its engines throbbing as it made its way north from Istanbul toward the Black Sea and the ports of Russia. Overhead ragged clouds raced, a touch of faint moonlight breaking through patches of torn gray. The water drew her eyes—black and seemingly still on the surface, yet with those deep and treacherous currents stirring beneath.

Somewhere in the village a man began to sing, and she heard for the first time the minor-keyed lament of Turkish music, repetitive and strange to Western ears, yet somehow haunting.

Again a sense of isolation swept over her. She was out of touch with all she knew and was sure of, abroad upon currents that might take her almost anywhere. Mrs. Erim, for all her calmly authoritative ways, was a woman with depths not easily read. The younger Nursel was also a puzzle, with her devotion to Anabel and her slight air of reserve that overlay all small courteous efforts toward a guest. She had yet to meet Dr. Erim, the brother. And tomorrow there would be the man she had come to see—Miles Radburn. Loneliness and confusion engulfed her. Had she been right in this quest? Was there an answer to be found? She left the veranda door slightly ajar, turned off the heater, and got into the big comfortable bed, glad enough to be weary.

She slept heavily, wakening only now and then to strange sounds from the watercourse that flowed beyond her doors. Then waking not at all until the vociferous crowing of what seemed a thousand roosters began at the break of day.

# 3

FOR A LITTLE while Tracy lay beneath blankets and stared at a liquid shifting of patterns upon the diamond design of the ceiling. Through the opened slit of the veranda door a flickering snake of watery light made its way into the room and told her the rain was over, the sun up and shining upon the Bosporus. She lay still a few moments longer, listening to crowing cocks and bleating goats. Then she slipped out of bed and went to look outside.

The hills of the opposite shore were newly green after the rain, and the Bosporus was a dark deep blue beneath a lighter sky. In coves across the water streamers of mist drifted, thinning as sunlight reached them. She could see the weathered wooden houses of a small village opposite climbing steeply upward. Across the strait in the direction of Istanbul, a great triangle of stone walls with a huge round tower at each apex mounted the steep pitch of hillside— apparently a medieval fortress.

But the morning air was cold and she soon closed her doors upon the brightening scene. The sun would help. Already its light restored her lagging courage, steeled her in a sense of purpose. Soon now she must face Miles Radburn and this morning she would be ready for him. She must be ready for him.

Halide brought her breakfast tray, with rolls and syrupy black Turkish coffee. Tracy sat in bed against plumped pillows with the table over her knees and breakfasted in unfamiliar luxury, regretting only the continental meagerness of the meal. This morning she could have managed the pancakes and bacon and eggs of a good American breakfast.

The room no longer seemed haunted and the white cat was not there to lend a slightly melancholy presence. She had difficulty accustoming herself to the room's vast expanses, however. The modern furnishings did not really suit the room, and she wondered if Anabel had chosen them, along with the gold carpet, in order to brighten its shadowy gloom. She and Miles Radburn seemed to have lived here for some time as permanent and privileged guests. Quite evidently Sylvana Erim regarded herself as a patron of the arts and she apparently had the wealth, thanks to her Turkish husband, to indulge her whims on this score.

By the time Nursel Erim came to fetch her, Tracy had put on a gray-blue frock, simply cut to her small waist and slim figure. Her one ornament was again the gold pin that was something of a talisman. She had brushed her brown hair to the shining perfection that was her one pride, and swirled it into a high coil on the back of her head. She looked neat, if not gaudy, she decided—and promptly felt like nothing at all the moment she beheld the vision of Nursel.

This morning's version of the Turkish girl was simpler as to coiffeur and her heels were not so high, but she was no less smartly dramatic in tight black Capri pants and a blue Angora sweater that set her off to good effect. The sultans, Tracy recalled, had liked their ladies generous of curve, and while the dress might have changed from pantaloons to pants, the ample flesh was there and roundly enticing.

"Mrs. Erim wishes to speak with you," Nursel said. "She awaits you in Mr. Radburn's study."

"Is—is he there?" Tracy asked.

The other girl shook her head. "Always he goes for a long, very fast walk after breakfast. It is a British custom, I think? Soon he will return, but Mrs. Erim will see you first."

Miles Radburn's rooms were also on the third floor, overlooking the land side of the house across the drafty gloom of the big salon. Nursel escorted her to the door of the study and opened it for her. Beyond the expanse of a walnut desk piled high with books and papers Sylvana Erim sat in a leather chair. She said, "Good morning," pleasantly and indicated a chair. Then she moved a commanding finger that caused Nursel to close the door and obediently vanish. Mrs. Erim was accustomed, quite evidently, to a well-trained household. Tracy found herself wondering if tradition had trained Nursel to meek acceptance of this dowager rule. Away from Sylvana, the girl appeared to have more spark of her own.

"You slept well?" Sylvana asked of Tracy, and went on without waiting for an answer, gesturing widely with her hands. "You see? This, my young friend, is what you have come to contend with."

Tracy saw. She did not sit down at once, thus opposing herself in a small way to Mrs. Erim. It was better for her own courage if she did not give in too easily to this autocratic woman.

The huge room was no more tidy than the desk. Wall shelves were packed with books that lay in disorder, sometimes propped one against the next, sometimes in leaning stacks. In one corner stood a refectory table piled high with a conglomeration of papers and books, folders and portfolios. A large armchair of red damask held more of this hodgepodge in its stolid arms. The only oasis in the sea of disorder was a drawing table with slanted board that stood near veranda doors, a piece of work in progress upon it. At least the room boasted a tall, elaborate white porcelain stove that gave off a more comfortable warmth than that provided by an electric heater.

"I can see what Mr. Hornwright meant when he spoke of a housekeeper being needed," Tracy said wryly.

Mrs. Erim stiffened as if the words were a reflection upon her establishment. "He will allow the servants to touch nothing, you understand. He does not mind dust if it is not upon his drawing board. We manage to come and go behind his back, but you can see the difficulty."

Tracy could indeed. The task looked monumental in its most elementary steps, and, with the master of this confusion set in opposition to order, she had no idea of how she might proceed. Moving about the room, she paused before the drawing board where a long strip of cream-colored paper bore decorative Turkish script done in India ink.

Mrs. Erim noted her interest. "That is ancient Turkish calligraphy. Mr. Radburn has taken great interest in mastering the art of copying such script. Though, of course, he does not read it. But come—sit here, if you please. He will return soon and we must discuss this matter a little. I do not have good news for you."

Tracy sat down and looked at her hostess. Mrs.

Erim had discarded her flowing robe and wore a gray suit that bore, like Nursel's clothes, the stamp of Paris. Her long golden hair was caught into a coil on the nape of her neck and held by a silken snood. In the morning light her complexion seemed more glowing than ever. Again an air of calm assurance lay upon her. Clearly she expected those about her to fall in with her ways and Tracy braced herself a little. She must not let this woman intimidate her, or defeat her purpose in coming here.

"Last night I talked to Mr. Radburn after dinner," Mrs. Erim said. "He does not wish you to remain. He will not allow you to touch one paper of his material. But he agrees to speak with you. This, at least, I have arranged. When I asked that you be permitted to stay a week, he would not listen. The mood of the bear is upon him—and what can one do?"

Had Mrs. Erim worked for her or against her in this paving of the way? Tracy wondered. She did not trust the woman at all.

"Then I'll have to talk to him myself," she said, attempting a confidence she did not feel.

Mrs. Erim regarded her in silence for a moment. Then she rose in her graceful, unhurried manner and crossed the big room to the closed door of an adjoining room.

"Come," she said. "I have something to show you."

She opened the door upon what was obviously Miles Radburn's bedroom and stepped aside for Tracy to see. Here there was no confusion. The room appeared lived in, but crisply in order. The veranda shutters had been set ajar and morning sunshine poured in from a woodsy hillside beyond, warming the air a little and stage-lighting the room with a bright shaft that fell upon the bed.

Tracy spent no more than a glance upon the room itself, for her eyes were caught at once by a picture that hung above the carved headboard of the wide bed. It was the portrait of a young woman painted in a high, soft, silvery key—a little misty in its execution, except for the face which had been presented in slightly exaggerated focus. Tracy's fingers curled about the lower rail of the bed and she stood braced against the flood of emotion that washed over her. Somewhere, sometime, in one way or another, she had known the moment would come. Now it was here. From the wall her sister's face looked down at her, as elusive, as secretive, yet as strangely appealing as Tracy remembered, and almost as real as a living presence.

The picture showed a slender girl in a lacy white gown, her fair hair drawn loosely from her forehead and tied at the back of the neck with a silver ribbon. The curved cheek and jawline of the partly turned head revealed a breathtaking beauty. The mouth had been touched with pale color, unsmiling and wide, but not too full of lip. Only the eyes had been emphasized to the point of distortion. They seemed closed, and dark lashes lay smudged against pale cheeks. One saw at second glance that they were not wholly closed. The girl in the picture gazed from beneath lowered lids, a faint, green-eyed gleam just showing. It was a face that hinted of tragedy, yet all in the same instant perversely promised joy. It was a young face, yet never carelessly young, the whole done with misty fragility— from which the dark smudging of the eyes stood out in vivid, unsettling contrast.

"That is Anabel," Mrs. Erim said. "His wife."

Tracy stared at the picture and waited for the room to settle. She had known this intensity of feeling must come, but she had not expected the portrait, had not been braced for it.

"She is the reason why this book will never be finished," Mrs. Erim said calmly. "Only three months ago she died tragically, as you may know, and the shadow of her suicide lies heavily upon all of us. Your Mr. Hornwright thinks only in practical terms of how many pages of script, how many prints must be made from Miles Radburn's drawings. To persuade Mr. Radburn he speaks of the healing value of work, but he does not understand the evil truth about this shadow."

Tracy drew her gaze from the portrait abruptly. The room had steadied, her vision cleared. "What do you mean by the truth?" she asked.

"This is not your affair." Mrs. Erim spoke with calm assurance, as though she reproved a child. "Your duty is to return home and make Mr. Hornwright understand that there will be no book. Nothing else concerns you here."

So this was why she had been invited to the yali. If permitted to remain, this was to be her accomplishment.

"You are against this book, Mrs. Erim," Tracy countered. "Will you tell me why?"

The Frenchwoman shrugged. "As I say, I am a realist. I have a practical nature. To a man who was once a fine artist, this work is a method of burying himself alive. It is a ridiculous thing that a child like yourself has been sent to deal with such a problem."

Tracy looked again at the picture. "Do you mean that he loved her so much that he can't bear to live without her? That all work has become meaningless to him?"

The veneer of calm flickered for an instant and threatened to crack, while the bright color in Mrs. Erim's cheeks flamed more intensely.

"What absurdity! You do not understand. Certainly he had no love for her in the last years of their marriage. She was wicked, depraved, beyond hope. At the end he despised her. But it is difficult for him to face this thing in himself. This is why he prefers not to be alive. He buried himself in such meaningless work as he does now long before her death."

This was not the first time Tracy had heard her sister spoken of in scathing terms. Yet even after Tracy Hubbard had ceased to be an adoring small sister and was old enough to face the fact that Anabel was sometimes less than perfect, she had never wholly accepted this verdict. The enigma of her sister still troubled her, as well as the question of whether there was more she herself might have done; whether some action of hers might have averted the final tragedy.

"Why did she die?" Tracy ventured. "Why would a girl who had so much take her own life? A girl who was so beautiful!"

The moment the words were spoken she saw that she had gone too far in pressing for an answer. She had forgotten the need for caution. There was sudden wariness in Mrs. Erim's eyes.

"It is a childish thing to parallel worldly possessions and beauty with happiness," Sylvana Erim said virtuously, overlooking the fact that her own manner of living seemed to contradict this tenet. "You will do well to content yourself with the task for which you have come. I must remind you again that Mr. Radburn's private concerns are not your affair. This is true, is it not, Miss Hubbard?"

The time had come to step back from the line she had overreached. "Of course they're not my affair," Tracy said meekly. "It's just that you showed me the portrait and my interest was aroused."

"I show you the portrait only that you may understand the folly of your errand. You will be wise not to mention to Mr. Radburn that you have seen it."

Tracy could feel the warmth in her own cheeks. Once more she felt like a child who had been disciplined and did not dare to answer back. Before she could attempt a reply, there was a knock on the study door and Halide's voice called urgently in Turkish.

At once Mrs. Erim led the way back to the study, closing the bedroom door behind her. "He is coming now. I will wait to introduce you, then leave you in his hands. When you wish to arrange your plane reservation home, I will be glad to take care of it for you."

Tracy could have wished for more time to recover from the impact of the portrait and from this exchange with Sylvana Erim. She felt as though the label of her identity had been stamped upon her, and she wished for Anabel's well-remembered trick of gazing beneath lowered lids that never revealed all that she was thinking.

The study door opened abruptly and a man stood upon the threshold. He was tall and leanly built. That he had once been a soldier was evident in the straightness of his back, the carriage of his shoulders, yet there was nothing in his bearing to suggest that he welcomed with interest what any new day held for him. His rather craggy face achieved that curious effect of being handsome which strong though ill-assorted features may assume in certain men. He looked older than his thirty-eight years and his face evidenced a somber quality, suggesting a loss of the ability to laugh.

"You look well," Mrs. Erim said. "It is a good morning for your walk. Miles, this is Miss Hubbard, the young girl who has been sent from New York to see that you proceed in your work with great dispatch." Amusement lighted her eyes. "I will leave you to settle the matter between you," she added and went to the door.

Miles Radburn opened it in silence and closed it after her. Then he turned and looked at Tracy without expression.

"Why Hornwright sent you, I'll never understand," he said, and Tracy noted that his years in America had not banished the British inflection from his speech. "Nor do I understand why you came on after I wrote you at the hotel. Perhaps you had better sit down and tell me what this nonsense is all about."

Tracy seated herself beside his desk, mentally rejecting the label of "young girl" that Mrs. Erim had placed upon her. Even as a child, she had sometimes felt herself older than Anabel. Miles Radburn stayed where he was, his hands busy with a briar pipe and pouch of tobacco, his eyes indifferent, no longer upon her. He had added up her sum total, found it of no consequence, and was already dismissing her. The very fact served to stiffen her spine still more. She must think only of how she could persuade this man to let her stay.

When the pipe was lighted to his satisfaction, he shoved a heap of papers carelessly to one side and sat on a corner of the desk, swinging one long leg. The blue pipe smoke carried a not unpleasant tang.

"Begin," he said. "Recite your piece. I've promised Sylvana I would listen. Just that and nothing more."

She sat up resolutely and faced him. "Mr. Hornwright feels that you are doing an important and distinguished book. Turkish mosaics have a significant place in the history of the world's art and—"

"Spare me that sort of sales talk," Radburn interrupted. "I know why I'm doing what I am doing. I'm curious only to know why you are here. There was a Miss Baker whose name I suggested to Hornwright. Do you fancy that you can take her place?"

She'd had enough of being talked down to—

first by Mrs. Erim and now by this cold, rather frightening man.

"You're not ready for Miss Baker," she told him heatedly. "She would take one look at this— this mess!—and go straight home. Do you think she'd be willing to sneeze her way through all that?" Tracy waved a scornful hand at the refectory table, where the pile had reached so dangerous a height that an avalanche to the floor was momentarily threatened.

Radburn glared at her out of gray eyes that were without warmth, though he was clearly capable of anger.

"I can find anything I want at a moment's notice," he said. "I want no one coming in and mixing things up."

"Mixing things up!" Tracy echoed, forgetting that she was here to placate, to coax and cajole, to somehow endear herself so he would allow her to stay. "I never heard anything so silly in my life. Look—look at this!"

She left her chair like a small and impetuous cyclone and dived into the pile on the table with both hands. The avalanche tottered for an instant and then a good part of it went sailing off into space to scatter itself about the floor at Tracy's feet. Her indignation left her as abruptly as it had risen and she found herself regarding in horror the destruction she had wrought. She did not dare to look at Miles Radburn.

There was a long and deadly silence, broken by an explosion of sound. It was a sneeze. And having started, Mr. Radburn could not stop. He sneezed twice, blew his nose violently, unable to speak, and then repeated the explosion four more times in rapid succession.

Out of the past a sudden memory of her father's outraged face flashed into Tracy's mind and she suppressed a desire toward incongruous laughter.

"You're behaving just like my father!" she cried. "He wouldn't let anybody touch a thing in his study. But he couldn't really find what he wanted, the way he claimed. I was the only one who could straighten out his papers and keep them in any sort of order. So maybe I do have some experience that would be useful to you."

His sneezing spell subsiding, Mr. Radburn flourished his handkerchief. "Perhaps you can begin," he said coldly, "by picking up everything you've sent off onto the floor."

Tracy looked down at scattered pages of manuscript and drawings. "Where would I put it if I picked it up?" she asked reasonably. "Surely not back on the summit of the mountain?"

A dark flush had engulfed Mr. Radburn's somber features and there were beads of perspiration on his forehead. Unexpectedly, Tracy felt sorry for him. After all, she thought, with that perversity of humor that so often seized her at inopportune moments, how did one deal with an intruder who behaved as she had?

"I'm sorry," she said contritely. "But you were way off somewhere with your made-up mind and I had to get you to listen to me, to pay attention. I think I can be of some help without disturbing you as much as you think. I enjoy setting things in order and I don't chatter or make loud noises. You can pretend I'm not here. Besides, I do have a stake in this, you know."

"Why should I interest myself in your stake?" he demanded. "I have not asked you to come here."

Tracy went on as though she had not heard him. "I've been working for a couple of years at *Views*. It's a wonderful, exciting place where things are happening. Someday, if I'm useful enough, and enough of a burr under someone's collar, they'll let me into editorial work. I begged Mr. Hornwright to send me on this assignment. I thought I could do a sort of housekeeping job before Miss Baker came. If I go home empty-handed, it's likely that I'll be fired. Especially if I go home within a day or so of when I got here."

Everything she was saying was true. If it was not the whole truth, it must nevertheless sound convincing.

"This is a responsibility I refuse to accept," Radburn said. "It's not my affair."

Tracy regarded him almost pityingly. He looked like a man in whom all light and warmth had been wiped out. She turned from him and knelt on the floor before the scattered papers. There was an empty space beneath the table and she began depositing the sheets one by one in orderly heaps in that single clear space. Typed pages in this pile, carbon sheets in that. Penciled notes over there and sketches here. A special place for what appeared to be finished drawings of tile and mosaic detail. When the man behind her left his desk and moved restlessly about the room, she did not look at him.

"I am a short-tempered man," he said at length, and she knew that his voice came from near the veranda doors, where he must have paused before his drawing table. "I lack patience and I have no particular fondness for catering to women. I do not swear at the servants, but I am likely to swear at you if you annoy me."

Tracy looked up from a lovely mosaic pattern done in varying shades of blue. "If you swear at me I'll talk back," she said. "I don't like being sworn at. It will be more peaceful if you just ignore me and let me work." She turned the drawing over and saw the lettering on the back: *Sultan Ahmed.*

"This is from Sultan Ahmed's Blue Mosque, isn't it?" she said eagerly. "I must see that before I leave Turkey. And I want to visit St. Sophia—

Ayasofia." She looked up at him and intensity was once more in her voice. "Mr. Radburn, will you let me stay for a week at least?"

He did not swear, though for a moment he looked as though he might. Then, to her astonishment, since she had not thought it possible, a fleeting smile lifted the grim corners of his mouth.

"One week," he said. "I will bribe you with a week. Otherwise you are likely to tumble the books from my shelves and engulf me in wreckage. Didn't your father ever swear at you?"

"My father is a gentleman," she told him with dignity. "And I was very young in those days. He only spanked me."

"An excellent solution," said Miles Radburn, and went grimly back to his painstaking calligraphy work on the drawing board.

Silence fell upon the room. Somewhat shakily Tracy settled herself cross-legged on the carpet, careful not to let her weight creak the old, old boards of the floor. She lifted her papers without a rustle. The occupation of her hands gradually calmed her, and she thrust back the small surge of elation that sought to possess her. A week would never be enough. Not only for this task— but for the other more important one that had brought her here. The questions she must have an answer to, for her own peace of mind. At least she had made a beginning. Mr. Hornwright might be astonished if he saw her now, but he would not be wholly displeased.

The work was unexpectedly absorbing. At least Miles Radburn had identified each sketch on its back. Before long she had a pile of Blue Mosque drawings alone, and others were beginning to emerge. The Mosque of Suleiman the Magnificent, of course, as well as numerous unpronounceable mosque and palace names she had never heard of—each with a pattern of its own. The variety of tile designs was amazing and endless. She made no attempt to read manuscript pages, but simply piled them up. They would have to be arranged by subject matter later. More than once she pressed a finger hard beneath her nose to avoid a sneeze. A dust cloth would be needed before any of this material could be put into a file, but for now she would be still as a mouse and continue her sorting.

While she worked she tried not to think of that portrait on the wall of Miles Radburn's bedroom. The enigma loomed larger than ever, and there was pain as well in any thought of her sister. Now she must deal only with the task at hand.

The morning passed quietly. Radburn worked at his drawing board and paid her no attention. No one came to disturb them, and when Tracy finally stole a look at her watch she found that it was nearly twelve o'clock.

"I'm going out for a while," Radburn said

abruptly. "I presume someone will tell you what to do about lunch when the time comes."

He did not glance at the neat piles emerging beneath the shelter of the table, but went out of the room and closed the door firmly behind him. Tracy seized the moment to jump up and stretch widely. She would have to find some more comfortable way to work. Another table certainly, and a chair would have to be provided. Perhaps Nursel would help her. She would ask nothing of Mrs. Erim, who thought Anabel wicked and depraved, and who wanted to see Tracy Hubbard go home as soon as possible.

It was Nursel who at length came tapping on the door to summon her to lunch. The Turkish girl had changed from Capri pants to a full print skirt that gave her a flower-patterned grace of movement. She stood for a moment looking in astonishment at the heaps of sketches and papers beneath the table.

"He allowed you to do this? But it is a miracle!"

"He didn't allow me," Tracy admitted sheepishly. "I just started doing it and he didn't know how to stop me."

"Then you are not to go straight home as Mrs. Erim expects?"

Tracy shook her head. "I have a week. Then we'll see."

"Mrs. Erim will be surprised," said Nursel guardedly.

"And not pleased, I think," Tracy said.

Nursel made no comment. "Luncheon is ready. My brother and I would like you to dine with us, please. You have yet to meet Murat. Mrs. Erim dines in her own rooms in the kiosk. Come downstairs when you are ready."

Back in her room—Anabel's room—Tracy peered into the dressing table mirrors and found cobwebs in her hair and smudges on her nose. Her hands were grimy, and she set Miles Radburn down another notch in her estimation for being a careless and untidy man. Yet the bedroom had been as neat as a military barracks. There had been no disorder to distract from the effect of that stunning portrait on the wall.

If he had despised Anabel, why had he hung her picture there? The question persisted in Tracy's mind—one of the questions to which she must find the answer. But there was no time to puzzle now, with Nursel waiting for her. There was still the fourth member of this household to meet, and she must be careful during this meal. Careful to make no slips, careful to appear nothing more than they believed her to be. At least she was relieved to know that she need not face Sylvana Erim again immediately. There was a shrewdness about the woman that would seize upon any slip Tracy might make.

When she had washed in cold water and rid herself of smudges, she went down to the second floor. Nursel took her into a room which was apparently used as both living and dining quarters and which, she explained, she shared with her brother. Again there was a large Turkish stove to help against the chill. While Sylvana, the foreigner, had turned to old-fashioned, becushioned Turkish luxury in her rooms, the younger two had furnished their salon as though they could not decide between European and Turkish furnishings, and thus did justice to neither. As Turks, they had excellent taste, while their adaptations of much that was European left something to be desired. There were Middle Eastern touches of tilework and mother-of-pearl, fine carpets on the floor, and, in contrast, rather heavy graceless furniture of walnut or mahogany set stiffly at attention. Along one wall shelves displayed a collection of small art objects behind closed glass doors.

"My brother is busy in his laboratory so we will not wait for him," Nursel said. "There are times when he does not come to meals at all. He has made a study of diseases of the Middle East and at present he is working on a new drug for the treatment of a certain virulent eye disease."

"Will Mr. Radburn join you at lunch?" Tracy asked.

"Who is to know?" Nursel spoke lightly. "Our guest does as he pleases."

They sat at a table set for four, and a servant

brought hot clear soup with crescents of vegetables in the broth.

"I must warn you that there is a crisis," Nursel said as they began to eat. "My brother does not ordinarily lose his temper. Perhaps he is not always a reasonable man, but he has a good disposition and is very kind when he is not angry. Today he is very angry with Mr. Radburn."

She would have left the matter there, but Tracy, eager to learn whatever she could of Miles Radburn, questioned her openly.

"What has he done to make your brother angry?"

Again Nursel's dislike of the artist was evident. "Yesterday Murat wished to use our caique to cross the Bosporus for an important appointment, but Mr. Radburn had taken it himself. My brother was most inconvenienced. There is a small motorboat also, but Ahmet Effendi had gone on an errand across the Bosporus in that. Murat is still much disturbed." Nursel's dark eyes danced with sudden sly mischief. "I must warn you that it is better for a woman to cast down her eyes and take no sides when my brother is angry. While he is a modern Turk and a great admirer of Mustapha Kemal, I can tell you he is given to the old beliefs when it comes to women. I am supposed to be emancipated. But you will see."

Her words and manner suggested that Murat's

sister had a mind of her own that was not altogether acquiescent, for all that she seemed to move in obedient meekness about this twin establishment.

As they were finishing their soup, Dr. Erim appeared. He was a man of medium height, darkly handsome. Though he was a number of years older, the stamp of family resemblance marked him as Nursel's brother and his eyes were as large and lustrous as hers—true Turkish eyes. Thick black hair was brushed back from a fine forehead and his nose had an aquiline look that gave his face a faintly sinister cast.

He bowed over Tracy's hand gallantly, clearly a man who appreciated the company of women. He was more friendly toward her than anyone else in this house had been, with none of Nursel's suggestion of holding herself off even as she went through the gestures of hospitality. He asked Tracy pertinent questions about herself and why she was here, yet with no suspicious probing. Though he did not seem to take her work with *Views* seriously, he at least treated her as a woman. A fact that was somewhat reassuring after Miles Radburn's cool dismissal of her. At the same time she found Dr. Erim's attentive manner a little disquieting. This was a game she'd had little practice in playing. For Anabel it had come naturally, but Tracy had always recognized that she could not be another Anabel.

"It is pleasant that you have come to visit us in Istanbul, Miss Hubbard," Dr. Erim said. "Even though I fear this trip will prove a waste of your time."

"I've already begun work for Mr. Radburn," Tracy told him. "Why is it a waste of time if I help in the preparation of material for his book?"

Murat Erim shrugged. "This is work which should be done by a Turk. Mr. Radburn is an outsider. It is not possible that he will understand our ancient mosaics as a Turk would understand them."

Tracy found herself speaking up in defense of Miles's project. "Mr. Radburn seems to have done a great deal of research. The editors of *Views* feel that the book will be an important one."

"No doubt, no doubt," said Dr. Erim blandly and let the matter go.

During the meal he did most of the talking. He explained how the *dolmas* were made with vine leaves stuffed with savory rice, nuts, and currants, and extolled the Turkish predilection for flavoring everything with lemon juice. Tracy helped herself from the plate of freshly cut lemons on the table and found that a few drops improved the flavor of lamb.

While they ate, Dr. Erim spoke of his sister too, mentioning her almost in the same breath with the food, and as though she could no more hear him than could one of the vegetables on his plate.

72

"Nursel is an example of what Turkey is doing for women," he said proudly. "Today is not like the old times. Everything is possible for women now. You know that my sister received training to be a physician?"

Tracy looked at the Turkish girl in surprise, but Nursel shook her head, deprecating her brother's words.

"Please—Murat knows I did not continue with my studies. My father and my two brothers overestimated my ability. They were too enthusiastic about arranging my life in the new pattern. I did not complete my training."

"Nevertheless, she is now most useful in my laboratory," Dr. Erim said. "That is, when I can persuade her to help me there. She is often busy with social events, or with doing her hair in the latest fashion, or in helping Mrs. Erim with her perfume-making." He sniffed the air and made a slight grimace. "Even my laboratory has taken to smelling of attar of roses!"

"Which may improve it," Nursel said, faintly mocking. "Guinea pigs and mice do not of themselves furnish a pleasant atmosphere. If you wish, I will help you this afternoon."

They were halfway through the meal when Miles Radburn appeared, and at once silence fell upon the table. The artist took his place without apology for being late, but he did launch at once into an explanation about the boat.

"Sylvana has told me you were inconvenienced," he said to Dr. Erim. "I'm sorry. I'd supposed the boat was free for the afternoon, and there was a matter I wanted to check as soon as possible."

There could be a burning quality concentrated in Murat Erim's dark eyes. He was restraining himself with difficulty, it appeared, though the reason for his annoyance seemed out of proportion to the cause.

"It would be better, perhaps, if you asked permission to use the boat first," he said, breathing a bit heavily.

"Of course I asked permission." Miles gave his attention to the soup. "Sylvana said it would be quite all right to use it for my errand. As I've said, I'm sorry if I inconvenienced you."

Dr. Erim stared at him, and Tracy thought uncomfortably that this was how hatred would look. She did not believe she had ever seen it exhibited so strongly in a man's eyes.

"There are times," Dr. Erim said, "when I forget that I am not master in my father's house."

Nursel flashed a sidelong glance at her brother and then looked at the food on her plate. Miles said nothing. It was as though, having made his apology, he had shut himself away from them, and Tracy remembered what Mr. Hornwright had said about a wall. Miles Radburn had gone behind one now and was indifferent to the others at the table.

Dr. Erim too fell into a silence that was heavy with resentment. Sitting next to him, Tracy noticed that he drew from his pocket a short string of yellowed ivory beads and began to play them through his fingers. Bead by bead, each one slipped along a cord until he reached the large finial bead that joined two ends of the strand in a sort of tassel. He toyed with the large bead briefly and then went on around the string again until the absent movement of his fingers seemed to calm him.

Nursel saw Tracy's interest and spoke to her brother. "Perhaps Miss Hubbard has never seen a *tespih* before. You must show her this one."

Dr. Erim started as though he had not noted the occupation of his hands, and held up the ivory beads with a faint smile. "We find that busy fingers often calm the mind and quiet the nerves," he said and handed the beads to Tracy.

The ivory was warm from his fingers as she ran the beads through her own. "Are they prayer beads?" Tracy asked.

Dr. Erim shook his head. "Not these. A proper strand of prayer beads must have exactly thirty-three beads in its length. These are shorter. I've heard the English call them 'fidget strings.' They are only for the therapeutic purpose of busying the hands. You will see them in the hands of men all through the Middle East."

"How strange that women do not need the

same outlet." Nursel raised her own pretty, well-manicured hands, wriggling her fingers. "I suppose we are expected to be so thoroughly occupied with household tasks that our hands are busy enough. Murat has many *tespihler* in his collection. You must show Miss Hubbard sometime."

"Why not?" Dr. Erim said. "Let me show her some of them now, while we wait for dessert."

With a key from his pocket he unlocked a glass cabinet against the wall and reached toward a shelf, where more of the beads were spread out in display or piled in glowing heaps of mixed color. He chose several strands at random and brought them to the table.

They were lovely things. Some of the less expensive were endlessly varied in their coloring. There were others of greater value made of ivory and amber. Some of the amber beads were still in their reddish, unaged state, while others were a golden, honey brown. All were smoothly rounded, without carving, to give a proper texture for the fingers. In the little heap on the table was a single tespih of black jet, gleaming darkly among the rest.

Dr. Erim reached into the heap and picked it up. "This is typically Turkish," he said. "A strand of black amber."

Tracy's fingers, moving idly among the beads, stilled. Perhaps it was only her imagination, but it seemed to her that everyone in the room was staring at the black beads in Dr. Erim's hands. Even Miles Radburn was paying somber attention. Ahmet, who had just come into the room with a tray of stemmed glasses containing rose sherbet, allowed his attention to flicker briefly over the glittering heap and focus on the black.

For Tracy, it was as if the sound of Anabel's voice echoed through the room. The high hysterical note of her sister's telephone call from Istanbul was so sharply clear in Tracy's mind that she half expected others in the room to hear and respond to it. Anabel had wailed something about "black amber"—though her confused words had meant nothing to Tracy. Now, in this house, the phrase had been repeated and it rang so insistent a note in her mind that Tracy could not let the moment escape without catching up these key words.

"What is black amber?" she asked.

Murat Erim dropped the black beads at her place. "It is a form of jet which is mined near our eastern border in a town called Erzerum. It is a popular stone often used for pins and other jewelry, as well as for making tespihler."

Tracy picked up the strand. The smooth jet shone intensely black in her hands, but, though she ran the beads through her fingers several times, they seemed in no way remarkable.

Dr. Erim returned the black tespih to the heap

and started to gather up the strands to make room for Ahmet's dessert plates. Then he paused and gestured toward the tespihler.

"You must choose for yourself one of these, Miss Hubbard. As a souvenir of Turkey. Please— any that you like."

Tracy thanked him, hesitating. She touched the black amber, picked it up, and it seemed to her that the room hushed, waiting. Carelessly she let the strand ripple through her fingers, discarding it, and chose an inexpensive string of gray-blue beads.

"It is very kind of you," she said. "May I have this blue one? It matches my dress."

"But of course," he said. "Keep it for yourself."

The moment of stillness, of waiting, was past. The room seemed to move and breathe again. Dr. Erim swept up the rest of the beads and replaced them on the shelves, locking the cabinet. Tracy held up her choice, allowing the tespih to dangle from her fingers, suddenly aware that Murat was looking, not at the beads, but directly at her with an odd, questioning expression on his face. Ahmet was no longer paying attention and Miles had again retired behind his wall. Yet Tracy had received the momentary impression that the attention of the room had been upon the black beads, and that Murat was interested in her rejection of them more than he was interested in the choice she had made.

Nursel broke the brief silence, making conversation almost nervously. "You must tell us about yourself, Miss Hubbard. What part of the United States are you from?"

Tracy dropped the tespih into her lap. Off guard, she answered readily. "I was born in the Midwest—in Iowa," she said, and at once could have bitten her tongue. But if it meant anything to Miles or the other two that she came from the state where Anabel was born, no one showed it and Tracy hurried on.

"I've always wanted to live in New York. I love the smell of printer's ink and I wanted to be in the center of publishing."

She knew she was chattering and found it difficult to stop. It was a relief when Dr. Erim, having recovered from his tiff with Miles Radburn, joined in the talk again. There was no further clash between the two men, and Miles still seemed unaware of how greatly he had annoyed the other. Tracy ate the delicately flavored sherbet and enjoyed a piece of *locum*— the richly sweet Turkish delight.

When they left the table, she turned hesitantly to Miles Radburn, but before she could ask about the afternoon he spoke to her curtly.

"I prefer that you let your—ah—housekeeping go for the moment. I won't be around to answer questions and I'd rather you keep out of my papers when I'm not present."

He did not wait for agreement, but went off toward the stairs. Ahmet held the door for Tracy, bowing as she came through, and she had a feeling that he understood Miles's words, indeed had a greater understanding of English than he pretended.

She returned to her room, feeling more than a little annoyed with herself. She had not needed Miles Radburn's presence that morning. She had asked him no questions. Yet only when she was angry enough did she seem able to face him with sufficient determination to gain her own way.

The gray-blue tespih was still in her hand and she studied it absently, thinking of the black amber. Had the sense of arrested attention she felt been wholly imaginary, or had everyone in the room really watched her when she held up the black beads just before she discarded them? The strand had seemed innocent enough in itself. Yet Anabel's frightened voice persisted in her mind. This too was part of the ominous puzzle that would not let her be until she found the answer.

She put the beads aside, ready now to face the thing she had been holding off throughout the morning. She must confront the fact of her sister's portrait on the wall of Radburn's room, with all the ramifications of why it was there, if, as Anabel had implied, he had turned against her. The urge to see it again was so strong that

80

Tracy's next step seemed inevitable. With Miles Radburn away, this was the time.

She opened the door of her room a crack and listened intently. The vast gloom of the salon had a thick feeling of unstirred emptiness. She could hear the voices of servants from the depths of the house, but there seemed to be no one up here. She opened her door wide and looked across the nearly empty expanse toward the door of Miles's study. It stood slightly ajar and she went toward it, moving quietly.

# 4

WHEN SHE REACHED the study she paused again to listen. The inner silence was complete. Cautiously she pushed the door to a wider angle so that she could look into the room. And paused in surprise, for it was not, after all, empty. The houseman, Ahmet, stood before Miles's drawing table, apparently studying the script upon it in utter concentration. When he finally sensed her presence and looked up, his dark face did not change. He stared at her with unblinking eyes, his expression telling her nothing. After a moment he stepped back from the board, made her his usual polite bow, and gestured toward the calligraphy with one long-fingered hand.

"*Hanimefendi*," he said, "—this word of Allah."

The explanation seemed clear. For an uneasy moment she had felt there was something wrong about the man's quiet, absorbed presence in this room, but there was no reason why he should not, as a good Moslem, study the word of the Koran that Miles Radburn had copied.

"Do you read the old Turkish script, Ahmet Effendi?" she asked.

He shook his head without indication that he understood and slipped past her from the room. So softly and smoothly did he move that she scarcely heard his tread upon the stairs, though she stood in the doorway looking after him. When she was certain he had gone, Tracy crossed the study to Miles's bedroom door and opened it. Her heart began to thud in her ears, but there was no one there, and she went to the foot of the bed where she could best see the portrait of her sister.

This picture, she felt sure, had never been exhibited. It must have been painted during the early time of Anabel's marriage to Miles Radburn. She knew enough about his work to recognize the excellence of the portrayal, though the picture was unlike anything else he had done. The misty-silver quality that lay over the whole, with the lovely, tragic face emerging from it, the eyes in dark, dramatic contrast, was totally different from the usual Radburn touch. Working in a manner that was wholly virile, he had nevertheless intensified the femininity of his subject. As always, he was a superb draughtsman, and the excellence of the painting gave its emotional effect upon the beholder all the more impact.

Out of childhood memory haunting lines of verse came to Anabel's sister, and she spoke them aloud whimsically.

> This maiden she lived with no other thought
> Than to love and be loved by me.

But that was Annabel Lee, and this Anabel had been mistaken in her loving. In his portrait the artist had caught the very essence of her being—a sort of gossamer tension that had always frightened Tracy. The same look had been upon her that day eight years ago when Anabel had come to Iowa to tell her fifteen-year-old sister that she was to be married.

Tracy had played hookey from school that day in order to meet Anabel's train. They had gone to lunch together in a drab little restaurant, where they could sit in a booth at the back and hope to pass unnoticed. Anabel had been gay and electric, yet as gossamer as mist—hard to pin down. Never had Tracy seen her look more beautiful, more magical, and her own heart had ached a little in the old way—not only with love, but with something of envy as well. To be like Anabel— the wish had been a part of her for as long as she could remember, though she knew its foolishness, knew it must be thrust back, contradicted. It had seemed to Tracy in those days that Anabel would always have what she wished, merely for the taking. While Tracy, following inescapably in her shimmering wake, must compete with a vision she could never live up to.

At lunch that day Anabel had eaten like a bird and talked in high excitement. "I posed for him, Bunny darling," she said, using a pet name for Tracy that went back to Easter rabbit days. "That's how I got to meet him. He thought I had interesting bones, or something. And some sort of quality he wanted to catch on canvas. Then he began to worry about me—the way people do." The high, light laughter made heads turn, and Anabel stilled it at once.

Yes—people had always worried about Anabel. Her mother had worried. Tracy's father, Anabel's stepfather, was the only one who had refused to worry. When Anabel had run away from home shortly after Tracy's twelfth birthday, he had not concerned himself. Indeed, he had probably been relieved to see her go. Tracy had hated him a little, and worried as much as her mother had.

Nevertheless, though their mother had suffered deeply—Anabel had always been her favorite— she had lacked the strength to stand up to her husband in Anabel's defense. Knowing this, Anabel would never come home. She wrote to

Tracy now and then—quick, brief notes that did not say very much, while Tracy wrote long, though sometimes laborious letters because of her instinct to preserve whatever tenuous thread still bound Anabel to a family, if only through her younger sister. It had seemed necessary for someone to care about holding onto Anabel, and Tracy had never stopped trying. On the occasions when Anabel had come west it was to see Tracy secretly, never her mother or stepfather.

At home, life had been difficult for Tracy. Her mother had always blamed her for the occurrence that had brought matters to a head and sent Anabel away from home. At the time, Tracy had accepted her mother's evaluation and blamed herself, indulging in an orgy of twelve-year-old suffering and self-reproach. She knew better now; knew that she had been no more than a chance instrument. The fact that she had behaved with childish jealousy was not something to brood over for the rest of her life. Eventually, Anabel would have taken the same step whether Tracy had played her role or not. This was the continuing puzzle of Anabel—that she must hurl herself headlong toward disaster, when to other eyes there seemed so little need.

After Anabel had left home there were new walls around Tracy, and watchful suspicion, as if they only waited for her to do something wrong. She, who was accustomed to being open about all she did, who expected to be trusted, found herself faced with doubt and distrust on every hand. All because Anabel had gone before. Her love for her sister had been increasingly mixed with resentment. She knew now that this had been a healthy, self-preserving emotion, and sufficiently justified. But at the time she had not understood and there had been a sense of guilt. Even now that old feeling of being somehow to blame because she had been jealous of her sister reached out of the past to give pause to the grownup Tracy and make her question her feelings toward Anabel.

That day in the restaurant Tracy had tried to take blame upon herself for what had occurred to drive Anabel from home. But, as always, Anabel would not listen.

"It would have happened anyway, darling," she had said with unusual frankness. "You mustn't reproach yourself. Not ever."

She had gone on to speak of her coming marriage to a man who knew "almost all" about her, and who loved her as she was. She had refused Tracy's plea to make things up with her mother.

"I don't want to," Anabel had said and the words were final. There could be stubbornness in Anabel too, though of the kind that sometimes slipped away and left you seemingly unopposed when you had really been defeated.

"I'm sorry, Bunny darling," she went on, "but I never want him to meet my mother or your father. He thinks I'm all alone with no one in the world to turn to—which is almost true. He likes it that way. That's why I can't even tell him about you."

Her decision had hurt Tracy, yet she had accepted it. Anabel had found someone new to worry about her, someone closer at hand who could really look after her. The relief to that very young Tracy had been considerable.

They were going to visit Miles's relatives in England, and then go out to Turkey for their honeymoon, Anabel told her. Istanbul had always fascinated Miles as a painter. He wanted to try something besides portraits.

"He's so—so accountable and wonderful," she told her sister in warm excitement. "I can depend on him. He won't let me hurt myself. For the first time in my whole foolish life I'm going to be happy. And safe. When we're on our way, I'll send you something, darling, so you'll know everything is fine. Something that will make you think of me whenever you wear it."

Anabel had kept her word. By airmail had come the little feather pin that Tracy had worn ever since. A pin that said to her: "Here's a feather for your cap, Bunny darling. Wear it and remember me. You haven't done such a bad job raising me!"

So Tracy had worn the pin and warmed to the thought of Anabel's happiness, reassured that everything would now be all right for the sister she adored. Even then she had begun to suspect the flaw in Anabel that was like a crack in fine glaze—something for which there was no cure. But she closed her eyes to the flaw and kept her love and loyalty intact.

Now as Tracy touched her fingers to the pin in the familiar way and looked up at her sister's face, tears burned her lids. Anabel had not been safe, after all. Toward the end she had apparently been far from happy, and according to her Miles had not proved as dependable as she had expected. The faint green gleam of Anabel's eyes peered beneath the smudge of dark lashes and there was no telling what they saw, or what the girl behind them was thinking.

A voice spoke abruptly behind her, a bleak chill in the sound. "May I ask what you are doing in this room?"

Tracy whirled in dismay to find Miles Radburn in the doorway. There was more than a winter chill in his face. Anger burned beneath ice, and Tracy felt alarmed. Anabel had warned her of danger, and, though Tracy had somewhat discounted her sister's hysteria, she was suddenly afraid. She snatched at the first straw that offered.

"I—I'm sorry. I know I shouldn't have come in

here. But Mrs. Erim showed me the picture this morning, and—and I couldn't resist coming to look at it again. It must be—I mean I've seen some of your other portraits—and this must be one of your finest."

"The picture is not on display, Miss Hubbard," Miles Radburn said. "If you are to stay for the week I've promised, you will have to resist such impulses. I suggested, I believe, that you stay out of my study this afternoon."

Tracy nodded mutely, unable to force words past the tight feeling in her throat, hardly able to see him through the blur in her eyes. He stood aside to let her return to the study. Then he went to his drawing table and seated himself on the high stool before it. She had been dismissed.

At the door to the salon she paused with her hand upon the brass knob. There was something he ought to know, and she could at least tell him this.

"When—when I came in a little while ago," she faltered, "Ahmet was here, studying that calligraphy strip you're doing. When I surprised him, he said those were the words of Allah and went away."

Miles did not trouble to look at her, nor did he comment. He simply waited for her to go, and if he had any interest in Ahmet's actions, he did not reveal it.

Tracy managed the toe latch at the bottom of

the door awkwardly, and as she did so the white cat slipped past her into the room. With an air of being entirely at home, the animal sprang upon Miles's desk, moving so gracefully, so lightly, that not a paper was disturbed. There she seated herself and stared at the artist out of wide green eyes. Anabel's cat. The cat to which her sister had given Tracy's nickname of "Bunny." Out of loneliness, perhaps? Out of an aching for someone from home to talk to?

Miles raised a hand as if to cuff the animal from the desk. Outraged, Tracy moved first. She caught the white cat up in her arms and faced him defiantly.

"Poor Yasemin!" she cried, her cheek against the cat's pricked ears.

"That's not its name," said Miles sharply. "It's called—"

"Bunny," Tracy provided. "I know. That's a silly name for a cat. So I've renamed her. She's my cat now. While I'm here, that is. And any man who would strike a cat—"

He swore then. Quite loudly and firmly. Good British oaths that had the sound of a seafaring nation behind them. Tracy fled with the cat in her arms and heard the loud slamming of the door behind her.

She carried Yasemin back to her room and sat down with the small warm thing in her arms. She was in real trouble now. If ever Miles Radburn

90

guessed who she was, he would send her straight home. She was sure of it.

"If only you could tell me about Anabel," she murmured to the cat. "Yasemin, what am I to do?"

Yasemin, however, had received enough of cuddling and human emotions. She scratched Tracy on the wrist, squirmed out of her arms, and leaped to the middle of the bed. There she washed herself neatly, sponging away the human touch with rasping tongue and firm pink paws.

Tracy stared at the scratch absently. What had happened might have been funny, she supposed— his getting furious and swearing at her over a cat. But it was not funny because of Anabel. Not only because of the phone call, but because of the letter she had received from Anabel more than six months ago.

Her sister had written that she and Miles had returned to Istanbul at the invitation of a good friend who had entertained them in her home during their honeymoon in Turkey. Miles was not painting just now, but he had developed an interest in Turkish mosaics. Mrs. Erim had offered him a base from which to operate in his research, and certain living arrangements had been made with her. All this by way of explanation. What Anabel wanted was to have Tracy drop everything and come out to Istanbul at once for a visit.

"If you'll come, I'll own up to having a sister," she had written. "I need you, darling. Things are going terribly wrong and I know it would help to talk to you."

It was not the first time Tracy had received such a summons. A few years after her marriage, Anabel had paid Tracy's expenses to New York one summer and Tracy had gone for a few weeks' visit against her parents' wishes. The way her sister looked had alarmed her. She had been thin and highly nervous. Flashes of the old gay Anabel had alternated infrequently with an Anabel who had only complaints about the dull life she led and resentment of what she regarded as her husband's neglect. Miles was away in England at the time. Had he been in New York, Tracy would have tried to see him, in spite of Anabel's wishes. As it was, she had discounted her sister's lamentations to some degree and tried to calm her and talk a little sense into her. For the most part the visit had been ineffectual.

Yet, strangely enough, Tracy had never lost her belief in some deep-rooted worth in Anabel. The good qualities were there, if only one could get at them. She was talented in so many ways. She could sing and dance, and if she had possessed a drive toward achievement she might have succeeded in the theater. Perhaps her most remarkable gift was the one of making life seem gay and carefree to those around her. She possessed a talent for laughter and for the generating of laughter. Even Nursel had felt this and had spoken of their running off to be free of sober faces and a restriction upon laughter. Yet the Anabel who had this gift for life was being destroyed by another Anabel. For some of the world's gifted there seemed to be this strange pull toward self-destruction that those who loved them could only watch in bewilderment and try, however hopelessly, to oppose.

Tracy knew only that she must hold to that slender tie by which Anabel allowed herself to be bound. After the visit to New York, she had continued to write the letters her sister seemed to want. It was all she could do.

Eventually she had been old enough to escape the impossible atmosphere that had been built up around her at home. By the time she moved to New York, however, Anabel and Miles were living out of the country and there were no meetings with them in the two years she had been in the east.

When Anabel's letter of summons had come six months ago, Tracy had felt both sympathetic and annoyed. She knew very well that Anabel loved to exaggerate and dramatize, and she suspected that nothing practical could be accomplished by flying to Istanbul with such dispatch as Anabel requested. Tracy might hold her hand and listen to her grievances and perhaps help her temporarily to a better balance. She wrote firmly to Anabel and she did not go to Turkey. She would come later, she promised. If she left now, while she was still a trainee in a new department, the company might not want her back. Anabel must understand how important this job was to her.

Anabel had not answered her letter, though Tracy had written again, promising to manage a trip during the summer. There had been a silence of months—which was not unusual. Tracy, absorbed and happy, free for the first time in her life, had put worry about her sister aside. Anabel would forgive her eventually, and Tracy had let the thread between them slacken.

Then, only three months ago, had come that wild and confused telephone call. Tracy had hardly recognized her voice, so upset had Anabel sounded.

"I never knew it would come to this!" she wailed over the wire. "I never knew Miles could be so wickedly cruel!"

This sounded like more of the usual thing and Tracy broke in, trying to quiet her, to make sense of what she was saying, but the girl at the other end of the wire ran on incoherently, and there had been a true note of terror in her voice.

"I need you desperately, Bunny. I shouldn't ask you to come—perhaps it would be dangerous for you to come. But there's no one else I can turn to.

I must talk to someone. Someone who can get me away from here!"

Tracy spoke to her sternly then. "Anabel, listen to me! Get hold of yourself and tell me quietly what's the matter."

Anabel took a breath of air in a big gulp and went right on. "It's the black amber again! It turned up yesterday and I know it's the end of everything. The secret is hidden with the Sultan Valide—remember that, if you come. And don't let anyone know you're my sister. If they don't know, they won't touch you. Bunny, I'm afraid— I don't want to die! Bunny—"

She broke off and there was a moment's silence in which Tracy pleaded with her to speak quietly, to explain. Then Anabel said in a whisper, "Someone's coming up the stairs." There was a long silence. Tracy held her breath, trying desperately to hear what was happening all those thousands of miles away in Istanbul. Then had come the most terrifying thing of all. Anabel had not spoken again, but she had whistled softly, incongruously into the telephone—the mere snatch of an old nursery rhyme: *London Bridge is falling down, falling down, falling down . . .* She whistled that much of it before the phone went dead.

The snatch of tune had taken Tracy back to her childhood in an agonizing wave of memory. When she and Anabel had lived at home, there had been many a secret signal between them in the form of nursery tunes they both knew well. *Here we go round the mulberry bush* . . . meant, "All's well. The storm is over." But *London Bridge* was the panic call. It meant, "Here comes ultimate disaster. Get ready for the roof to fall in." And it was never used except for desperate emergency.

That day, over the wire from Istanbul, Anabel had given her the disaster signal, their own secret "Mayday" call—and hung up the receiver.

Tracy tried at once to call Istanbul back. It had taken forever, and when someone speaking English had come on at last it was to say that Anabel was unable to come to the phone. Tracy asked for Miles, only to be told that he was out of town. In the end she had given up without identifying herself. She had tried to stem her own terror by telling herself that this was just the sort of wildly dramatic trick Anabel loved to play. But the conviction had persisted that this time the game was real.

The next day the news of Anabel's death had been in the papers, of front-page importance because of Miles's name.

Tracy had broken a long silence and telephoned her father in Iowa, only to be told that this was exactly what he had expected. This was the road down which Anabel herself had chosen to travel. It was the end she had deserved.

She cabled anonymous flowers for Anabel's grave and she began planning at once to get to Istanbul. She could not let her sister's sudden death, on the heels of that confused phone call, go unchallenged, unquestioned. Yet for once Anabel's words had bred a certain caution in her. She knew instinctively that if she went out at once, announcing herself as Anabel's sister, the questions would go unanswered. And she had a responsibility now. She had not gone to Anabel's help. She had regarded the earlier letter as the usual cry of "wolf!" But this time something had been dreadfully wrong and she could not rest until she knew what it was. She had never accepted whole-cloth the things Anabel had said about Miles. But now she must get to Istanbul and learn about him for herself.

She had lacked money for an immediate trip, or even credit to borrow for so wild a venture when she could not admit to being Anabel's sister. Then Mr. Hornwright had opened a door and she had dashed through without looking back.

As Anabel's half sister, she had been able to come here under her own name and identity, since even Anabel's maiden name was different from her own. As long as this incognito held, she would be safe from whatever threat Anabel had hinted at. The leads she had to follow were few: Anabel's outburst against Miles, which though not especially new, was more extreme. A reference to "black amber" and to someone referred to as a Sultan Valide who was in possession of a "secret." On the surface all wildly improbable. Yet Anabel had been frightened. Anabel had died. Driven to suicide by what degree of desperation? And by whom?

From what she had seen of Miles Radburn, he seemed the most likely instrument. She could imagine him driving a woman almost crazy. Particularly if she were so foolish as to love him. Yet there was the paradox of Anabel's picture on his wall. And there was Tracy's own voice of reason which told her that not everything Anabel said and did could be taken at face value.

If only there was someone to whom she could turn with trust and confidence. Now, sitting in the room that had been Anabel's she thought again of Nursel. The girl had seemingly been Anabel's friend and she was certainly no friend of Miles Radburn. But to what extent she might be trusted Tracy did not know. It was possible that Nursel might become an ally in her search for the truth. She needed an ally badly in this maze of hidden motives and secretive behavior, yet she did not dare to trust anyone yet.

There were as many undercurrents in the murk of these problems as there were out there in the stream of the Bosporus, where Anabel had ended her life. Tension and dislike were evident between Dr. Erim and Miles Radburn. There was tension as well between Murat Erim and his sister-in-law, Sylvana, who held more power in this household than the brother and sister felt she should.

As Tracy sat there, turning futilely within the perimeter of her own thoughts, Halide tapped at her door. The maid carried a small pile of books in her hands and, when Tracy called to her to enter, she trotted into the room and deposited them on the table with a smile. Yasemin seized the opportunity and moved like lightning, flying through the open door as though she had waited here a prisoner.

When Halide had gone, Tracy looked wonderingly at the four titles. The books were all about Turkey. One was a modern guidebook which she had hurried through at home. Another was an account of Atatürk's campaign and reforms, and there was a book about the ancient peoples of Turkey. The fourth volume was an account of Ottoman Empire days, detailing the stories of fantastic wealth and power, with its deterioration into corruption and greed and shocking cruelty.

Mrs. Erim might have sent her the first two, and possibly the fourth, but surely only Miles Radburn would have in his possession the third volume. She opened to a flyleaf and saw that his name was written there and in the others as well.

Was this an apology for his loss of temper? she

wondered. For the space of a moment she softened toward him and then smiled wryly at herself. She must never forget how attractive this man had seemed to Anabel in the beginning, and how wrong Anabel had, admittedly, been about him. It would be safer to dislike him intensely, to remember him as coldly frightening, as a man who could strike out violently at a cat. Somehow, she must dig in her toes and stay, but she must not be drawn into friendliness toward Miles Radburn.

Thus bolstered in her own determination, she sat down and opened a volume at random. She forced herself to read and tried to think about what she was reading. This was an account of Turkey's earliest inhabitants, the Hittites—a people of some consequence in the ancient world. They had been mentioned in the Bible. The lady named Bathsheba, who had led David astray, was a Hittite. Indeed, the Hittites had in their day rivaled the Egyptians and the Babylonians in importance. Behind them in Turkey they had left friezes and statues of remarkable beauty. After the Hittites had come the Semitic invaders and the conquerors from the West—from Greece and Rome. There had been a great intermingling of races so that Turks were Indo-European, with a dash of Mongolian thrown in.

All of which was undoubtedly fascinating to

know. But the persistent echo of a nursery rhyme kept time with the words as she read, and Tracy could not care less about Turkish history at the moment. Indeed, she could not sit still in this room for a moment longer. She flung down the book and jumped up to get her coat. The afternoon was growing late and she must get outdoors and release this restless anxiety that would not let her be still. Only physical effort would serve. She'd had enough of the four walls of Anabel's room.

There was no one in the upper salon. The door of Miles's study remained closed. The white cat was nowhere to be seen. Tracy ran lightly downstairs to the marble corridor that bisected the ground floor and found her way to the door on the land side. Turning from the paved driveway that ran between yali and kiosk, she followed the path along the hillside above the Bosporus until it ended at a small gate set in the stone wall that surrounded the property. Beyond, the main road, having curved around Erim grounds, resumed its direction, running north, paralleling the water, though not close to it.

She expected the gate to be locked, but it was only latched, and she opened it and went through. The sun had dipped partially behind the hills of Thrace across the water, but there was still time for a stroll before it grew completely dark. She followed the scrubby grass along the road's edge so that she need not worry about passing traffic. The nearest village, apparently, was on the other side of the Erim property. Here were pleasant woods, still winter sere, though green shoots were beginning to push through the brown grass underfoot.

Curving, the road dipped toward the water and brought her at length to a large and ornate wrought-iron gate hung askew on dilapidated hinges, permanently ajar. To Tracy's mind there was always something both intriguing and touching about a ruin. She could not resist this one and stepped through the gap in the broken gate.

What had once been a fine garden spread before her in wild disarray. Vines and creepers and weedy shrubs had made a tangle of the place. All about were great plane trees and horse chestnuts with their candled blooms ready to bud anew with the coming of spring. A monstrous rhododendron hedge that would later be bright with blossoms had grown unrestrained, forming a wall that darkened the far side of the garden on the right. Straight ahead shallow steps led down to the water, their marble shimmering rosy-white in the lengthening rays of the sun. Beyond, dark water swept softly past.

The house rose on her left and, for all that it stood in ruin, the stamp of former wealth and eminence lay upon it. It was no ordinary house—

there was too much marble showing through the curtain of shabby vines that overhung it. Once it had risen two stories above the basement floor, but she could see that toward the water the roof had fallen in upon the upper story and most of the wall on the water side had crumbled into the Bosporus. Yet a good part of the house stood intact, and she ventured toward the flight of marble steps that led to the marble framework of an empty door.

At the foot of the steps the pattern of a great circular mosaic lay partially revealed. It would be beautiful, she thought, if it were uncovered, but now it was earth-encrusted and weed-grown with the tangle that reached to the very steps. So romantic an invitation as the doorway offered was not to be resisted.

Tracy climbed the marble steps. The wooden door had rotted upon its hinges and fallen inward. She stepped over broken timbers and found herself inside the ruin. What remained of graceful arches that had framed windows on either side of the door revealed a fretwork of fine carving. Part of the ceiling was gone and the roof above as well, so that the house stood open to the water. What had once been a palace on the Bosporus had become a haven for lizards and mice, a nesting place for birds.

Worms and termites and general rot had broken the floor of the great central room in a number of places, and she stepped with care. One wall had bloomed with painted flowers that were now faded to a pale, dreamlike beauty. There was tarnished tilework over a doorway, and she studied it in the graying light from the water. Her sorting of Miles Radburn's drawings had given her a new interest in such things.

The rear of the house seemed fairly sound and further rooms stretched away in sheltered darkness. The sun had set by now and dusk was coming more quickly than she had expected. The chill in the air had intensified and a curious uneasiness possessed her in this haunted place.

Tracy hesitated on the threshold of a farther room, seized by a desire to flee from this crumbling, eerie place. Stepping cautiously, she went through the doorway into the next shadowed room beyond.

# 5

AS SHE MOVED ON, filled with uneasiness, yet held by a strange desire to persist, she felt something soft beneath her foot. When she bent to pick it up, she saw that it was a silk scarf. Its colors were washed out in the dim light, but it seemed to be a woman's scarf and she wondered at its presence here. She put it into the pocket of her coat and went on.

Around the turn of a dim hallway where a

staircase led upward, she came to a sudden halt. Had she heard something? Was there someone else wandering about this ghostly place? The woman who had dropped the scarf, perhaps?

As she hesitated, a sound of whispering came suddenly clear, and then ceased to be whispering as someone spoke angrily aloud. Tracy drew back beneath the shadow of an arch, dismayed. The presence of others here seemed somehow less innocent than her own. The words were in Turkish. She could make out only that there seemed to be a man and a woman, and that they were arguing heatedly, their voices distorted and strained. The arguers must have been two or more rooms away, and Tracy started warily back along the course by which she had come, seeking the opening to the big main salon. Upon its threshold she paused, hesitating to step into the open where light from empty windows on the water would touch her clearly. As she paused, the man's voice rose above the other, speaking a name sharply. "Hubbard," he said and rushed on in Turkish, enclosing her name in words that had a menacing ring.

Her own name spoken in this atmosphere of angry conspiracy was terrifying. All the warnings of Anabel's letter swept back. Wanting only to escape unseen, Tracy started heedlessly across the floor, forgetting the rotting wood underfoot. As she stepped down hard, a board cracked, throwing her sharply to her knees. She could feel the scrape of splintered wood across one shin, the smarting of pain.

The noise of her fall betrayed her. Immediately the voices stilled. There was a breathless pause, followed by the sound of running feet, the hurried sounds of flight. She could not see them go, but they must have fled through another door and into the garden, rushing away in the gathering darkness. A guilty flight, it seemed, and she was glad they had gone without approaching her.

She gave her attention to her own predicament and pulled herself out of the hole into which she had fallen. She was examining her torn stocking, feeling gingerly of her skinned leg when a sound nearby made her look up sharply.

There was a fourth person there in the ruins. A man stood silhouetted against water and fading sky. There was something ominous about the motionless way in which he stood looking at her, faceless with his back to the light. He had made no sound when the others had fled, and she wondered if he had been there all along, spying upon them. She could only stand where she was, waiting for him to move, to speak. He broke the silence by addressing her in Turkish and coming toward her. She saw then that it was Ahmet. She did not trust or like this soft-spoken, silent man, but at least he was not a stranger. The hand she had touched to her leg was sticky with blood, and she held it out for him to see.

"I've hurt myself," she said. "Can you help me?"

He understood the gesture at least and came at once to assist her, moving with quiet assurance. "Come, please, *hanimefendi*," he said, and she limped out of the house and toward the gate, leaning upon his arm. As they walked slowly along the road, he muttered to himself in his own language. Since all Turkish sounded explosive to Tracy's unaccustomed ears, she could not tell whether he was commiserating over her injury, or complaining because she had interrupted the meeting of two he seemed to have been watching.

They had gone only a little way when a man appeared walking toward them. He moved at the pace of an evening stroller and, as she drew near, Tracy saw that it was Murat Erim. Ahmet greeted him, gesturing toward Tracy's bleeding leg.

"You have hurt yourself?" Dr. Erim said, hurrying to her in quick concern.

She explained that she had come for a walk and had been unable to resist exploring the ruined palace. It had been foolish of her to trust the floors, and of course she had fallen. As they walked back, he questioned Ahmet in Turkish and the man answered at considerable length. Before he had finished, Dr. Erim broke in upon his words, directing him to hurry on to the house.

"We will have warm water and bandages waiting," he said when Ahmet had gone off at a trot. "My sister is well versed in dealing with such injuries. Do not concern yourself. It is fortunate that Ahmet followed you, feeling that you might lose your way in a strange place. I had wondered at finding our side gate unlocked. It is where you came through, is it not?"

She had a sudden feeling that he might be dissembling, that he was abroad for some private reason of his own and was testing her in some way.

"It is where I came through," she admitted, and did not explain that the gate had been opened by someone ahead of her.

The houseman had apparently said nothing of the two who had taken flight, and Tracy did not contradict his account.

At the house Dr. Erim took her to Sylvana's rooms. Mrs. Erim had been working in the laboratory, but she left her perfume distilling to come upstairs. When she saw Tracy's scraped and bleeding leg, she sent Ahmet at once to find Nursel. Evidently Dr. Erim did not use his medical training in such matters and, when he saw that she was in good hands, he went away.

When Nursel came, bringing her first-aid kit, the wound was duly bathed and bandaged. Sylvana asked questions of her, but again Tracy kept her own counsel. She had happened upon some sort of hornets' nest and it seemed wiser to say nothing until she was sure of her ground. The fright she had felt over hearing the angry mention of her own name lingered. Her knowledge that two people whose identity she did not know had been discussing her heatedly under strange circumstances was no more reassuring than was the fact that Ahmet had been surreptitiously observing them.

When the bandaging was done, Sylvana Erim herself accompanied her to her room, gave her tablets for the pain, and suggested that she go to bed at once. It would not be necessary to get up for dinner—the meal would be brought to her. From now on, said Sylvana, Miss Hubbard must remember not to run about in unknown places after dark.

When Mrs. Erim had gone, Tracy got ready for bed. Now that she was alone, anxiety swept back again. The fact that she had blundered unheedingly upon that clandestine meeting seemed to remove a little of the safety of her incognito. They could not know who she was, but if she stumbled upon some secret and gave cause for concern, her way might be all the more difficult in this house. Besides, what was their interest in her that her name should have been mentioned? Had it something to do with her working for Miles Radburn?

Just before she got into bed, she remembered

the scarf in her coat pocket and brought it out. It was of finely woven silk, with stripes of dark plum color that alternated with cream and ran its entire length. The pattern had a faintly familiar look, but she could not remember where she might have seen it. She could not recall that Nursel or Sylvana had worn such a scarf since she had been here.

Sylvana's medication began to relax her, making her drowsy. She lay down on the bed without turning off the light and thrust the scarf beneath her pillow, too groggy now to puzzle about it. The tablets took quick effect and she fell soundly asleep.

She must have slept for two or three hours before Nursel tapped on her door and came in, followed by Halide with a tray. Tracy wanted only to wave the food away and go back to sleep, but Nursel insisted that she have something to eat. She supervised the matter of getting Tracy up against her pillows as if she were a helpless invalid, and set the bed table across her knees. Then she dismissed Halide and drew up a chair beside the bed.

"Now," she said pleasantly, "while you refresh yourself, you must tell me all that happened when you were injured. There is something strange here. I have said nothing to Sylvana or to my brother, but I do not think you have told them all the truth."

Tracy drank hot broth and found that the fog was clearing a little. With Nursel she felt less cautious and tongue-tied, and since the girl saw through her evasion, as the others had not seemed to, she gave her an account of exactly what had happened. There had been a man and a woman in the ruined palace, both engaged in angry discussion. And Ahmet had been there too, apparently watching them unseen.

Nursel listened intently, her slender hands clasped about her knees, a look of concern in her huge dark eyes.

"I do not know what Ahmet Effendi could be doing—watching someone away from the house. This does not seem like him. He is not a good-tempered man, but he is very loyal."

"Why don't you ask him and find out?" Tracy said.

Nursel shrugged. "One might as well ask the Egyptian obelisk in Istanbul. Ahmet Effendi does not talk if he does not wish to talk. But I suppose it is his own affair if he wishes to spy on persons outside of this house."

"What if those two were someone from this house?" Tracy asked.

"Why do you think that?"

"I have no way of knowing," Tracy admitted. "But I heard someone mention my name. It was as though they were arguing about me in some way."

"About *you?*" Nursel echoed. "But this is very strange. You are sure it was your name you heard spoken?"

"I'm sure," said Tracy. She reached beneath her pillow and pulled out the scarf. "This is something I found when I went into the ruin."

The Turkish girl looked at the scarf as though it were alive and dangerous. "Please," she said in some agitation, "it is better if you do not tell this story to anyone. Not even to my brother. It will be better if you forget all this, if you know nothing about it."

"Then you know whose scarf this is? You know what this might mean?" Tracy asked bluntly.

Nursel's agitation seemed to increase. Her eyes were luminous with something like fear. "No, no, no—I know nothing! It is only that these matters are of no concern to you. Soon you will go home to New York, Miss Hubbard, and that will be for the best. This is not your affair."

Tracy wanted to say, "It is my affair. Whatever is going on here is my affair—because I am Anabel's sister." But she could not risk going that far with this girl whom she knew so slightly, for all that she had been Anabel's friend.

As if to conceal her agitation, Nursel rose and went to the balcony doors, opened them slightly, and stood looking out across the water. When she spoke again the course of her words took a surprising turn.

"Why did you go to this place—the palace ruins? What drew you there?"

"Why—nothing special," Tracy said. "I went for a walk and I stumbled on the gate by chance. I was curious and went inside—that's all."

Nursel nodded thoughtfully. "It is strange, but Mrs. Radburn, who was also an American, loved this place. Often when she was unhappy she went there alone. Sometimes I accompanied her, when I thought she should not be by herself."

Tracy lay back against her pillow, her eyes closed. She had no taste for the food on the tray. Was Nursel making some deliberate connection between her and Anabel? But that wasn't possible. No one had known of Anabel's sister. Nursel turned back to the room with a slight gesture, as if dismissing the whole affair. Tracy opened her eyes and spoke cautiously, watching the other girl, trusting her not at all.

"This morning," she said, "Mrs. Erim showed me the portrait of Anabel in Mr. Radburn's bedroom. The face in the picture seemed so lovely. Was she like that—Mrs. Radburn?"

Nursel returned to her chair beside the bed. "She was like that—and not like. Often she had the charming quality of a child. She wanted always to be gay and lighthearted. She wanted to be the heroine of her own little plays. Yet she was married to him—so dark and heavy and serious. Oh, I could tell you stories about the year they lived here! Have you seen the fortress on the other side of the water in the direction of Istanbul?"

"I noticed the towers this morning," Tracy said.

"That is Rumeli Hisar. A very famous place in Turkish history. It was built to guard the Bosporus from the invaders, though its purpose failed. There is a similar fortress on this side, but smaller and not so interesting. One time we took Anabel to Rumeli Hisar for a picnic—all of us. My brother and Sylvana, even Miles. That was one of her wild, gay days. Something reckless would get into her when she would be like—like a knife"

"What do you mean—like a knife?"

Nursel turned back to the room. "Very sharp and cutting in her ways. She could hurt without thinking. Perhaps more like a sword than a knife, with the ring of steel about her. Yes—that is it! Like a blade hidden by folds of silk, ready to cut when one least expected it. That day at the fortress she wanted to go to the very heights. Miles forbade her. He said she had no head for high places. But Anabel told him she could fly to the top if she chose, and she proved it by running up those long flights of steps that lead through the garden inside. We sat watching her and I was frightened. I cried out that someone should go after her, and Murat started the climb, but Miles stopped him. He said to let her go or she'd never

114

get it out of her system. Perhaps he wanted her dead even then. It was a day in the springtime and the pink Judas trees were in bloom along the Bosporus. There is one that grows on a hillside outside the enclosure of the fortress walls. Anabel said she must see it from the very highest place. So she went up there, running like a gazelle, never looking back, never looking down. From the notch in the wall she could see the tree and she called to us that it was beautiful, enchanting, we must all come up there to see it."

The story thread broke off, and Tracy heard the emotion in Nursel's voice as she lowered her dark head.

"Never have I had an American friend, except when I was young and went to the American girls' school at Arnavütkoy across the Bosporus. That was where I learned to speak English. My friend was a girl of my own age whose father was an American naval officer. But she was not like Anabel. No one else could be like Anabel."

*No one else could be like Anabel,* Tracy thought, and closed her eyes briefly. No one else had the wonder and excitement that had been Anabel's, or her extreme attraction for danger.

"How did she get down from the wall that day?" she asked.

"It was a dreadful time. I will never forget. She turned to call us to come and see the view from the opening in the wall. And when she turned she

115

was forced to look down. The wall is high and narrow at that place, and there was a moment that caught at my heart. I thought she would fall before our very eyes.

"Miles saw what had happened and he shouted to her to lean back against the wall and wait there for him. He started up at once, but she did not wait. She wavered toward the steps and stumbled part way down the first level before she fainted there on a narrow ledge. It was only by good fortune that she did not roll over the edge. He reached her and brought her down from the heights. I could almost admire him then. He was strong and sure and he carried her all the way to safety before she wakened and began to struggle. Then I did not like him for long!"

Her words had a sudden ring of spite in them as she continued.

"When Anabel recovered she was hysterical— weeping, terrified. Miles slapped her across one cheek. Brutally, cruelly. Never, never will I forgive him for that blow. Or for his actions—not only that day, but later."

One of Tracy's unpredictable and independent voices suddenly sounded in her mind. She had listened in dismay and she could have wept for Anabel, who was frail and fragile and never one to pit her strength against heights. Yet perhaps her sister had asked for stern treatment. What else could Miles have done, once he got her down, but shock her out of her hysterical state with a good slap?

"Did she quiet after he slapped her?" she asked Nursel.

The dark eyes widened in surprise, as if the other girl had expected indignation. "But of course. She wept afterwards—more softly. She was terrified of him, as she had every right to be—though I did not know this at the time. I did not know how much he wanted her dead."

The voice of justice was insistent, even though Tracy would have liked to shut it out. She was, after all, on Anabel's side. But the voice would not be still.

"It doesn't seem as though a man who wanted his wife dead would hang her portrait on the wall of his bedroom where he must look at it every day."

"Ah, but that is most easy to understand," Nursel objected. "What do you call it—the bed of thorns, the hair shirt of your Christian martyrs? He has a need to punish himself for what he has done. He is not without conscience, for all his wickedness. Part of the penalty he pays is to be unable to paint again. He will pay forever—but never enough. Never enough to bring Anabel back to life."

Nursel covered her face with her hands and was still. On one finger a star sapphire winked in the lamplight.

Again Tracy longed to say, "Anabel was my

117

sister. If you were her friend, be my friend too. Help me to find the truth." But she did not dare. Though Nursel seemed increasingly frank, the time had not yet come. It was better to wait and be wise.

Nursel took her hands from before her face abruptly. Her eyes were sorrowful and there was a lingering tinge of fear, but there was no wetness on her cheeks.

"Give me the scarf," she said, suddenly urgent.

Tracy had thrust it beneath her pillow and she did not reach for it. "You do know who it belongs to. Why do you want it?"

"It is not wise for you to keep it," Nursel said obliquely. "It is possible that you might do great injury to the innocent if you tell others all that happened today. If you give me the scarf, it will be replaced where it belongs and no one will be the wiser."

Tracy hesitated, then made up her mind. "I'll give it to you. But not now. I'll give it to you before I leave for home."

Nursel was not satisfied, but she made a small despairing gesture. "You do not understand. Never mind. You are not finishing your dinner. I have disturbed you with my talk. Sylvana will be displeased if you do not eat everything. Come— the lamb is delicious."

Tracy wrinkled her nose. "I'm not hungry. Please take it away."

As Nursel rose to lift the tray from the bed table, someone knocked on the door and Miles's voice said, "May I come in?"

For an instant Nursel looked startled. Then she smiled at Tracy. "It is a new day in Turkey. Sometimes I hear my grandmother's voice and I forget. Will you speak to Mr. Radburn?"

She did not want to, but she could hardly refuse. "All right," she said grudgingly.

Nursel opened the door and the white cat flicked around Miles's legs and leaped into its corner chair. He ignored the animal and came to stand at the foot of Tracy's bed.

"I've just heard about your fall," he said. "I hope the damage isn't serious."

Was he too going to question her? Tracy noted again what a chill gray color his eyes were, how there was in him a lack of any light or human warmth except when he was angry.

"Only a scraped shin," she said. "I'll be all right tomorrow. I really don't know why I've been sent to bed."

"I suggest that you forget about work and rest tomorrow," he told her. "I'm going to the city in the morning and I don't expect to be at home at all. Take the day off and do as you like."

"What I'd like," said Tracy, raising her chin obstinately, "is to get to work and finish the job I've come here to do."

"I prefer not to lock my study against you,"

Radburn said. "Have I your promise that you will stay out of my rooms until I return?"

Remembering the way he had caught her—an intruder staring at Anabel's picture that afternoon—a flush swept into Tracy's cheeks and her determination crumbled. She could see his plan clearly enough. He would keep her away from his work and he would find new excuses every day until her week was up. Then he would send her home. At the moment she did not in the least know how to oppose the pressure that was being put upon her on all sides.

He seemed to gather agreement from her silence and gave her a stiff-necked nod. "Good night," he said abruptly and went out of the room.

Nursel made a rude face at the closing door. At least she had recovered from her upset emotions over the story she had told.

"I know what we shall do," she announced. "Since you are free tomorrow, you must come to Istanbul with me. I have an errand to perform for Sylvana, and there is a small jewelry shop I must visit for Murat. If your leg is well enough, perhaps you will wish to come with me to these places. There will be time to visit a mosque, perhaps. You must not leave Istanbul without seeing something of its wonders."

Since nothing could be accomplished here, Tracy accepted the invitation, but her sense of frustration increased. She was being forced to

120

mark time on every hand. No door opened to answer the questions about Anabel which so troubled her. The few days granted for her stay already seemed to be slipping away with nothing achieved. At least time spent with Nursel need not be wholly wasted.

"I will leave you now." Nursel broke in upon her thoughts. "Sleep well, I am sorry that I burdened you with my unhappy memories. You must not give them a thought. It is all over now. Except for him."

This seemed an odd way to put it.

"What do you mean—except for him?" Tracy asked cautiously.

For a moment Nursel looked as though she would not answer. Her lips tightened and in her eyes Tracy had a disturbing glimpse of an anger that seemed brightly corrosive.

"I have not forgotten," Nursel said. "I do not mean to forget. One day he will make a mistake—and I will be waiting."

She picked up the dinner tray with its half-eaten meal and bore it away. When the door closed after her, Tracy sank limply back against the hard pillows. She was fully awake now, her thoughts ready to skitter back and forth and around in circles. Nothing that she had seen since she arrived in this household formed a logical, discernible pattern. On every hand there were contradictions.

Ahmet had been one of the three in the ruins of the old palace, but who were the others? Could the woman have been Nursel? Was that the reason for her interest in the scarf Tracy had found? As far as the two voices were concerned, there was no identifying them. They had been distorted in angry disagreement, and she could not guess whether the woman was someone she had met or a total stranger. It was the same with the second man. It might even have been Murat himself, pretending afterward to approach along the road, pretending to be surprised by the open gate. Since the language had been Turkish no accent had been identifiable.

The scarf was perhaps the main clue. Tracy drew it from beneath her pillow and once more studied the plum-colored stripes. Without warning a memory of where she had seen such material returned to mind. There had been a cushion or two in Sylvana Erim's salon made of this very stuff. But where that fact led, she had no sure idea.

Wasn't it probable that the roots of whatever was happening here now went back a few months ago to the time when Anabel had been alive? There was the dark hint of some desperate act behind her sister's death. "I don't want to die!" Anabel had cried—and gone almost directly to her death. If someone in this house was responsible, then reverberations of whatever had happened might continue for a long time after. Particularly if opposing forces of suspicion and concealment were still fighting some underground battle. If only she could know who concealed, and who suspected, so that she could safely choose sides. But friend, or foe, all wore masks, and with a wrong move on her part the ground could open under her feet with greater disaster promised than the physical fall she had taken through a rotted wooden floor that afternoon.

Since the answers were not easily to be found, she must stay out the week and longer. She must find the courage not to be bullied by either Miles or the dominating Sylvana. Nor must she be lulled into too-ready confidences with Nursel. Or flattered by the attractive Dr. Erim's suave, sympathetic attention. She must remain aloof from them all and in possession of her own will until she knew enough to take necessary action—if action of any sort was still possible.

Across the room the forgotten Yasemin settled more deeply into her chair, purring contentedly. The white cat had once more made Anabel's room her own.

# 6

IN THE MORNING when Tracy wakened she found her leg somewhat sore and stiff. But Nursel's bandage was still neatly in place and the discomfort would be minor. She was already looking forward to a trip to Istanbul and a space of time away from this house with its uneasy secrets.

When she was dressed and ready for breakfast, she started toward the stairs, noting on the way that the door of Miles Radburn's study was ajar. She thought of speaking to him before he left and went to the door. But the study was empty. Balcony doors stood open and a cool morning breeze played through the unheated room. As she looked about, the wind caught a sheet of paper and drifted it across the floor.

Tracy went to pick it up and then stood still in shocking surprise, staring at the space beneath the long table where she had left her stacks of sorted papers. The area was in complete confusion. Not a pile remained intact. Papers and drawings had been whirled helter-skelter, some thrown face down, some face up—all mixed together hopelessly.

The wind had done this, she thought, and went to close the doors. But when they were shut and the room empty of sound, she stood beside the tumbled papers and drawings and knew that no breeze could have created such disorder as this, and in only one part of the room. It was not the normal, heaped-high disorder of the table top. None of those papers had been touched, nor had those on Miles's desk.

Could he have done this in a moment of angry

impatience? she wondered—to discourage her, to make her want to leave? But the act did not seem in character with what little she knew of Miles Radburn. He would surely be open in his opposition. He would not resort to anonymous trickery like this. There was something spiteful about the act. But who was she to suspect? Not the shy and timid Halide. Not Nursel, who was beginning to seem a friend. Though at times the girl appeared capable of spite. And surely this was not the sort of thing Sylvana Erim would stoop to. Who then?

Ahmet, perhaps? Moving softly, secretly, aware that she knew of his secret watching in the palace ruins, taking this small revenge? But the act seemed less like an intent to pay her back than like a deliberate threat, a warning. It was as if someone said to her quite clearly, "Stop this pretense of work and go home. We do not want you here."

Tracy hooked her thumbs into the waistband of her skirt, turned her back on the scene, and went downstairs. In bright morning sunlight she felt more angry than fearful. She had been pleased with her small sorting task, and it was thoroughly aggravating to have hours of careful work go for nothing. She would not be stopped as easily as this. When she came home from the trip with Nursel, she would go straight to work and sort everything all over again. What had been done was not serious—just annoying.

As she reached the second floor she heard the sound of voices from the dining area and she went abruptly into the room, driven by the strength of her own indignation. She hoped to find Miles Radburn at breakfast, but he was not at the table. Only Nursel and her brother were there, discussing some matter earnestly in Turkish. When she walked in they both looked up with a surprise that told her the expression she wore might be on the combative side.

"I've just been in Mr. Radburn's study," she told them. "I found all the sorting work I did yesterday thrown into disorder. Have you seen Mr. Radburn? I'd like to hear whether he knows about this. Who would do such a thing?"

Nursel and her brother exchanged a quick look in which there was some meaning Tracy could not catch.

"Mr. Radburn left early for Istanbul," Nursel said. "We know nothing of this."

Dr. Erim rose to seat Tracy at the table, but he did not speak. In spite of his formal courtesy there was a change in him and he did not seem at all like the sympathetic man who had brought her home last evening after her fall. There was a smoldering in his dark eyes and he looked at her with an uncomfortable intensity. Something was very wrong. Tracy sat down feeling suddenly shaken.

"What is it?" she said. "What's the matter?"

Nursel recovered herself first. "You have taken us by surprise, Miss Hubbard. You are angry. It is distressing that your work has been disturbed. We are shocked, of course."

Murat Erim took no placating cue from his sister. Though he had not finished breakfast, he did not seat himself again.

"Perhaps it is better if you go home at once, Miss Hubbard," he told her shortly. "It seems that only trouble awaits you here in Turkey."

"But why should I go home?" Tracy asked, dismayed by this unexpected attack. "It's true that what I found just now upset me and made me angry. But I can straighten out the mess with a little more work. It doesn't make me want to give up and go home—if that's what was intended."

Dr. Erim put his napkin down with careful restraint, bowed to her without replying, and went out of the room.

Tracy turned blankly to Nursel. "What have I done? Why is he so upset? I should think he would want to know who has played this mischievous trick."

The Turkish girl did not answer at once. She gave her attention to breaking a roll, to buttering it delicately. Halide came with Tracy's breakfast and she waited until the girl had gone away. A notion was beginning to turn itself over in her mind.

"Did you tell your brother what really happened in that ruined place last evening?" she asked Nursel. "Did you tell him that I heard voices there? That I heard someone speak my name?"

Nursel seemed alarmed. "No—no, I have said nothing. It is another thing than this that disturbs him. Please—you must pay no attention. My brother has moods. Sometimes he is angry with me, sometimes with Sylvana, or with the servants. It means nothing. As you can see, he is not a happy man. Unfortunate circumstances have come upon us since the death of our older brother."

She paused as if uncertain of how much she might say, then came to a decision and threw reticence aside.

"According to our Turkish law what a man leaves when he dies must be divided equally between members of his immediate family. Thus Sylvana, Murat, and I share equally in ownership of the yali. However, Sylvana prevailed upon our brother to circumvent the law during his lifetime by building the kiosk in her name, by turning much of his personal fortune which he amassed, not by inheritance but in his own exporting business, into outright gifts of money and jewelry to her. There was little left for Murat and me besides this house. We are dependent on Sylvana for most of what we have. And she holds

128

the purse strings tightly. My brother is not one to live happily accepting what should rightfully be his from the hands of this Frenchwoman. Thus you will see that he may be easily upset."

"I can understand how he must feel," Tracy said. "But I still don't see why he should be angry with me."

Nursel sighed. "He does not mean to be inhospitable, Miss Hubbard. Please forgive us and enjoy your breakfast."

Tracy ate her rolls and coffee in silence and Nursel sat with her, making no further attempt at talk. She seemed pensive and subdued this morning. Perhaps she was already regretting her outspoken confidences to Tracy last night.

"Will you tell your brother," Tracy said, "that I have no interest in anything except the purpose for which I have come here." That was true enough. She needn't elaborate.

"And what purpose is that?" Nursel asked gently.

"Why—my work for Mr. Radburn, of course," said Tracy, but a faint prickling ran along the skin of her arms as if something had brushed her lightly in warning.

Nursel nodded. "Of course. I am sorry there has been this little upset. I will of course speak to the servants and see if I can find out who has played this unkind trick. The young girls who work for us are sometimes like merry children."

Tracy said nothing She did not think this was the prank of a merry child.

"In any case," Nursel went on, almost in pleading, "let us forget the matter now and use our day pleasantly. Let us enjoy ourselves on our trip to Istanbul. Let us be happy this morning. This morning I wish to be like—like Anabel, with only the desire to be gay."

The coaxing words were hard to resist and Tracy's annoyance began to fade. "I agree," she said. "Let's not spoil the day."

Nursel cheered up with startling suddenness. Perhaps her air of meekness was something she used to keep out of trouble and to hide her own feelings. A girl who could be devoured by bitter anger at one moment, and in the next be close to sentimental tears, offered a riddle that was not to be easily solved.

The two set off soon after breakfast. Though it was late March, the day was a gift from spring— brightly warm and sunny. Budding promise showed along every tree branch, and overnight the grass had gained a fresh patina of green. Nursel drove as though she liked the feeling of the wheel in her hands and there was a new eagerness about her once they were away from the house, as if she too delighted in flinging off the shackles of its secretive atmosphere.

As Tracy stole a look at her, it was hard to believe that this poised and fashionable young woman was the same emotion-driven girl who had told her so much last night. She looked very beautiful today. Not a wisp of her smoothly lacquered hair stirred in the breeze from open windows, though Tracy's brown bangs were ruffled beneath the curve of her blue suede beret. The dangling earrings Nursel wore caught glints of sunlight and danced with every movement of her head, giving her an air of careless light-heartedness. The clips at her earlobes were circled by tiny blue stones, and the lower teardrops of silver framed larger stones of the same flawless blue.

"How pretty your earrings are," Tracy said.

Nursel smiled at the compliment and, when she slowed the car for the next turn, she reached up to pull the trinkets off and held them out to Tracy.

"Please—they are yours. Wear them in happiness."

"Oh, but I couldn't take them!" Tracy said in dismay. "I didn't mean—"

Nursel dropped them into her lap. "It is a Turkish custom. You cannot refuse or you will offend me. If I did not like you, I would not give them. May I call you by your first name, please? As you will call me Nursel."

"Of course," Tracy said, touched by the friendly gesture.

"You know, do you not, that we Turks have

131

possessed last names for only a handful of years? Before that there was great confusion. Now we are westernized and we have chosen last names for ourselves. But we still cling to the use of first names. It is more comfortable."

"Thank you, Nursel," Tracy said and clipped the pretty things to her own ears. She loved the dancing feel of the earrings against her cheeks. Anabel had worn earrings like this, and never the dull button variety Tracy permitted herself. For a moment Tracy felt almost as elegant as Nursel, as glamourous as Anabel.

With a graceful gesture, the Turkish girl had endeared herself. Nevertheless, Tracy wished that a faint reservation did not mar her feeling toward the other girl. Earrings or no, Tracy could not be wholly comfortable with Nursel Erim. She had the feeling quite often that the Turkish girl was hiding something.

Nursel gave her an approving look as she clipped on the earrings. "They become you," she said. "And of course the blue color will keep you from harm. Or so the ancient Turkish belief tells us."

In Turkey, Tracy recalled, blue was the color used to ward off the effects of the evil eye. She had already seen babies and small children with blue beads woven into their hair or worn as necklaces. Car radiators sometimes wore a string of such beads, and donkeys often wore them around their necks.

The car had left the ferry and was following a main thoroughfare of modern Istanbul. A long strip of plane trees, still bare of leaves, divided the two lanes of traffic, and great concrete government buildings flying the Turkish Crescent and Star rimmed one side of the avenue. As the road dipped toward old Istanbul across the Golden Horn, Tracy sat up eagerly to watch for the famous skyline.

The Golden Horn was that curving, narrow strip of waterway that opened from the Bosporus and bisected Istanbul, separating the old from the new. There were two bridges across it—one the newer Atatürk Bridge, the other the ancient Galata, which they were now approaching. Across Galata Bridge had traveled the caravans of the ancient world. Today the horses and camels had given way to motor vehicles of every description, packed in close formation as they streamed back and forth across the water.

As they drove toward the beginning of the bridge, the skyline came into sight and Tracy drew in her breath. With rain and fog banished, it was a magical thing—a great pyramidal mound of solidly packed buildings from which rose the domes and minarets of a myriad of mosques. There was little color, Tracy saw. Istanbul was a gray city, even in the sunlight. But the grace of its minarets, the perfected architecture of dome rising upon dome, gave the whole an almost ethereal grace.

They slowed for the bridge traffic, and Nursel identified a structure here and there. To the left, near Topkapi Palace, which the French had called the Seraglio, rose that marvelous structure built by the Emperor Justinian in the year A.D. 537—the divine St. Sophia, once a church, then a mosque, and now a museum to house the relics of its own great history. Somewhat higher was the Blue Mosque, while nearer the center was a far vaster building—the mosque of Suleiman the Magnificent.

They were on the bridge now and traffic ran bumper to bumper, with a stream of pedestrians crossing by means of the walks on either side. The waters of the Golden Horn were filled with boats of every description. Below the bridge on the right ran what seemed to be a street paralleling the bridge at water level. Here fishing boats were drawn up and men peddled their fresh wares to purchasers on the bridge.

"A portion of the Galata floats on pontoons," Nursel explained. "It is opened only once each day. At four o'clock every morning it swings open to let boats in and out of the Golden Horn. Two hours later it is closed again and traffic is once more allowed to cross. To see the bridge at dawn when it is open, to see it close and the traffic flow across again is a wonderful thing.

Once my brother brought me here for the sight."

On the far side as they left the bridge, the narrow cobbled streets of Stamboul, as the British had called the old quarter, swallowed them and it was necessary to drive slowly, for now there were donkeys and peddlers and pedestrians crowding every thoroughfare. Yogurt sellers, candy peddlers, purveyors of drinking water vied with each other for the right of way. Boys, with brass trays hanging from chains and laden with tiny coffee cups, ran about skillfully without spilling a drop. Nursel drove into the maze of streets and up the hill to find a place to park.

"We are near the Covered Bazaar," she said. "We will go there first and I will complete my errands."

Once they were on foot in the steep, cobbled streets, Tracy caught the smell of dust that was the smell of Istanbul. The slightest stirring of air sent the dust that lay between cobblestones and along every ledge and gutter edge into a swirling dervish dance.

They crossed the courtyard of a lesser mosque where pigeons thronged, being fed by passers-by. Beyond rose the arched entryway to the Covered Bazaar. Set in stone above the pointed arch that gave final entrance to the bazaar was the insignia of the Ottoman Empire, with its emblem of crossed flags. The stream of men and women that went in and out of the entrance wore European dress for the most part, and the faces were those of any cosmopolitan city where races mingled. Here and there Tracy saw men carrying tespihler in their hands, or with strands of beads hanging partially out of pockets.

Once through the arch, they were in the maze of the bazaar itself. It was, Tracy found, a city of tiny shops gathered beneath arching stone roofs that had been stained and weather-beaten by the years. At intervals high windows let in a watery semblance of daylight. For the most part, however, the lighting was by electricity, and the small glass window of each shop glowed with warm light. Off the first stone corridor other corridors opened, and still others upon those, until Tracy was soon lost in the web.

The shops were apparently gathered into communities, each group selling one type of goods. They passed window after window heaped high with gleaming golden bracelets— vastly popular with girls from the villages, Nursel said, since they still counted their worth as brides by the number of gold bracelets they might string upon their arms. There were shops where nothing but slippers and shoes were sold, and where the smell of leather was strong. There was a street of copper shops, another that sold only brass, and there were endless rows of small jewelry stores.

It was into one of these that Nursel went on her first errand. So small was the shop that its exterior consisted of no more than a narrow show window and a door. Inside was a small counter behind which there was room for a single shopkeeper. The space before the counter could hold no more than two customers comfortably at one time. The young man behind the counter greeted Nursel by name and at once brought stools for his guests. He was tall and well built, with bright, intent dark eyes and a smile that showed the flash of fine teeth.

"This is Hasan Effendi," Nursel said.

The young man bowed gravely and murmured in English that the *hanimefendi* did his shop honor.

Tracy sat upon her stool and studied the fascinating array within. Every inch of the tiny space held shelves on which were displayed beads and brooches, rings and amulets and tiny ornaments.

"You have the tespih for my brother, Hasan Effendi?" Nursel asked.

The young man reached into a drawer behind him and laid upon the glass counter a tespih strung with beads of fine green jade. Nursel studied them with interest.

"Murat will be pleased," she said and gave them to Tracy to see. "These will be a valuable addition to my brother's collection."

The string was like others Tracy had handled yesterday—a short string with finial beads and no clasp. In her fingers the jade felt exquisitely smooth and was cool to her touch. When Nursel took them back and asked the price, a gentle, almost teasing bargaining began between buyer and seller. The good-natured banter quickly concluded, Nursel paid the sum agreed upon and put the small package in her handbag. Then she spoke to Tracy.

"You will excuse us, please, if we speak in Turkish? Hasan Effendi is the son of Ahmet Effendi and I have a message for him from his father."

While they spoke together, Tracy studied the young man with new interest. His good looks and well-built frame held little resemblance to the wiry Ahmet. Until he began to frown. Then they seemed kin at once. She did not like the way he scowled, or the somewhat harsh note that came into his voice. Once more Nursel cast down her eyes in the old meek way, though this seemed a little strange when the man on the other side of the counter was a shopkeeper and the son of a servant in the Erim household.

It was possible that he sensed Tracy's surprised interest upon him, for he suddenly broke off, smiling, and reached into a box beneath the counter.

"Perhaps you would like to see the tespihler I

will soon send to Mrs. Erim, *hanimefendi*," he said, and cast a handful of bead strands upon the counter before her.

Tracy leaned closer to see the colorful array. Automatically she looked for black amber, but there was none in this collection. Nursel, after a glance, seemed to dismiss the display with indifference.

"I am sure Mrs. Erim will be pleased to have them, Hasan Effendi," she said politely. "She is eager to assist you in the success of this shop, just as she is eager to help her villagers."

The look of Ahmet was in the son's eyes again—a little sullen, darkly resentful. But he did not answer. As they left the shop, he came with them to the door and stood looking after them as they walked away.

Once they had turned a corner and were out of sight of the shop, Nursel flung off her air of meekness and became herself again.

"It is very difficult for Hasan Effendi," she said. "Our elder brother sent him to school for a time, but after he died Murat did not wish to continue Hasan's education, for there was so little money. Nor is Sylvana interested in spending the money—though she could afford to. So this young man is forced to work in a small shop. He is ambitious, however, and perhaps he will one day finish his education and become an attorney."

"He seemed angry with you when we left," Tracy said, probing.

Nursel seemed undisturbed. "It does not matter. It is nothing. The behavior of Mrs. Erim infuriates him. Perhaps this is a good thing. Come—we will go this way. I have now an important purchase to make for Sylvana."

As they walked down still another corridor, Tracy saw that along the edge of the walk marble heads and busts, a broken pedestal or two, portions of a marble pillar had been piled carelessly—all fragments with the stamp of age upon them.

"Shouldn't some of these things be in a museum?" she asked in wonder.

Nursel's shrug was expressive. "Who is to know how such things find their way into the bazaars of Istanbul? All through Turkey there are ancient ruins still to be excavated. Undoubtedly pilfering goes on. Ah—here is the place I am looking for."

She had stopped before a shop that was larger than the others, perhaps a combination of three or four thrown together. The show windows were dusty and far less cluttered, displaying only a few fine articles of silver, copper, and brass. It was as if this shop knew its own worth and was above tawdry commercial display.

As Nursel entered, the shopkeeper came respectfully to greet her. He signaled to a boy to bring wooden chairs for the guests, and they were seated in the bare main aisle. The shop was rather dark and the smell of dust lay heavily upon it, yet Tracy sensed that all about were objects old and rich in value.

The boy who had brought the chairs disappeared, to return shortly with a copper tray on which were set small cups of Turkish coffee. Tracy sipped the thick, bittersweet brew determinedly.

When they had been refreshed and Nursel and the shopkeeper had exchanged courtesies, he brought out the treasure for which she had come. The object was large and fairly heavy and he bore it before him with a ceremonial air. A sharp word to the young boy sent him scurrying to fetch a table upon which it could be placed and a cloth with which to dust it.

Tracy saw that it was a very grand and dignified samovar. Its copper luster was tarnished and dull, but beauty of form remained. Above the large water compartment rose tiers or racks and lids and a tall copper chimney. Below was the curving base on which the whole thing rested. A handle over the spout was fanned and ornamentally embossed, fancy as a peacock's tail. On either side of the tank were strong handles by which the heavy piece could be lifted.

The boy handed the dustcloth to his master,

backed fearfully away from the copper beauty, and bolted to the rear of the shop.

Nursel smiled. "He is afraid. He knows the story of this samovar. It is perhaps more than two hundred years old. In the old times the finest samovars came from Russia, but this was made in a village in Anatolia. You can see how beautiful the workmanship is. Always we Turks have valued artists and, when the Sultan of that day found so fine an artisan in a small village, he brought him and the samovar he had made to Istanbul. There the man was given an important place at court and encouraged in his work. Unfortunately, he was one who enjoyed intrigue. Perhaps he was not as clever at court affairs as he was clever with his hands. It seems that he came to a sad end and his head floated down the Bosporus in a basket."

Nursel walked around the samovar, touching it respectfully now and then.

"The most romantic part of the story comes later," she went on. "The samovar was given at last to the Sultan's mother, the most powerful woman in the Empire. For many years it graced her summer palace on the Bosporus. Unfortunately, she was stabbed to death and the samovar outlasted her. Later the samovar was placed in the Topkapi Palace museum. Many years ago it was stolen from the museum and disappeared, only to come to light recently in Istanbul's bazaars. What a marvelous treasure for Sylvana to own, though I wish that Murat had found it first."

Tracy regarded the samovar with interest. "Won't it be returned to the museum?"

Again Nursel made her graceful little shrug. "Perhaps it will be. But for now Sylvana may enjoy it and she will also enjoy making Murat envious." She sighed as though she foresaw further tensions at the yali with the coming of the samovar.

There was no bargaining here. Apparently the price had been arrived at between Sylvana and the shopkeeper, and Nursel had only to pay him the not inconsiderable sum.

When they returned to the car, the shopkeeper accompanied them, bearing the treasure wrapped carefully in Turkish newspapers and tied with string. The boy, it seemed, would not carry it. He had run away to hide until the samovar was gone from the shop.

When the large package had been placed in the back of the car, Nursel suggested that there was time for Tracy to see the Blue Mosque before lunch. They drove a short distance and then parked again.

"I am sorry I cannot go in with you," Nursel said. "I must not leave Sylvana's treasure alone in the car. But you may enter and look around as long as you wish. I am content. There is no hurry."

The great mosque was a pyramid of domes rising upon domes, with the largest one crowning the top. At each of the mosque's four corners rose a slender minaret, encircled by small bands of balcony, as rings might encircle a finger. The two extra minarets—six was a greater number than any except those possessed by the great mosque in Mecca—stood somewhat to the side.

Tracy's eyes were filled with the soaring grace of the architecture and she stood looking up at the domes for a long while before she walked across the wide courtyard to the entrance. She had read that Sultan Ahmed had so admired Justinian's St. Sophia that he had copied the outer form of it in this mosque.

Near the entrance an aged Turk pointed to large soft slippers she could put on over her shoes, and held out his palm for her tip. Shuffling in the ungainly coverings, she stepped into a world of flying arches and vast domes, all floating in a shimmer of blue light. Far above, high windows circled each dome and graced each arch, flinging sunlight into the heart of the mosque, only to have its gold transfused by the expanse of mosaic until the air seemed blue as an undersea cavern. Tracy stepped onto soft layers of carpet, dozens of which were arranged in orderly rows, covering every inch of the floor. A sense of spreading, soaring space was all about her, not only overhead, but all round at floor level. There were no pews to break up space as was the case in a Christian church. The carpets were there to be knelt upon, and only four enormous fluted columns interrupted the open vista.

So varied was the decoration of tilework, with its flaunting of blue peacock tails, its stylized reproduction of blue roses and tulips and lilies, its giant inscriptions from the Koran that adorned pillar and dome and arch, that the eye soon wearied and Tracy ceased to see detail, but was absorbed into the vast blue atmosphere.

The hour was nearing for prayer, and the Faithful, having performed their ablutions in running water outside the mosque, were coming in to kneel upon the carpets, gathering in a mass toward the front of the edifice. There were no women among the worshipers who faced Mecca. The men who passed Tracy paid no attention, undoubtedly accustomed to tourists and intent upon their own purpose. A low, carved stand in the form of a giant X held a huge Koran, its worn pages open to be read by whomever pleased.

Overhead wires had been strung across the space, and from these hung glass lamps which had once contained oil and wicks for the lighting of the interior, but now boasted unromantic glass bulbs for electricity. In her huge slippers Tracy shuffled beneath them toward one of the outer galleries, her senses dulled by the very blueness and the vast assortment of detail. The wall pulled

145

in her perspective a little and she rounded a turn of the corridor to come to a surprised halt. A few feet away a man stood before an easel, intent upon his painting. She saw that it was Miles Radburn.

She stood where she was, watching him, uncertain whether to advance or go quickly away before he saw her.

# 7

AN UNEASY PRICKLING stirred at the back of Tracy's neck and she smiled ruefully. Her hackles were rising, undoubtedly, at the very sight of this man. She moved nearer, trying to walk without scuffling, in order to see what he was doing before he discovered her there watching him.

His dark, rather saturnine head was bent toward the work in progress on his easel. He was, of course, painting in blue—an assortment of blues that made up one of the far-flung peacock panels over his head. Meticulously he was filling in tiny wedges and feathery curves, and she marveled that he could do such work. Once he had been a painter of men and women, known for the swiftness with which he could cut through exteriors to the essence of his subject in quick strong strokes. He had done just that in his painting of Anabel. How could he turn now to this painstaking detail, so lacking in any human quality?

He must have sensed her presence, for he looked around and recognized her without welcome. Tracy braced herself. She did not like the uneasiness she felt with this man, the inclination to flee from something half feared and not understood. For this very reason she stood her ground.

"Touristing?" he asked. "What do you think of all this?"

She did not believe he really cared what she thought, but she tried to give him a true answer. "It overwhelms me. I get tired of trying to look at it all at once. I suppose I keep wanting to see a human face somewhere in all that sea of abstract design."

"The Moslem religion forbade the depicting of humans or animals," he reminded her. "Mustapha Kemal changed all this, but it's why artists used to turn to architecture and mosaics to express themselves. They produced some of the finest work of this sort that's ever been done, as a result." He waved a hand toward the interior of the mosque. "Of course a lot of what you see there now is stenciling. Unless you look closely, you can't always tell it from the real tile. Many of the less famous mosques have finer work preserved in them."

He turned back to his painting and she watched

him for a few moments longer. When it appeared that he had nothing more to say to her, she intruded upon his silence.

"Did you happen to go into your study before you left this morning?"

He answered carelessly. "Only when I first got up. I had no time after breakfast. My stuff was in my car and I wanted to get an early start."

"I went in," she said quietly. "Someone had gone through the sorting I did yesterday and whipped everything into complete disorder."

She had his attention now. He stared at her, his face expressionless.

"That means it has begun again," he said.

His words had no meaning for her, yet they had an ominous ring.

"What do you mean? What has begun again?"

"The work of our evil genius. Our poltergeist, or what have you. Was any damage done to my papers and drawings?"

"Not as far as I could see," Tracy admitted. "It was as though a child had mixed everything up."

"It was not a child." He continued to regard her with an odd concentration. When he spoke again his words took her by surprise. "Those earbobs you're wearing—I suppose you found them in the bazaar?"

Startled, her hands flew to the earrings she had almost forgotten. "Nursel gave them to me. I admired them and she took them right off and handed them to me. She wouldn't let me refuse."

He nodded. "You have to be careful what you admire. The Turks are a wildly generous and hospitable lot. But you shouldn't wear the things. They don't suit you."

"But I like them," she said, beginning to breathe hard.

He set down his palette and brush on the folding stand beside his easel and came over to her. Before she knew what he meant to do, he pulled off the clipped earrings and held them out to her.

"That's better. Now you're all of one piece."

She was both outraged and disconcerted as the earrings dropped into her hand. Suddenly old memory was strong. It was as if she were a young girl again and her father had just thrown her first lipstick into a wastebasket. The words he'd spoken so long ago rang in her ears as if she heard them now, "Don't try to look like your sister Anabel. Just be yourself."

But she was not a child now, she thought indignantly, and Miles Radburn had no authority to tell her what she might wear. Nevertheless, the old feeling of having made herself ridiculous— because she could never be like Anabel— possessed her as it used to do, shattering all self-confidence.

"What do you mean—all of one piece?" she

faltered, hating the very uncertainty of her words.

He went calmly back to his easel and began to put his painting things away. "Don't blame me for seeing as a painter sees. How is your barked shin?"

"It's all right, thank you," she managed in a choked voice.

He continued without looking around. "You ought not wander around old ruins in the dark. If you get into trouble so easily, perhaps you'd better not stay in Turkey until your week is up."

This was exactly what Dr. Erim had said at breakfast, and she found she was tired of being told to go home. She walked away without another word, her chin stiffly atilt. She would not be scolded and frightened, and she would not go home.

Halfway across the courtyard she clipped on the earrings again. They set up a small defiant dance against her cheeks, and she told herself that it made no difference if Miles Radburn was right. Even if she wasn't the type for dangling earrings, even if she was no match for Anabel's memory, he had behaved in an outrageous manner. She would wear what she liked and do as she pleased. But he had spoiled her delight in the baubles and she would not readily forgive him.

He must have put his painting things away

rather quickly, for he caught up with her before she left the courtyard.

"There's something you ought to see," he said. "Hold on a minute."

She reminded him coolly that Nursel had been waiting for her quite a while, but he brushed her words aside.

"You wanted to see something of Istanbul. Look up there."

They were close to one of the minarets, and she looked straight upward at a tiny balcony that circled one needlelike finger near the top. The tower seemed unbelievably tall and thin, and the man who had climbed the stairs within it and stood upon the balcony seemed small as a puppet figure. The muezzin wore no robes and carried no trumpet. In his black business suit he stood within the high circle and cupped his hands about his mouth. His long, wailing cry was almost lost to them on the wind, so they heard only a faint warbling. Then he turned and cried out again, and this time the call to prayer came toward them and they could hear the liquid sound of the words:

"*Allahu akbar! La ilaha ilia' llah!*"

"'God is most great . . . there is no God but God . . .'" Miles Radburn repeated softly.

Tracy found that she was unexpectedly stirred by the sound. Her indignation was fading in spite of herself.

151

"Even this is passing," Miles said, as the man completed his calls and disappeared into the darkness of the minaret. "There are a good many mosques these days where you'll find the muezzin sitting comfortably on the ground, warbling into a microphone. Can't say I blame them. I climbed a flight of stairs inside a minaret once. Those fellows have to keep in trim, even if their flocks are falling off."

"There seemed to be a great number of men coming into the mosque," Tracy said.

"Mostly of the older generations, I suspect. It's too bad some of the younger Turks are turning away from religion—with nothing to put in the place of what they're chucking out."

"There were no women," Tracy mused. "I saw only men kneeling on the carpets inside."

"The women are in separate niches at the back," Miles said. "You'll always see a few sitting cross-legged, keeping out of the way of the men but no less devout. Shall we go along now and find Nursel? Perhaps you'll both have lunch with me."

The earrings bobbed against her cheeks, but she no longer felt defiant. She did not particularly want to lunch with Miles Radburn, but something in her had quieted, temporarily at least. An unspoken truce had been declared. An uneasy truce, perhaps, because his strange words about a poltergeist lingered at the back of her mind, as well as his quick changing of the subject after he had spoken.

Nursel was waiting patiently in the car. She accepted Miles Radburn's invitation to lunch with the guarded courtesy she adopted toward him. Tracy had a feeling that Miles himself did not suspect how thoroughly he was disliked by Nursel Erim. Further evidence, perhaps, of the blank side he turned toward the feelings of others. Further evidence of the barrier he placed between himself and the world.

Again they drove a short distance and left the car in an open place not far from the Spice Bazaar. When they got out, Nursel explained to Miles about the samovar—that she dared not leave it behind.

He lifted the ungainly package out in its newspaper and string wrapping. "I don't suppose this is the same one . . ." he began.

Nursel broke in quickly. "Yes—it is the same. Sylvana purchased it long ago. She waited to bring it home because it might remind you of unhappy things. But now a little time has passed."

"Yes," Miles said, "time has passed. We'll take it with us and see that no harm befalls it. Though I gather that it has weathered history better than those who have owned it."

Together they walked through crowded streets. Near the Spice Bazaar the roadway was filled with cars and taxis, with carts and horses and donkeys, with teeming humanity. Awnings overhung open stalls where spices were sold and flapped in the wind above fruit stands. The Istanbul smell of dust was pleasantly cut by the scent of Eastern spices and the odor of ripe fruit.

The restaurant in the Spice Bazaar to which Miles took them was very old. They climbed narrow stairs to a room at the top and were shown to a table near a deep window that overlooked Galata Bridge and the Golden Horn. A glass chandelier hung from the dome of the ceiling and there was blue and black tilework around the walls.

The menu was in English as well as Turkish, and Miles ordered for them—swordfish on skewers, alternating with bits of bay leaf, tomato, and lemon slices. Tracy looked out the window toward the buildings across the Golden Horn in newer Istanbul, where an ancient fire tower topped a mound of less picturesque buildings that graced the old quarter.

"We build only in stone now," Nursel said. "No longer are wooden houses permitted. Istanbul has burned down too many times."

On a nearby wall hung the familiar picture of Mustapha Kemal—Atatürk—that Tracy had begun to see everywhere.

Nursel saw her eyes on the picture. "My father fought with the Ghazi, as they called him—the Victor—in the campaign that saved Turkey.

Ahmet Effendi was with him in those days also. My older brother and Murat and I grew up on stories of those times. Ahmet Effendi would have given his life for my brother, as he would for Murat also."

"But not for you?" Tracy asked.

Nursel smiled. "I am a woman. It is not the same. Still he is loyal to any of our family. Even to Sylvana."

She began to discuss the current political situation with Miles, and Tracy found herself watching him as she listened. Even now, when he had invited them to lunch, he remained somewhat absent, lapsing into an occasional moody silence almost in the middle of a sentence. She had again the feeling that she was looking at someone who had ceased to be alive. Ceased deliberately.

The swordfish, when it came, was delicious. Mediterranean waters and those of the Marmara and the Bosporus all offered their wares to Istanbul, and fish was a favorite food with the Turks.

Not until the meal was half over did Miles put a sudden question to Nursel, giving her his full attention for the first time.

"You know about what happened this morning?" he asked.

Nursel stared at her plate. "Yes, Tracy has told me."

"It sounds like the old game starting up again."

"Perhaps it is a warning." Nursel smiled, attempting to treat the subject lightly.

"It won't be easy for anyone to frighten Miss Hubbard away," Miles said. "I suspect she'll make a stand."

"Of course I will!" Tracy felt the earrings dance vehemently against her cheeks. His unexpected support braced her to further resist leaving.

He did not let the matter drop. "From what quarter do you think such a warning might come?" he asked Nursel.

"I make only a small joke," the Turkish girl said. "I do not know who does this thing." But she sounded uneasy.

"Last time there were hints dropped that it might be Anabel playing these tricks," Miles pointed out. "What happened this morning seems to indicate that it couldn't have been."

Nursel spoke quickly. "I have never believed this of Anabel! But, please—it is better not to talk of such things. This—poltergeist, as you say, is only mischievous. He does no harm."

"He frightened Anabel half out of her wits," Miles said. "Tracy is made of sterner stuff. Perhaps she'll frighten him." He flashed his unexpected smile upon Tracy. "After all, she has managed to intimidate me. Perhaps your Turkish spirits had better look out for themselves."

This was no longer a joke to Nursel. "One must not speak aloud the name of evil," she protested.

A spark seemed to have been lighted in the bleak inner landscape of Miles's being and now it burned more intensely.

"I don't agree. I'm inclined to think that evil has a name—a human name. Perhaps there are times when it's better to cry it as loudly as possible—even from the rooftops. Once the name is known, of course."

Nursel said nothing more, withdrawing herself pointedly from so distasteful a subject. Apathy fell upon Miles again. They finished the meal with little conversation, but Tracy could not forget the glimpse she'd had of unexpected fire in the man who had been Anabel's husband.

It had been surprising to see his indifference kindle into something verging on excitement. True, it was a dark excitement and Tracy had the uncomfortable feeling that a hint of violence might lie beneath the surface. Yet it showed him alive and not wholly indifferent to what happened around him.

When the meal was over and they left the restaurant, Miles carried the samovar to Nursel's car, packing it away again in the rear seat.

"I believe I'll start home myself," he said. "I need to get on with that strip of calligraphy I'm doing for Sylvana. And I want to have a look at our mischief-maker's new trick."

Tracy caught him up at once. "In that case, I'll start cleaning up the muddle as soon as you've looked it over. Then I can get on with my work."

For an instant he seemed disconcerted. As they drove off, Tracy glanced back and saw him staring after the car with an expression that seemed part annoyance, part dismay.

On the trip home, crossing on the ferry, and driving along the road on the Anatolian side, she and Nursel talked idly and at random, not touching again on the subject of Miles Radburn or the disturbance in his study. Questions teemed in Tracy's mind, but she dared push them no further at the moment.

When they reached the yali Halide came to carry the samovar upstairs.

"Come with me while I take it to Sylvana," Nursel suggested. "It will be amusing to see her open it. She has coveted this for very long."

As the three climbed to the second floor of the kiosk the door of Sylvana's salon was flung suddenly open and a sound of angry voices reached them. Dr. Erim appeared abruptly at the head of the stairs and it was clear that he was enraged. Though the argument was in Turkish, there was no mistaking Murat's anger or Sylvana's indignation.

As he started down the stairs, Halide squealed and ducked out of his way with the samovar and Tracy drew back against the rail to let him pass.

Nursel reached a hand toward her brother, but he brushed it aside and rushed downstairs. Whatever had occurred, the quarrel had been thorough.

"I am sorry," Nursel said. "I must go to him. I must learn what has happened. This time she has pushed him too far. Please—you will take the samovar upstairs to Mrs. Erim."

Thus directed, Tracy and Halide climbed the remaining steps. Tracy had no desire for an encounter while Sylvana was in a temper. Her own presence in this household was too uncertain, too tenuous. There was, however, no avoiding what was to come. Sylvana stood in the open door of her salon, clearly struggling to regain control of herself. Her air of calm was gone and she seemed at the point of angry tears.

She glanced impatiently at Tracy, then saw the package in Halide's arms. She seized upon it as a distraction.

"Good—you have brought home the samovar!"

There was no opportunity for Tracy to slip away. She was waved into the room in Halide's wake and could only watch uncomfortably as the maid placed her burden upon a table and Sylvana began to rip away its covering. The great, handsome thing emerged into view, and at once assumed an aristocratic air, as if its presence made any place a palace.

As Sylvana walked about the samovar,

exclaiming raptly in French, her hands clasped in admiration, the fury of her quarrel with her brother-in-law died out a little. Her color remained higher than usual and she was far from tranquil, but the samovar was indeed serving as a distraction.

"It has been neglected," she said, touching the plump sides with admiring hands. "Of course I shall not use it, but the exterior must be polished to a fine gloss. This I will do myself."

She spoke to Halide in Turkish, apparently explaining to the village girl where the samovar had come from, perhaps something of its story, for Halide's eyes began to widen. Suddenly she backed away as the boy in the shop had done, and ran out of the room.

Sylvana laughed, something of her surface tranquillity restored. "Our girls from the villages are still fearful and superstitious," she told Tracy. "They cling to the old ways in their customs. You notice that Halide keeps her head covered. That is because it is still regarded as unseemly to let a man see one's hair."

She circled the small table upon which the samovar stood, admiring it anew, pointing out to Tracy the art that had gone into its creation.

"The Anatolian Samovar!" she said softly. "That is the name by which it is called. Of course such a thing is not in itself evil, as Halide imagines. It has merely been witness to much wickedness. Legend has it that the Sultan's mother was drinking tea made from this very samovar on the afternoon when she was stabbed to death. The ruins of her summer palace where she died are only a short distance from this house."

"The ruins I explored yesterday?" Tracy asked.

"Yes—the very same. How is your injury?"

"It doesn't bother me," Tracy said.

Sylvana's attention could not be drawn for long from her new treasure, and she continued with her story.

"The accounts of tragedy that surround the samovar go on and on. The strangling of a young prince occurred in its presence. With all the princelings there were in the harem, there was much jealousy and those who stood close to the Sultan were always in danger of their lives. Both because of ladies who wanted their own sons to succeed to the throne, and court officials who feared their power might be usurped. All the Bosporus area has a history of wickedness to curdle the blood. It is said that a man died much later when the samovar was stolen from the museum. How fortunate that I am a French-woman and am able to savor such stories without being frightened by them!"

Tracy's attention had begun to wander. Now that she was here, she remembered the scarf she had found in the ruins last night. Her glance moved about the room, seeking. This was surely the place—yes, there was the pattern among cushions on a divan below the windows. A pattern of plum-colored stripes.

She picked up the cushion. "What very pretty silk this is."

Sylvana nodded absently. "Yes—it is from Damascus. I bought a length of it last year."

"It would make a lovely scarf," Tracy mused.

Sylvana patted the samovar and circled it possessively, her interest upon her treasure.

"I don't suppose you have any of this material left?" Tracy persisted.

Sylvana glanced indifferently at the cushion. "No, it has all been used. The last of it went into a scarf. A gift I made for Nursel." Then her attention seemed at last to focus upon Tracy. "I understand that Mr. Radburn will permit you a week here after all. You are working? How does the task progress?"

"Not very fast," Tracy said. "There are too many interruptions." She watched Sylvana's face, wondering how much she knew of what had happened in Miles's study.

"It surprises me that he has consented to have you remain. Perhaps, Miss Hubbard, there is something about this work of yours you have not wished to tell us?"

Tracy had no idea what she meant, but she was on guard at once. "I don't understand," she said.

162

"No matter." Sylvana's smile was enigmatic. "I must not keep you when you are so busy. Thank you for bringing me the samovar."

Thus dismissed, Tracy left her presence, newly concerned. She followed the covered passage back to the third floor of the yali. On the way she pulled off her coat and when she reached the upper salon she dropped it on a chair, drew off her beret to run her fingers through her hair. The earrings tapped her cheeks lightly and she pulled them off, tucked them into the beret. It wasn't necessary to prove her independence by wearing them now.

# 8

AS TRACY WALKED toward the door of Miles's study she saw that he had left it open to the warmth of the springlike day, and through it she could see him working at his tilted drawing table. Again he seemed completely absorbed. He was working in black ink, as he converted the intricate details of a photograph into the large, decorative calligraphy.

He glanced up and saw her in the doorway, caught the expression on her face.

"You're watching me the way you did in the mosque this morning. What does that look on your face imply?"

"I'm sorry if I stared," she said as she went into

163

the room. "You were concentrating so hard that I didn't want to interrupt you."

He made a sound of exasperation. "There's more to it than that. What were you thinking just now?"

His mood had changed completely from that of lunchtime. He was neither smiling nor darkly excited. Once more she felt uncertain, but at least she would not dissemble.

"I was wondering how you can work at that sort of thing. It's as though someone who has created cathedrals turned to copying a hedge maze."

For a moment she wasn't sure whether he would fling his brush at her angrily and dismiss her from the room, or simply retire behind his granite barrier. He did neither. To her considerable astonishment he laughed out loud. The sound was not altogether cheerful, but it was better than his scowl.

"Hornwright should know just how you've tackled this job. I'm not sure he understood what he was inflicting upon me, or the risk he was taking in sending you out here. At least you speak up, however foolish your conclusions may be. But I must ask you to remember that I am your problem only as far as this book is concerned."

Her own sense of humor revived with disconcerting unexpectedness and she found herself smiling at the picture he had evoked.

"I'll try to remember," she told him cheerfully.

"Good!" he said, sounding stiffer than before in the face of her good humor. "Now perhaps you can get on with your housekeeping. I can't endure that disturbance under the table much longer. I prefer my own forms of disorder."

She knew he meant his words to sting and was all the more determined to remain unruffled. She went to the table where the morning's mischief still awaited her, pulled up her skirt, and sat down cross-legged like the women in the mosques. She would not think of the spite behind this havoc for the moment. She would simply sort things back into their respective heaps and leave all other problems for later. The problem of Nursel, for instance, and the scarf that belonged to her.

The room was quiet except for the faint rustle of papers. As she worked, Tracy found herself once more interested in the project itself. She dipped into manuscript pages concerning the work of the Seljuk Turks, and read a little here and there. Apparently the Seljuks had left behind tiles and mosaics of surprising beauty in their mosques and mausoleums. Coming before Islam, there were even occasional human representations and animal pictures in some of their work. In their pigments they had used a great deal of turquoise and white, dark blue and indigo and gilt. A pink shading seen in some of the mosaic panels, as Miles pointed out, in his text, was due to an ingredient used to hold the tiles together. Several reproductions in color revealed the imaginative beauty of Seljuk work.

So complete was her absorption in seeking out drawings which matched the text that she was startled when Miles spoke to her.

"When I came into the house a while ago, I heard what sounded like a bang-up fight going on between Sylvana and Murat. Do you happen to know what was wrong?"

She was surprised that he would question her on affairs of the household. "I've no idea what it was about," she said. "Just as Nursel and I came upstairs, Dr. Erim burst out of Mrs. Erim's salon and rushed off. Nursel went after him and I haven't seen her since. Halide and I took the samovar to Mrs. Erim, and she seemed terribly upset over what had happened. Though of course she made no explanation to me."

Miles returned to his calligraphy and again there was quiet in the room. Tracy's work went faster now as she reached material she had sorted before. When Miles spoke again it was in a milder, more reasonable tone, as if he wanted to persuade her of something.

"I suppose that the recording of details about mosaics and their history may seem like mere copy work and note-taking, yet it's a task that needs to be done. So much is falling to ruin and

166

accounts ought to be preserved. Until a comparatively few years ago there was no written history in Turkey, you know, and there hasn't been enough consulting of what archives exist. Few translations have been made. I'm not doing this alone. A number of people are helping me get this record together. When it's finally in a book, the result will be worth accomplishing."

Tracy looked up. From her place on the floor she could see across the top of the intervening desk to where he sat on a stool, bent above his drawing board. Shadows emphasized the craggy features of his face and marked the unhappy slant of mouth corners, hiding the coldness that so often repelled her. An odd warming toward him stirred in her and she saw him as a man more dedicated than she had guessed. A man who worked with integrity at the assignment he had given himself.

Hesitantly she ventured a question. "But couldn't almost anyone do the actual copy work and free you to get on with the writing of the book?"

"This particular work happens to interest me," he said, his tone dry.

She considered him more sympathetically than she had ever expected to, wondering how to probe and explore, how to discover the true identity of the man who had been Anabel's husband. Perhaps a bold frankness was the only way to smoke him out from behind his wall.

"Mrs. Erim thinks there will never be a completed book," she said, "and that you don't really want to write it. She wants me to go home and tell Mr. Hornwright that it will never be done—so that he will call the whole thing off."

"What do you think?" he asked.

"How can I tell? You sounded just now as though you believe in this work. But you don't seem to move it ahead very quickly."

She wondered what he would say if she told him that Nursel believed the work was a hair-shirt process—a sort of punishing of himself for his treatment of Anabel in the past. But she had gone far enough for the moment and she did not dare put the thought into words. In an odd way she found that she was more reluctant than before to goad or bait him. She had begun to consider him not only as Anabel's husband, but as a man in his own right.

"Mrs. Erim may have her reasons for not wanting to see this book finished," he remarked. "The same reasons, perhaps, that led to this quarrel with her brother-in-law. It's possible that she's right and you are wasting your time here, Tracy Hubbard."

She no longer believed that Mrs. Erim was right, but before she could say so, he glanced toward the door.

"Listen!" he said.

From the direction of the stairs came the sound of high heels clicking briskly along. Miles bent above his board again. Tracy caught the scent of Sylvana's rose-drenched perfume as she came to the door of the room.

"I may speak with you, Miles?" Mrs. Erim asked.

Tracy had never listened to her voice before as an entity in itself. She noted its faintly querulous note, and a slight stridency in the higher pitches. It did not seem as tranquil as her manner.

"Of course—please come in," Miles said.

"There is a little trouble," Sylvana murmured as she entered the room. Clearly she had not seen Tracy sitting on the floor watching her over the top of the desk. Her air of composure had returned. From her blond hair drawn into its neat, heavy coil on the nape of her neck, to the tips of her smart black pumps, she looked undisturbed. If one did not listen to the faintly importunate note in her voice, one would think her wholly poised.

"First," she went on as Miles waited, "I think this American young girl must go home at once. It surprises me that you have permitted her to remain, when—"

"The American young girl is right over there," Miles said, cocking an eyebrow at Tracy. "Perhaps you would like to tell her why you think she should go home?"

Sylvana Erim was not in the least disconcerted.

She glanced calmly across the desk at the top of Tracy's head and gestured her toward the door.

"If you please? I wish to speak to Mr. Radburn alone."

Tracy looked at Miles as she stood up. "I'd really like to know why Mrs. Erim doesn't wish me to stay."

"I am sure you know my reason very well," Sylvana said.

Miles nodded toward the door. "Suppose I call you when we're through."

Mrs. Erim came at once to stand beside the drawing board, paying no further attention to Tracy. As she went out of the room, Tracy heard her exclamation of pleasure.

"This is beautiful work! The best you have done, my friend. The buyer in New York will be enormously pleased. There seems to be a sudden demand for Turkish calligraphy to use as decoration."

Tracy closed the door softly and sped across the salon to her own room. She had endured enough for one day. Somehow she must draw into the open at least one of these currents that flowed beneath the surface of life in this house. Sylvana, she knew, would tell her nothing. Dr. Erim appeared to be angry with her for some reason. But there was still Nursel, and it was time for the Turkish girl to be brought into the open.

In her room Tracy unlocked the drawer and took out the scarf she had found last evening in the palace ruins. With it folded into her purse, she went in search of the girl who had been Anabel's friend.

Nursel was not in her own room, but when Tracy questioned Halide on the lower stairs the maid gestured in the direction of the laboratory in the kiosk.

Tracy had not been in this lower section of the hillside house before, except to climb the stairs. The area seemed to be made up of a large main room, brightly lighted, with two or three smaller rooms opening along one side. The big room was rimmed with cabinets, and there were tables of equipment and shelves on which labeled cages of mice and guinea pigs were kept, lending a slightly zooey smell that was lessened by the hovering aura of perfume. At the far end Dr. Erim worked with two young assistants and he did not look up as she came in.

A light burned in one of the small cubicles and Tracy heard someone humming a plaintive Turkish tune. Tracy looked in and found Nursel, dressed in a white lab jacket, working intently with a glass measuring phial. She glanced up and smiled at Tracy.

"You have come to visit me? Good. Please come in."

Tracy stepped into the small room, where a

171

strong odor of sandalwood for the moment dominated weaker scents. On wall shelves were innumerable glass bottles, labeled and grouped in perfume families—the animal, the flower scents, the plant perfumes.

"Do you distill the oils yourselves?" she asked.

"Sometimes in spring and summer Mrs. Erim does this," Nursel said. "But it is a difficult process and it is simpler to work with essential oils and extracts already prepared. For me, it is the blending, the combining of scents that is interesting. Tell me what you think of this."

She unstoppered a small flask and put a dab of scent on the pulse place on Tracy's wrist. It was necessary to leave the atmosphere of sandalwood and step outside in order to catch the delicacy of lilac, very light and fresh.

"Lovely," Tracy said as she returned to Nursel. But she had not come here to talk about perfume. "Are you very busy? I'd like to have a talk with you, if it's possible."

"I thought you had returned to your sorting," Nursel said. "Has Mr. Radburn grown restless again?"

"Mrs. Erim wanted to see him alone. I think she wants to convince him that I should be sent home at once. Do you know why she feels this way about my being here? After all, it was she who invited me out in the first place."

Nursel bent above a glass tube, pouring

carefully. "Perhaps I can guess. But I do not think she will give Mr. Radburn her true reason for wishing you to go home."

Over her shoulder Tracy glanced toward the end of the long room. Dr. Erim seemed wholly concentrated on his work and betrayed no evidence of noticing her at all.

"Could we go somewhere else to talk?" she asked Nursel.

"But of course." The other girl finished her immediate measuring and put a stopper in the glass tube. "This will wait." She sniffed at her fingers and wrinkled her nose. "These essences which Sylvana prefers are too heavy for me. Wait—I will cleanse my hands and we will go where no one will be near."

She washed her hands in a basin and then reached for a sweater from a rack, handing it to Tracy.

"Put this on—it is a little cool outside. I have my coat near the door. Come—I will show you something."

She did not speak to her brother as they left the building, and he paid no attention to their going. Outside they followed an uphill path through the woods until they reached the summit of a small hillock, still on Erim property. Here a little summerhouse had been built, with arched doorways and open latticework walls. During warm weather it would make a charming haven

173

of cool shade. Nursel stood outside its door and directed Tracy's attention to the view.

From this height a great stretch of the Bosporus could be seen in the sunny afternoon—a winding strip of navy-blue ribbon separating Europe from Asia. In the direction of Istanbul a filmy haze hung low like the concealing veil of a harem beauty. Nearer at hand across the strait the stones of Rumeli Hisar shone golden in the light, unlike the black aspect the fortress took on after the sun had set.

"It is beautiful—our Bosporus, is it not?" Nursel said. "But how strange the currents are down there. The Black Sea is not very salty and it causes a cold surface current to flow down the strait toward the Sea of Marmara. From the Marmara a warmer, more salty undercurrent flows in the opposite direction toward Russia. Different kinds of fish are caught in these two bands. If you look from your window at night, you will see boats with bright gasoline lamps being held over the sides to attract fish into the nets. But enough of such matters—you have not asked to speak with me because you wish to know about fish. Come, here is a rock where we may sit in the sun and talk."

The rough stone surface had been warmed and dried during the bright afternoon. The two girls sat upon the boulder and were quiet for a little while. There seemed no way to go about this delicately, Tracy thought. She drew the silk scarf from her handbag and held it out.

"I'll return your scarf to you now. I know from Mrs. Erim that it is yours."

The other girl hesitated for just an instant. Then she took the scarf and opened the striped length. The plum- and cream-colored folds ran like liquid through her fingers, dropped into a pool of warm color in her lap.

"You were the woman in the ruined palace yesterday, weren't you?" Tracy said.

The girl's dark head bent over the scarf and she did not look up. At last, when Tracy thought she might not answer, she said softly, "Yes, it was I."

"Ahmet was there," Tracy said. "He was watching you. And there was a second man. All rather secret."

Nursel's head came up and she looked at Tracy with her bright, dark gaze. A gaze less gentle now, a look in which there was no meekness.

"Secret—yes. But not the affair of anyone else."

"Except that you were talking about me," Tracy said. "I've been wondering why ever since. Whoever spoke my name was angry at the time."

"And you do not know why?" Nursel asked.

"How could I know why? Was it perhaps Mr. Radburn who was with you? Or your brother?"

Nursel sighed and began to ripple the scarf

175

through her fingers as though she needed to keep her hands busy, as men did with their tespihler.

"If I tell you something, will you keep my secret? Though because of Ahmet Effendi, perhaps it is a secret no longer. He does not approve. If I tell you this, I put myself in your hands. Give me your promise that you will say nothing."

"I'm not likely to run to Mrs. Erim, or to your brother, or Mr. Radburn with confidences," Tracy said.

For a moment longer Nursel studied her, as if probing for an answer as to whether or not Tracy could be trusted. Then she nodded.

"An American promise is better sometimes than a European promise. Perhaps you will be my friend, as Anabel was my friend. The man who came to meet me in that place last evening was Hasan."

Tracy repeated the name blankly. "Hasan?"

"You do not remember? In the Covered Bazaar today—the small shop where I bought the jade tespih for Murat. Hasan is Ahmet Effendi's son."

Tracy recalled the young man at once, remembering the distrust she had felt as she had listened to the harsh note in his voice as he spoke to Nursel. She remembered too that there had been what she recognized now as a certain familiarity between him and Nursel.

"I wish to marry Hasan," Nursel confessed.

"But his father is old-fashioned and does not think such a thing suitable. My brother would be furious. He does not know. He has a great sense of position and he would oppose my marriage and I could do nothing unless I ran away. But Hasan is in no position now to afford a wife. Later, perhaps. Waiting is hard, but I must wait and let no one know until the proper time comes. Then I will laugh at anyone who tries to interfere. I do not like this—that Ahmet Effendi was watching. Soon I must speak to him. I must persuade him that we will wait."

"Would Mrs. Erim be against this too?" Tracy asked.

Nursel made a small sound of scorn. "Sylvana would be happy to see me leave the yali. She would like to turn us all out and fill the house with her friends and her entertainments. There is no loyalty in her toward the family of my father or older brother. Murat opposes her, while Ahmet Effendi remembers that our brother cherished this woman and brought her into our home. That he gave her everything it was possible to give. Ahmet Effendi's first loyalty was to our brother, after our father."

Nursel's bitterness was intense, and it seemed a release for her to put it into words. As she listened, Tracy glimpsed the anger and pain that underlay Nursel's attitude of meek obedience toward Sylvana, and toward her brother as well.

She touched the other girl's arm in sympathy. "I'm very sorry. You have my promise that I won't tell anyone. But I still don't understand why you were speaking about me in that place."

"It is because you have brought a new unrest into the house. Because where you are trouble will follow. Like the thing that was done to your work this morning. I do not like such a happening. It is like a beginning of what happened before, and it is very disturbing."

"Do you think it could have been Sylvana who played that trick?" Tracy asked. She had not thought this likely before, but after witnessing the end of Sylvana's quarrel with Dr. Erim, and after the brief scene in the study just now, she was less than sure that tranquillity was the true keystone to Sylvana Erim's character.

Nursel drew up her knees and clasped her hands tightly about them. "Sometimes it is better not to think. Not to see."

"I don't like to play ostrich," Tracy said. "What did Mr. Radburn mean this morning when he spoke of a poltergeist? What do you mean when you say the tricks have begun again?"

"This I do not wish to speak about," Nursel said. "When such tricks were played before they were a prelude to trouble. Perhaps to death."

"The death of—of Mr. Radburn's wife?" Tracy asked.

"The death of your sister," said Nursel softly.

178

For a moment the quiet in that high, sunny place was intense. For a moment it seemed to Tracy that she could not have heard the word Nursel had spoken—"sister." But there was no mistaking the way the other girl was watching her, her eyes darkly intent and questioning.

"How long have you known?" Tracy asked.

Nursel sighed softly, as though it might be a relief for her to let this secret be known.

"I knew from the moment when Sylvana phoned me in town and told me to go to the hotel to pick up an American whose name was Tracy Hubbard."

"You knew—and you said nothing?"

"It seemed that you wished to keep this a secret," Nursel said. "I gave you many opportunities to tell me and you said nothing. I feared you would suspect from my manner toward you. I could not be easy."

"But how could you have known? Anabel told me often that she let no one know she had any family."

"Yes—she explained this to me." Nursel plucked at the folds of silk in her lap. "She said nothing until the last time I saw her. The very morning of the day she died. She was wildly unhappy, distraught, not herself. Miles had been wickedly cruel to her. He had gone away from her in her time of great need. She sent me after him. She sent me to the airport to bring him back before he could leave for Ankara. But I was too late. Before I agreed to go, she was nearly hysterical. In that time she told me of her little sister in America. The sister she had sent for—who would not come to help her. The sister who had failed her."

"I suppose that's true," Tracy said and did not explain about the crying of "wolf."

"Then why do you come here now? Why do you come under this pretense of working for Miles Radburn? Why do you come here to fool us all and pretend that you know nothing of Anabel?"

It was difficult to face Nursel's accusing look. Difficult under the circumstances to know what course to take. The ground had jarred open beneath her feet.

"There are reasons," Tracy said. "It's a long story."

Nursel waited, but Tracy did not go on. She could not bring herself to speak of Anabel's hysterical phone call.

"You've kept my identity to yourself?" she asked Nursel. "Even though you knew who I was at our first meeting, you didn't tell the others?"

"Not at once," Nursel said.

Tracy sat up straight, bracing herself. "Who else knows of this now?"

"I am sorry." Nursel sounded acutely apologetic. "It did not seem proper to me that

Murat should not know. Last night I told him the truth. He is indignant that you should play such a trick upon us. That is why he was not very polite to you at breakfast."

"Now I can understand. You've told no one else?"

"Murat thought Sylvana should know also, since, in a sense, this is now her house. So he tells her today while we are in Istanbul."

Tracy remembered the veiled allusions in Sylvana's speech and understood them now. Probably at this very moment Sylvana herself was telling Miles Radburn, and Tracy could not believe that he would keep her here one moment after he knew the trick she had played upon him.

Nursel spoke gently, as though she guessed Tracy's thought. "I do not think Sylvana will tell Miles the truth about you. She would be afraid he might want you to stay, that you might ally yourself with him as Anabel's sister—against her."

"But why? I don't understand—"

"Because she does not want him to finish this book. In the beginning it was an excellent excuse to offer him her home, her hospitality—because he was doing this worthy record of Turkish history. But now it takes all his time, all his attention. He cares for nothing else. And this she does not like. It is because of Miles that she quarreled with my brother today. Murat wishes him to leave this house. But Sylvana waits for him to forget Anabel and accept the tranquillity and peace with which she wishes to surround him—at her own price."

Tracy stared at her, waiting.

"She is infatuated with him—that is what I mean."

This revelation was somehow the most disturbing of all.

"She's older than he is," Tracy objected. "And how could he—after Anabel—?"

"How upset you are, little one," Nursel said, sudden amusement brimming her eyes. "You are not, like Sylvana, a realist. You have indeed been an ostrich since coming to Istanbul. Sylvana claims her age is forty-one. She is only three years older than Miles. As my brother's widow, she is a wealthy woman. She can offer this man the safety of a cocoon in which to dull his sense of guilt. In the end she will have her way. Unless Murat can stop her. About Sylvana we can do nothing, but the prospect of having Mr. Radburn in our house forever is not a pleasant one. If I marry Hasan, I will escape. For Murat—what is there? He cannot bring himself to take a wife under circumstances as they exist. Of course he could go to Ankara, as the Turkish government wishes him to do. He would be given a fine modern laboratory connected with our best hospital. But he will not go. This is our father's home—it should belong to Murat. He is determined to stay and drive Miles away. Perhaps even Sylvana."

This was all readily understandable. There was only one part of it that Tracy could not accept.

"I think you underestimate Mr. Radburn," she said firmly. "I can't believe that he would take Sylvana seriously."

"So—you too are falling under his spell? This I do not understand. I do not like this man myself. And I have seen what he has done to Anabel—to your sister. It is a sad thing if you follow in her steps."

Tracy dismissed Nursel's words with an indignant exclamation and went at once to the question of Anabel.

"That's ridiculous. But tell me what it is he did to her. You've mentioned his cruelty and said several times that he is wicked—but you haven't explained."

Nursel flung the bright scarf about her shoulders and stood up. "We have talked enough of such things. I have no proof. If proof could be found I would tell you. Otherwise it is only the making of empty words. The air is cool up here. Let us return."

Tracy rose quickly and put out her hand. "Wait! There may not be another chance soon for us to be alone. Tell me how she died that day—I've never known any more than what was in the newspapers. Why was she out on the Bosporus alone in a boat?"

"This we have never understood," Nursel said. "Except that she meant to die. He had left her in anger and she did not wish to live. This is the only explanation possible. She took a boat from our landing—not the big caique with the engine, but a small motorboat, a boat for short travel, or for fishing. It was misty, dark and cold and rainy. She did not use the motor, we think, but rowed out into those swift currents, where she lacked strength to handle the boat. It had capsized long before they found it. Her body was recovered the next morning, below Rumeli Hisar. All that night we waited anxiously—with Miles gone to Ankara, and no help from him."

Tracy stared at the blue strip of water, winding so peacefully toward Istanbul, with its treacherous, reverse current underneath, flowing back to the north. Tears were wet upon her cheeks. Anabel had always lacked physical strength. She had been delicately made, finely boned—the fragile gossamer girl of Miles's portrait. She would have known that she'd be helpless out on that stream. What extreme desperation had driven her to choose that way to die?

Standing here on this hilltop, with the very waters in which her sister had drowned flowing at her feet, the intensity of feeling in Tracy made her faint and a little ill.

Nursel was watching in some concern. On impulse the other girl leaned to kiss her lightly on either cheek in the Turkish fashion.

"Please—you must not grieve," she said. "I do not know why you have come here secretly, but perhaps in time you will tell me this."

Tracy braced herself determinedly, blinking away both tears and faintness. She owed it to Anabel to find courage in herself and to go on.

"For one thing I'm here because I have a job to do," she said. "I'm sure Mr. Hornwright would never have sent me here if he'd known I was Anabel's sister. And I don't think Mr. Radburn would like it if he knew. Is it necessary to tell him?"

"*I* will not tell," Nursel promised. "I also believe Sylvana will not tell. But Murat will consider it his duty to inform Miles of this. He does not like the man, but he will do what he believes to be correct. Not at once, perhaps. He will examine the matter carefully with his scientist's mind before he acts. So perhaps there is a little time."

"If Mr. Radburn has to know, I'd rather tell him myself," Tracy said. "But not right away. I need a few days' grace first." Time, she thought—time to fight her way through the mists that still engulfed Anabel.

"Then you must speak with Murat yourself," Nursel said. "If you like, I will arrange this for tonight. Sylvana is having a small dinner party in her house and Miles will be there. I, also. But Murat will not attend her parties. There will be time for you to speak with him alone after dinner this evening."

As they started down the hill together, Nursel slipped a hand through the crook of Tracy's arm in a gesture almost affectionate. It was as if she wished to transfer something of her feeling for Anabel to Anabel's sister.

On the way back to the house Tracy asked one of the questions that remained unanswered. "I still don't know why you were talking about me with Hasan in that place yesterday, or why you both sounded so angry."

"You must understand," Nursel said. "It is necessary for me to discuss with Hasan all that is of importance to me. So of course I have told him this thing about you. He argued with me that I must tell the others. He was angry with me that I did not at first wish to do this. Today at the bazaar he reproached me again. A man does not always understand that a woman's small fibs may be necessary."

"But why should he feel that way about me?" Tracy found it disturbing to realize that this young man should harbor strong convictions about her when he did not know her at all.

"Hasan never liked my friendship with Anabel," Nursel admitted. "He wishes me to have no friendship for her sister."

Another thought occurred to Tracy. "Then Ahmet must know about me too—since he was listening to you yesterday."

"It is possible this is true," Nursel said absently, more concerned with the fact that Ahmet must have overheard her personal words with Hasan.

Somehow Tracy felt more uncomfortable about Ahmet's knowledge of her identity than about having Sylvana and Murat know who she was. From the first Ahmet had seemed the traditional plotter of Turkish legend, and she could not free herself of this impression.

As they walked down the hill, Nursel, at least, flung off her pensive mood and became once more lighthearted. As lighthearted as she had seemed this morning, Tracy recalled, when she was going into Istanbul to see Hasan.

"You must not disturb yourself," Nursel told her comfortingly. "I do not always do what men may tell me to do. I have the new independence."

Tracy wondered about that. Perhaps Nursel's independence was mostly wishful thinking. When Murat ordered, she seemed always ready to perform, used by him perhaps more than she herself realized.

"But what about Ahmet?" Tracy persisted. "Now that he knows about me, do you think—"

"Do not worry," Nursel broke in with reassurance. "Since Ahmet Effendi detests Miles also, you need not fear that he will tell him anything. Everyone will now wait in silence—to see what you will do. Except perhaps Murat."

The picture of that silent waiting carried no reassurance for Tracy. As they reached the kiosk and she left Nursel to her perfume blending and returned to Miles's study, Tracy found herself thoroughly dismayed by the fact that for a good part of the time that she had been in Istanbul the people whom she trusted least had been fully aware of her identity. After all her reluctance, Anabel must indeed have been distraught to give away her secret at the last moment.

That Miles did not yet know offered little comfort. This meant that the moment of telling him could not be postponed too long, or someone else would speak to him first. Yet it must be postponed for a little while, lest he send her home just when she was beginning to get a clearer picture of the relationships within this house.

Her immediate hope for concealment now lay in Murat Erim's hands. But it would be hard to face a man who was already indignant about her deception and ask a favor of him. The immediate prospect was thoroughly unsettling.

# 9

MILES HAD given up work on the strip of calligraphy and was sitting at his desk, reading and jotting notes with a pencil. He barely looked up when she entered and he did not question her long absence.

She was glad enough to slip in unnoticed and return to her work. The interview with Nursel and its resulting revelations had left her shaken. One of the things she liked least, though she had flinched from considering it at the time, was Nursel's implication that Tracy herself might be falling under the spell of Miles Radburn.

This, of course, was ridiculous. Because she could not always trust Anabel's claims, Tracy had tried in the beginning to be open-minded about him. Once she had met him, antagonism had flared between them and she had been at a loss to know what his true feeling toward her sister might have been. Today he had surprised her several times, leaving her further confused by the riddle he posed. But that did not mean she could be charmed by him, as Anabel had been charmed in the days before her disillusionment. This was not the problem.

The problem that confronted Tracy was how to explain why she had come here without letting anyone know that she was Anabel's sister. In her confidence that no one could know of her existence, she had painted herself very neatly into a corner from which there now seemed no easy escape.

"If you're going to sit under a table in this ridiculous fashion," Miles said abruptly, "you might at least stop sighing. I can hardly think for your breathing. Come along and we'll find you a chair. Maybe that will help."

It was uncomfortable to meet his eyes, she discovered. The role she had been playing in this house was no longer a safe disguise. She felt thoroughly self-conscious and all too easy to read.

Miles went into the central salon, picked up the round table, and bore it back to his study, velvet covering and all. Tracy chose the most solid of the four straight chairs and followed him. He planted the table in an empty space with an air of furious impatience, and she put the chair beside it. When she had gathered up some of the papers and drawings under the long table, she sat with her back to Miles and went to work. She was careful not to sigh, and she tried not to think about anything but Turkish mosaics.

They worked the afternoon out in silence. After a time Miles put aside his book and began to write busily with a pen. Not until it was past five o'clock did he stack several sheets together and bring them to Tracy.

"I presume you can type?" he said. "Perhaps you can prove your usefulness and copy these pages for me when you have time. There's a typewriter in the corner over there—one that speaks English. You've made me feel guilty about the manuscript part of this book. If you're to stay on for a time and protect that job of yours at *Views*, we'd better prove that there's something here for you to do."

She heard his sudden kindness in surprise. "I'll type it right away," she said and glanced at the handwriting to make sure she could read it. The strong script was legible and familiar. She remembered it well from the curt note he had sent to her at the hotel.

"I'm going to stop for now," he said. "I want to get out for a good walk before I have to dress for Sylvana's dinner tonight."

He stood for a moment beside her chair, as though waiting for her to look up at him. She recalled that he did not like to leave her in this room when he was out.

"Would you like me to stop now?" she asked.

"That's not necessary if you want to work a while longer." He drew a key from his pocket and laid it on the table beside her. "I've found an extra key for this room. You can keep it, if you like. Bolt the balcony doors when you leave, and lock the study door after you. Then there'll be no more interference with your work."

She looked at him, puzzled over his changed attitude, feeling increasingly guilty. "What did you mean about a poltergeist? Who do you think did this?"

"Poltergeist is as good a word as any for a mischief-maker. Perhaps it will stop now. I see no reason why anyone should try to frighten you into leaving. Let's forget about it unless something else happens. There seems to be no real harm behind it."

Tracy wondered, remembering that both Miles and Nursel had spoken of Anabel being frightened into desperation. Besides, there was a reason why someone might want to drive her away. A reason Miles knew nothing about—the fact that she was Anabel's sister.

He left her to her work, and the sense of his unexpected kindness stayed with her. He had, after all, considered her future at *Views* and was trying to safeguard it for her—while she was tricking and deceiving him in a way that could only bring his anger and contempt upon her when he discovered the truth. Nursel's hinting had been ridiculous, but nevertheless Tracy found that while she might not mind Miles Radburn's anger—that was something she had already dealt with—his contempt would be something else. She turned from the thought of it with a distaste that surprised her.

After he had gone she had bolted the veranda

doors. Now and then as she typed, she glanced uneasily at the open door to the study. Once when the clatter of typewriter keys was still, she thought she heard footsteps in the salon. But, though she went to the door and looked out, no one was there.

At length she finished her copy work and returned to her room. She was glad to have Yasemin slip in with her for company. The fact that everyone in this household except Miles knew she was Anabel's sister made her seem far more alone than before, and doubly vulnerable. What else could anyone think except that she was here because Anabel had told her something, because she was following some definite lead? They could not know how very little had been given to guide her. Only that mention of black amber, of some secret and Anabel's desperate cry. "I don't want to die!" she had wailed—and gone out on the Bosporus in a boat she could not handle.

By now Yasemin had accepted Tracy. She permitted herself to be stroked and petted and finally settled down to dreaming in Tracy's lap, offering an illusion of companionship. The two of them stayed quietly where they were until Halide brought a tray to the room, with a note from Nursel.

Murat was working late in the laboratory tonight, Nursel had written, and would eat over there. So perhaps Tracy would prefer to have this early tray in her room. The servants would be very busy later with Sylvana's nine o'clock dinner party. Nursel had talked to her brother and he would see Tracy at eight-thirty. She was to go to the living quarters Nursel shared with her brother. He would await her there.

Tracy was grateful for this smoothing of her way and glad that she need not face Dr. Erim at dinner. For the moment she must put aside her fearfulness about the encounter and find a way to pass the time.

Again she and Yasemin shared a meal, and afterward Tracy picked up one of the Turkish books Miles had loaned her and began to read of Ottoman times, of the legends and scandals that clung to those days. She found a rather gruesome elaboration of the story Nursel had told her on her first trip across the Bosporus in the car ferry—about the harem ladies who were dropped into the shallows off Seraglio Point when they displeased or bored a reigning sultan. There had been one such sultan who had made a thoroughly fresh start by ordering a hundred concubines tied up in sacks that were well weighted with stones at the feet, and gathered and tied tightly below the chin so that no struggling would be possible when they were dropped into the Bosporus. Sometime later a diver had gone down into these waters and found the hundred ladies all standing

194

up on the bottom, their long hair streaming in the current, swaying as if they performed some macabre dance.

The story was too vividly told for comfort and it added much to Tracy's uneasiness in a room that overlooked the Bosporus. When it grew dark, she went out upon the balcony and stood watching the night scene once more, reminding herself that the Ottoman Empire was long gone and Istanbul today was probably no more wicked than any other modern city.

Out on the dark waters she saw fishing boats moving, and the lights Nursel had described that would attract fish. Voices came clearly across the water, and now and then the whistling of a passing steamer added utterance to other night sounds. On the far side Rumeli Hisar stood dark and lonely, its towers black against the sky.

The thought of Anabel was strong and constant. It would not let her be.

She was glad when it was time to face Dr. Erim. Any sort of action was welcome by now. She brushed her hair until it shone and renewed her lipstick. As a last touch she clipped on the blue earrings that had been Nursel's gift. To charm Murat? she wondered wryly. Or merely to keep away the evil eye?

Nursel's brother waited for her in their sitting room. When he opened the door at her knock, she saw that he had spread a number of objects from his collection over the surface of a carved ebony table. He held a small satsuma bowl, turning it in his fingers, playing with it as he had with his tespih. She sensed in him something of an Oriental love for objects that could be savored by touch as well as by eye.

As he invited her into the room, she saw that he was no longer the angry man she had seen today at breakfast. There was a gentle, almost poetic sadness about his dark features. She noted again how arrestingly handsome he was, how naturally graceful in his movements—and how aware of feminine company.

"First—I must apologize," he said. "This morning I was extremely disturbed. I fear I was rude to a guest."

"You had every right to be annoyed," Tracy said frankly. "I suppose I've done a very foolish thing."

He drew her to a chair and piled cushions behind her when she sat down. "It is your right to do as you wish. I was disturbed because I thought at first that Radburn had brought you here, knowing very well that you were Anabel's sister, and that he was keeping this fact from us."

"Oh, no," Tracy said quickly. "Mr. Radburn doesn't know. That's why I've come to talk to you—to ask you not to tell him."

He stared intently at the small bowl in his hands, then set it on the table next to a small brass Buddha. "This we must discuss a little," he said. "There are certain aspects of this affair I would like to understand."

"I'm not sure I can explain," Tracy admitted. "I've acted mainly on impulse, I'm afraid. When this opportunity to come to Turkey arose so suddenly, I was afraid to tell Mr. Hornwright that I was the sister of Miles Radburn's wife. He might have thought I'd be an unsettling influence and no help in moving this book ahead."

Murat nodded gravely, watching her with an uncomfortable intentness. Suddenly he moved to bring a standing lamp closer so that its light would fall upon her, reveal her every expression. The inquisitor testing a prisoner? she thought wryly. His words surprised her.

"No—I can see nothing of Anabel in your face. Not the slightest look of her. Your expression is different, your way of speaking. There is no resemblance that I can find."

"That's true," she agreed. "People have always pointed it out. And I've always wished I were more like her. I've never seen anyone as beautiful as Anabel."

He did not disagree, or deny, but his sudden smile was for her and not for Anabel. "I can see that it would be difficult for any girl to have a sister, even a half sister, like Anabel. But I think you can make yourself very interesting and

197

pretty. I am glad to see you wearing such feminine earrings this evening."

"Nursel gave them to me," she said shortly.

"They become you. It is possible that in your growing-up years you have tried not to be prettily feminine because you believed you could not compete with Anabel. Is this not so?"

The conversation was taking so unexpected a turn that Tracy could only stare at him in astonishment.

Again his smile lifted for a moment the sadness that seemed to touch him tonight. "You are surprised that I compliment you? But why? You are a most feminine person. But you must be a little more frivolous, a little more fashionable, perhaps, in your dress."

"I can't ever be like Anabel," she said.

"No, you cannot be like Anabel. Your long hair, with the coil at the back becomes you, and such touches as the earrings you are wearing. Perhaps a dress less severe? You will forgive me for speaking frankly? Nursel can teach you much."

Tracy thought of Miles snatching off the earrings because they did not suit her, and the memory made her laugh. She was no longer angry because of what he had done. It seemed amusing that in this one day two men had reacted in so opposite a fashion to a pair of dangling blue earrings.

Her sudden smile must have touched a near-the-surface sensitivity in the man, for he winced. But at almost the same instant a much louder burst of laughter came from beyond the glass doors that bordered the veranda on the uphill side. Tracy glanced toward them and saw that lights glowed brightly all through the second floor of the kiosk and the chatter of voices and laughter was reaching them with the arrival of each new guest.

Murat frowned and went at once to close the draperies, jerking them in annoyance across the glass.

"She is forever entertaining," he said. "She knows everyone in Istanbul. The French ambassador is here tonight, and several government officials. Tonight she will be showing them the samovar, boasting of her find, proving once more how clever she is. When it should not belong to her at all."

Tracy pondered that. "You mean because it should be returned to the museum?"

"That, of course. Though, since she has considerable influence in high places, she will be permitted to keep it for a time. No, there is another reason."

He hesitated as though he could not decide whether to continue. Then he fixed Tracy once more with his keen, dark gaze that was so different from Miles Radburn's. Miles's cold look seemed to glance off without penetration. It was as though he seldom saw the one he looked at. This man's eyes hunted for the meaning that was essentially a part of the person who held his attention. Tracy felt uncomfortably that it would be difficult to keep a secret from him.

He pulled a carved chair away from the table and turned it so that he could sit astride it, facing her, his arms folded upon its back.

"I will tell you," he said. "I will tell you why that woman has no right to the samovar. She stole it from Anabel Radburn."

Tracy waited, suddenly alert and wary.

Murat studied her reaction as intently as though, without speaking, she might tell him something. "Perhaps I have said this too strongly. It was your sister who first found the samovar, dusty and unnoticed in a shop in the bazaar. From the first it seemed to speak to her. There were times when one suspected that she had some sixth sense few others possess. She managed to unearth the samovar's story and it enchanted her. At once she wanted Miles to buy it for her. The shopkeeper recognized tardily that he had a treasure in his hands and asked a fantastic price. Radburn did not care for the thing or its history, and he would not pay the price or bargain with the man. He did not want to encourage such whimsies in his wife. He said she could not have it—though he nearly broke her heart over the denial. Some months later it disappeared from view in the shop, and Anabel was forced to stop going to Istanbul to visit it. She had made a habit of this. We knew of it, though she did not tell her husband."

Murat's hands sought for a cigarette and lighted it. "You do not smoke? Good. Turkish women, like Turkish men, smoke too much today. Nursel—and Sylvana as well. I prefer a woman who does not smoke. But to return to the samovar. Anabel stopped begging for it, and there was peace again during the few days before her death. Only recently I learned that Sylvana had gone to Istanbul and made a payment on the samovar, knowing well that Anabel had set her heart upon it. She left it hidden at the back of the shop until she could bring it home without offending Mrs. Radburn.

"After your sister's death, she hesitated to produce it immediately and remind Miles of the unhappy quarreling over it. But now she has come into the open and has it for herself. Not that she truly appreciates it as a work of art. She is simply one to covet what others value."

So Nursel had not understood her brother's attitude about the samovar, Tracy thought. She had believed he would envy Sylvana for possessing it.

"I do not like to see that evil object come to my father's house," Murat went on darkly. "Though perhaps it was ordained from the first to be brought here."

"Do you believe that?" Tracy asked.

He smiled a little tightly. "I am a Turk as well as a scientist. We are an emotional people, Miss Hubbard. Outwardly we may at times seem stolid and reserved. We are not explosive and given to expressing our slightest feelings without inhibition, as are the Greeks who live among us. But we have existed with the idea of Kismet too long not to have a certain fatalistic cast to our thinking. It is perhaps a thing that holds some of our people back from making faster progress. Though I believe we learn to do for ourselves today and do not always wait for God to act. Perhaps there is something I can do about this samovar."

"So it won't cast its evil eye upon this house?" Tracy asked dryly.

He shook his head. "You are making fun. It is clear that you are not at all like Anabel. She had great belief in evil as an entity in itself."

"I think she believed in goodness too," Tracy said quickly. "She loved to give happiness to those around her. When she was young there was always gaiety and happiness wherever Anabel was. She believed that happiness was something she could hold in her hand, and she was always reaching for it."

"Yet in the end she opened her fingers and let it slip away," Murat said.

Tracy wanted the discussion to go no further. It

was time to push her reason for this interview, to extract from him the promise she needed.

"As I've said, I'm here tonight to ask you not to tell Mr. Radburn who I am. At least not right away."

"I have no liking for Radburn," Murat said. "I do not care whether he knows about this or not. Except that he is still a guest in this house and that even an unwilling host has certain obligations. Perhaps you will tell me now why you have come to Istanbul under a pretense and still do not wish this man to know your identity."

She tried very hard to sound convincing. "It's just that I'd rather tell him myself. But not right away. If I can get into this work a little more deeply first, then perhaps he will let me stay."

"Why are you so determined to stay?"

"Because I have a job to do," Tracy told him, aware that she had begun to sound a little dogged.

"I see. We travel in circles and again you do not wish to tell me the truth. Perhaps it is none of my affair. No matter—I have something for you." He went to the cabinet where the remainder of his collection was displayed and took something from it, brought it to Tracy. The object was a small, tightly corked glass vial filled with a pale liquid.

"It is perfume," Murat said. "You may open it if you like."

She twisted the cork from the neck of the bottle and sniffed the light fragrance. It had a touch of sweetness without being cloying, and there was a woodsy scent to it that reminded one of some cool, mossy place where ferns might grow, warmed indirectly by the sun.

"This was Anabel's formula," Murat said. "She told me the recipe. There is oak moss in the base, a touch of ylang-ylang, and other ingredients as well. Your sister was fascinated by Sylvana's work with perfumes, but my sister-in-law would not trouble to teach her anything after a first attempt. Anabel's hands moved too swiftly, with too great carelessness, so that she broke some of Sylvana's equipment. After that, only Nursel would trouble to teach her. In a sense it was a game Anabel played, though she had some talent for it, I think. To encourage her I ordered from her an essence—for a lady whom I described to her. That small bottle of scent was the result. You may keep it, if you like. The lady was imaginary, based perhaps on Anabel herself."

Though Tracy had refixed the cork, a hint of delicate fragrance lingered on the air. It was as light and gay as Anabel herself had once been and she found it hard to swallow past the lump in her throat. The man was watching her with his air of gentle sadness, and she was suddenly aware of a possible significance behind everything he had said and done in this room tonight.

"You were fond of my sister, weren't you?" she said in wonderment.

At once the gentleness was gone and the sadness with it. He was on guard against her, alert and ready to deny.

She spoke again, quickly, as she stood up. "I'm glad to have this. Thank you for it. Will you at least let me tell Mr. Radburn who I am in my own way? If you will, I'll waste no more of your time."

"Very well," he agreed, still watchful. "It shall be as you wish."

He came with her to the door, but when they reached it, he did not open it for her, but paused with his hand on the knob.

"Before you leave," he said, "perhaps you will tell me why you were eager to choose the black amber tespih yesterday, and then deliberately discarded it."

He saw too much. He sensed too much. Now she could see what had been done to her. Murat had calmed her, appeared to sympathize, complimented and advised her—and then he had struck home to the heart of the thing he wanted to know.

"I don't know what you mean," she managed. "I don't especially care for black jet—why would I choose it?"

"Yet you wanted *that* tespih. I saw the wish in your eyes and it made me curious."

The very flush in her cheeks was giving her away, but she could not reach for the doorknob with his hand still upon it and she had no answer for him.

"It is a very strange thing," he mused. "This affinity for black amber. Anabel chose the jet at once when I offered her a tespih from my collection. I wonder why? Did you perhaps receive a letter from your sister before her death? Did she tell you anything that might be useful to you here in this house?"

She was warned now. The smell of danger was in the air and she knew how careful she must be.

"Yes—Anabel wrote me a letter. She wrote that she wanted me to come to Istanbul for a visit. I couldn't make the trip at that time. Perhaps I failed her by not coming. So it was necessary for me to come now, even though too late."

"What you might call a sentimental pilgrimage?" He opened the door for her, bowing slightly. "I have enjoyed your visit," he said, and there was a note of mockery in his voice.

She thanked him again for the perfume and for his promise. The door did not close at once behind her, and she knew he must be watching as she climbed the stairs.

The third floor seemed bleak and cold and empty when she reached it. The dim chandelier scarcely dispersed the shadows. But she had left a light burning in her own room, and there light and warmth welcomed her. Yasemin had waited. The mangal was freshly stoked with hot coals.

Anabel's eyes had been faintly green, Tracy thought. Was that one reason Miles so violently disliked this cat with green eyes?

She sat down and uncorked the perfume vial again. Woods and moss and sweetness—gay as a light summer breeze. She had not thought enough of Dr. Murat Erim's role in this picture. Samovar and sweet perfume and black amber—a pungent mixture of Turkish intrigue.

At least she knew something about Dr. Erim that she had not known before. His very resistance to her question had given her the truth. Murat Erim had been in love with Anabel. Where that fact led she could not tell, except that it might account for Murat's antagonism toward Miles Radburn. Miles's own indifference toward the other man seemed to indicate either that Murat's interest in his wife had remained ineffectual, or Miles did not care one way or the other. Somehow she found the latter hard to believe.

In any event, each of those who knew that Tracy Hubbard was Anabel's sister was intent in his own way upon seeing her go home as quickly as possible. This fact left her all the more certain that she was on the verge of some discovery. A discovery that would surely have to do with the ominous leitmotiv of black amber.

Yet Miles, who still did not know her identity, was the one she feared most, and she could not yet bring herself to tell him the secret the others knew. She would do it. But not yet.

The next few days passed quietly enough. Since she had a key to the study and Miles no longer minded if she worked in the room alone, she could go and come as she liked and was thus able to keep busy. None of her neat piles of paper had been disturbed again. No further untoward tricks had been played upon her. When it came to Turkish history, her education was growing apace. Miles had put a great deal of work into this book, she was discovering. At least into the first half of it. In recent months, it seemed, he had slowed down, perhaps losing the impetus of his first interest.

Once or twice she managed to coax him into telling her something of the places he had visited around Turkey, about the discoveries that were still being made. Then his interest would seem to kindle. But it did not last and he would quickly fall back into listless plodding. Sometimes he would sit at his desk staring at nothing, or he would fling himself impatiently from the room and go for long walks along the Bosporus.

For several afternoons in succession he gathered up his painting equipment and simply disappeared. Yet at these times he went on no distant trips, for his car remained in the garage and he would return too quickly to have been far away. After such disappearances restlessness and impatience would lie more heavily than ever upon him. He offered no explanation and it was not for Tracy to question him, however much she might wonder.

Except for mealtime, and not always then, she saw little of Murat and Nursel. And she saw nothing at all of Sylvana.

The day of her twenty-third birthday came, but she mentioned the fact to no one. Anabel had made much of every birthday of Tracy's. Even after Tracy was grown, Anabel would remember and some surprise always arrived on time, revealing that affection and imagination had gone into the choosing of a present. Once or twice Anabel had been ill, but even then some token gift had come, to make Tracy laugh and think warmly of her sister.

This would be the first birthday with no Anabel to remember it. The knowledge that all the good and lovely things Anabel had once been in the young Tracy's affection were gone forever came sharply home, bringing with it a further realization of loss.

Tracy was glad to spend the day working quietly and to avoid the rest of the household except for Miles. He was deep in one of his long silences and seemed not to know that she was about. During the afternoon he went out, as usual not mentioning where he was going. Tracy worked alone until Halide came with a not unexpected summons to Sylvana Erim's quarters in the kiosk. Ever since her talk with Nursel several days before, Tracy had known this moment must come. Sylvana, being in possession of the truth, would not be content to let matters go indefinitely.

As she followed Halide, Tracy touched the feather pin that was one of Anabel's imaginative gifts. She felt closer to her sister today than she had felt for a long while.

# 10

SYLVANA'S SALON, though perfumed as always, was not aglow with lamplight this afternoon. Instead, all draperies had been drawn aside from the windows to allow full daylight to possess the room. Sylvana sat against piled cushions on her divan, not reclining as a Turkish lady of the past might have done, but with her straight French spine upright, and one arm resting upon an inlaid table beside her. The scene was arresting, not only because of the golden-haired woman in a saffron yellow gown, but because the Anatolian Samovar occupied the table beside her in all its copper splendor. The exterior had been burnished to a rich gleam, and highlights reflected the saffron of her dress.

"Please come in, Miss Hubbard," Sylvana said without moving her head. "It will not disturb Mr. Radburn if we speak together a little."

Today the scent of Parma violet engulfed her as Tracy entered the room. She saw that Miles had set up his easel near a window where the light was good and he stood with a brush in one hand, and palette in the other, his attention wholly concentrated on the canvas before him.

So this was what his recent afternoon absences had meant. Apparently he was painting again— painting Sylvana Erim and her samovar. It did not help Tracy's equanimity to find him there. With so present an opportunity, who was to know what Sylvana might have told him? Or what she might now say in front of him?

Tracy took her place on the lower divan where she had sat before on the day when men from the villages had displayed their wares for Sylvana.

"Mr. Radburn tells me that you are proving yourself of more help to him than he expected, and that your work progresses well." Sylvana spoke without disturbing her pose.

"I'm glad," Tracy said, and ran the tip of her tongue along her lips.

Miles paid no attention to either of them. He wore a frown between dark brows, as though he did not care for what he saw evolving upon the canvas.

"Perhaps you know by now just how much

211

longer this work will occupy you?" Sylvana questioned. "A week more, do you think? Two weeks?"

"I'm not sure," Tracy answered carefully. "Mr. Radburn has ordered a proper file for me from Istanbul. As soon as it comes I can arrange his material in folders with a cross index. In the meantime, I am retyping pages of manuscript that have been revised. There's still a great deal to be done. I understand that much more information must be collected, many more drawings made before it will be possible to select those that are most representative."

She was echoing Miles now, giving the very excuses he gave for continuing his work indefinitely.

Sylvana remained outwardly tranquil, but one hand moved in her lap, the gesture faintly impatient.

Miles spoke at once. "Keep your hand the way it was. I want that ring to show. It will be the only touch of green in the picture."

"He will not let me see," Sylvana murmured plaintively to Tracy, and turned her hand so that the great square-cut emerald flashed, its light caught and thrown back, coppery-green, in the plump, burnished sides of the samovar. "He says I must not see this portrait until it is completed. But to return to the matter of your work, Miss Hubbard. Once this file you speak of is arranged, perhaps Mr. Radburn will then be able to keep his own work in order. Or perhaps I may be able to help him achieve such order myself."

The woman's hands were quiet now, her blue eyes calm, but her lips had tightened just a little. It was not hard to imagine that Sylvana might harbor a special feeling for Miles Radburn. But if this was true, what was his response? Tracy found herself glancing at him quickly, almost anxiously.

He laid down his brush and stepped back from the canvas, regarding it with disapproval. "Get to the point, Sylvana. Tell Tracy what it is you want."

"The English are so blunt," Sylvana murmured, but there was a look about her that said a Frenchwoman might be blunt too if the purpose served her. "I will tell you then. Of course I do not wish to hurry you beyond reason, but I have invited several friends who are coming from Paris to visit me. As you can see, your room and the one next to it, both being on the Bosporus side of the yali, are considered most attractive to visitors. I am sorry, but—"

"You'll want me to move, of course," Tracy said.

Sylvana permitted herself a slight smile. "I am glad that you understand. Perhaps you will not be sorry to leave this particular room, Miss Hubbard?"

Tracy stiffened at this reminder that the room had been Anabel's.

"Why should she want to leave it?" Miles asked.

The answer came blandly. "The sounds of the Bosporus, the cold, the damp, of course. For myself—I do not care for those rooms."

"If you need the space," Tracy said, "I can return to Istanbul for the remainder of my stay. I believe there are buses that come out here. I can manage."

"That would be difficult and inconvenient," Miles said. "How soon are these guests of yours coming, Sylvana?"

Mrs. Erim raised an eyebrow in mild reproach, but she gave in with seeming grace. "It is possible that we can postpone this visit for a little while. I do not of course want to inconvenience you."

"That's fine," said Miles.

Tracy found that her fingers were tightly interlaced in her lap. The battle had been won, with Miles's help, but she did not feel particularly reassured. Sylvana Erim's full arsenal of weapons would not be wasted in vain display. Tracy did not think that this apparent surrender meant a great deal. She left her place, presuming that she had been dismissed, but Miles spoke to her again.

"Come here and take a look," he ordered.

214

"While I never let the subject of a portrait breathe over my shoulder and start objections before I am finished, I sometimes welcome an outside eye."

Though she wanted only to escape, Tracy stepped behind the easel to look at the picture. The portrait had not progressed very far, but the tones in which he meant to paint were indicated. There was to be no mistiness here. He was doing Sylvana Erim in shades of gold and copper that made the canvas gleam with light. Already the samovar's shape was evident, and a saffron flow of color that was the form of the woman on the divan. There was no detail as yet, and he had not touched her face. Tracy wondered if he were merely playing with color at this point in order to postpone the moment when he must come to grips with his subject and really paint.

"The thing doesn't come to life," Miles muttered. "The colors are good and so is the general composition—woman and samovar in that juxtaposition. But it doesn't live."

"Dear Miles—you must not be discouraged too quickly," Sylvana put in. "You have grown unused to the brush. This will come. You will recover your touch, and without doubt this portrait will bring you great fame."

"It's not fame I'm thinking about," Miles said. "It's the loss of interest in painting anything at all that troubles me. Theoretically, I want to paint. But, specifically, I don't find a subject that sets off the necessary spark of energy."

Miles's inference that he found her less than inspiring did not please Sylvana. She looked as though she might burst through her veneer of calm, thus further irritating Miles. Tracy spoke quickly to distract them both to a safer topic.

"How beautiful the samovar is now that it has been cleaned and polished. Are you planning to use it for serving coffee, Mrs. Erim?"

"Never! But certainly not!" Sylvana protested. "One does not give a museum piece common usage. Even the polishing I have done myself. There was a green film in some places—which has prevented corrosion of course. But the samovar has received rough treatment. There are scratches and dents. I have disturbed it as little as possible. It is enough to beautify the exterior."

Tracy was studying its detail for herself, and a small amusing circumstance caught her eye.

"Do you see?" she said to Miles. "There in the samovar?"

He stared at the great gleaming thing and a faint quirk lifted one corner of his mouth. "That's rather interesting," he said and picked up his brush.

Tracy stepped back, not daring to watch him. The reflection in the copper curves of the samovar was not flattering to Mrs. Erim. If he chose to develop it, she would be even less pleased.

Sylvana stirred against her cushions. "What is it? You must tell me what you see."

"Don't wriggle, please," Miles said. "I'll give you a chance to rest in a moment. Let me catch this first. And don't ask questions. If I pull it off, you'll see it in plenty of time."

Sylvana sighed and settled back. The emerald winked on her finger and repeated its green fire in the samovar's mocking reflection. Tracy noted for the first time that just below the tall chimney a circlet of blue beads had been hung.

"Why is it wearing a necklace?" she asked.

Sylvana smiled. "That is Halide's notion. It is the only way I can get the girl to come into the same room with the samovar. She thinks the blue will halt its evil emanations."

"I like the beads there," Miles said. "A good Turkish touch. I'm not sure Halide isn't right about the emanations. Nor am I sure the blue beads are strong enough magic to protect us."

He worked for a while longer and then stopped with an impatient gesture and began to put away his painting things.

"Nothing comes right today, and I've tired you enough for this sitting, Sylvana. Will you give me a hand with this stuff, Tracy?"

As Tracy moved to help him, Sylvana spoke with calm authority. "I wish to see Miss Hubbard for a few moments, please. I will send her to you later."

It was clear that the unpleasantness for which Tracy had braced herself earlier was coming, and she waited, standing once more with her thumbs hooked into the belt of her dress in her attitude of resistance. She caught Miles's amused glance upon her before he took his equipment away, but that merely strengthened her determination not to be put down, no matter what was coming.

As he left, Nursel slipped into the room in the manner of one who did not expect to be sent away, and Tracy wondered if she had come to watch the final performance, in which Anabel's sister was to be sent home.

Idly the girl paused beside a table where a box stood open. "I see you have received the new shipment of tespihler from Hasan Effendi," she said.

Sylvana nodded carelessly. "The demand for them in New York seems to be growing. I can help the young man a little by buying such things from him."

Nursel dipped her hand into the box and scooped up a bright handful of beads. Tracy watched as they slipped through her fingers. Among the blue and red and brown she caught a brief gleam of shiny black before the beads clattered into the box.

"Perhaps there are other ways in which Ahmet

Effendi's son could be helped," Nursel said without looking at Sylvana.

Tracy paid little attention to the older woman's indifferent reply. The dark refrain had been sounded again. Meaningless, or otherwise? There had been no black amber among the beads Hasan had shown them in the shop. At what point, in what manner had these been added? Their presence would seem of no significance if it were not for Tracy's memory of a voice on the telephone and the desperate whistling of a nursery tune.

Sylvana's attention returned to Tracy. She did not ask her to sit down, but spoke out frankly. "Murat has told me that you are the sister of that unfortunate girl who caused us so much trouble, so much grief."

"That's true," said Tracy and felt again the dryness of her mouth. "I'm Anabel's sister."

"May I ask why you have come to Istanbul without giving us this information in which we would all naturally be interested?"

Stiffly Tracy repeated the reasons she had given to Murat and to Nursel, and nothing she said rang convincingly in her own ears. Sylvana listened with calm attention, and the samovar beside her gave back an oddly malevolent reflection.

"You expect us to believe this story?" she said when Tracy finished.

219

"It's all true," said Tracy, knowing very well that it was true, but that it was not enough of the truth.

"I have thought of this for several days," Sylvana said. "I have taken no action because I wished to consider the matter fully. Since the truth is now known to everyone in this house, it would seem natural to me that you must now inform Mr. Radburn. But you have not done so?"

Tracy shook her head and stood her ground. She could only hope that the churning of unreasonable fright that had risen in her so suddenly did not show. The sight of black amber beads had been unnerving.

"You have kept silent because you know he would send you home at once? Is this not so?" Sylvana prompted.

"I don't know what he would do," Tracy said. "I have a job to finish here. When it's done, I'll tell him. Just before I go home."

"Do you truly think I will permit such a thing?" Sylvana asked. "You are a foolish young girl. Mr. Radburn has begun to paint again. This portrait may be his salvation. I will not have him upset by such an occurrence. Tomorrow I will arrange for your passage home by plane. You will leave on the day after. I make myself clear?"

Tracy took a long slow breath. "I've offered to move into Istanbul. There's no reason why I need to stay in this house if you want my room."

Sylvana made an impatient movement with one hand, breaking her outward pose of calm. The samovar at her elbow reproduced the movement in miniature in its smooth copper surface, adding a baleful interpretation.

"As I say, you will be on the plane day after tomorrow," Sylvana told her. "If you are not, I will explain the truth to Mr. Radburn myself and see that he sends you home. I think he will not be pleased with what I tell him."

The trembling of inner anxiety was about to possess her utterly, Tracy knew. All the cards were in Sylvana's hands and her bluff was being called. She made one last effort.

"What if I tell him myself, Mrs. Erim?"

"That is as you please," Sylvana said. "In that case, I will of course add my own comments. Perhaps it will be pleasanter if you leave as you have come—saying nothing. The disturbance, the—the trouble to you will be less."

Tracy made up her mind and started toward the door. "Never mind. I'll ask Mr. Radburn myself. I'll tell him you want me to leave at once. Perhaps he won't need to remain in this house to finish the book. It's surely possible for him to move elsewhere and get the work done. Since this painting is not going well, he may prefer a change."

Nursel gasped softly. Sylvana did not speak until Tracy reached the door.

"For a few more days then," she said in a choked voice. "A few days only. After that you will leave. It is not necessary to speak to Mr. Radburn of this now."

Tracy went quietly from the room. She had won another reprieve, but at some cost to herself. Inwardly she was shaking. She did not welcome Nursel's company when the Turkish girl came after her in a rush.

"That woman!" Nursel cried softly. "It is she who should be sent from this house. No one else. But, please—it is better if you do as she wishes. It is better if you go away soon."

"Why should I?" Tracy demanded. "Why do you want me to go home? Why are you on Sylvana's side?"

Nursel's answer came indignantly. "I am not on that woman's side. Never! But I think it can be that you are walking into trouble. I think you are not enough afraid of how Mr. Radburn may— may change you. There are matters which I understand and you do not. If you go now, perhaps all may be well. If you stay—then you must rely on fate and hope for the best."

Now that she was away from Sylvana, Tracy's sense of rising panic had died a little. "I will not go," she said.

Nursel gave up with a shrug. "But now you will tell Mr. Radburn the truth?"

"I don't know," Tracy said. "I don't know when

I'll tell him. From now on I'll just have to play it by ear."

The expression puzzled Nursel, but Tracy did not stay to explain. She could no longer hide her distress and confusion and she fled Nursel's company, hurrying downstairs and along the passage to the yali.

Miles was in his study cleaning brushes when she burst in upon him. He looked at her without pleasure.

"What now?"

"Mrs. Erim wants to send me home immediately," Tracy told him, sounding more than a little excited. "Everyone wants me to go home, including Nursel!"

Miles scowled at her. "Perhaps they're right. Certainly you're a disrupting influence for all of us. No—don't put your thumbs in your belt and turn in your toes like a pigeon. I like quiet, gentle women. And *you* are what Hornwright sends me!"

She could only regard him in outrage. On top of everything else, this was too much. She was on the verge of blurting out the whole truth when Miles tossed down his brushes impatiently.

"Stop looking as though you were about to explode. We've both had enough for today. Go put on your coat and tie something over your head. Hurry back and we'll go out to tea. You need a change and so do I."

"I don't want any tea!" Tracy cried indignantly. Tea—at a moment like this!

He pushed her toward the door without gentleness. "Well, I do. Now hurry up. And don't come back here looking like a bomb about to go off."

Again she fled, this time to her room. She was furiously angry with Miles Radburn. Which, at least, was strengthening. Indignation would help her to stand up to him. The time had come to tell him the truth and she must face the fact and go through with it. She repaired her lipstick and tied a scarf over her head with overly emphatic movements. Except for the flush in her cheeks and the brightness of her eyes, she was once more in control of her emotions. It had been ridiculous of course to let Sylvana upset her. Partly her reaction had been the fault of that samovar with its queerly malevolent reflection. Once she had seen the image, it haunted and disturbed her, though she did not know why.

Miles was waiting when she returned to the study. He had put on a jacket and a cap and he appeared eager to be outdoors and away from the yali.

Downstairs Ahmet hovered near the landing, watching as the boatman helped Tracy into a boat smaller than the caique. She was aware of the old man's watchfulness as Miles started the motor and they set off from shore. When she looked back she saw him standing there, as if observing their direction.

There were no larger craft going by at the moment, and their course was clear to the opposite shore toward which Miles turned the prow of the little boat. They moved at a slight diagonal, and Tracy sat on the wooden cross seat in the stern and lifted her face to the wind.

Beneath them the water flowed still and dark. At the moment the surface seemed deceptively unruffled, hardly appearing to move as the little boat slapped its way across the strait, leaving a churning white froth behind. The cool, clear air was reviving to breathe and carried with it none of the dust of Istanbul. Nor any hint of roses or Parma violet. Tracy felt calmer now and in better control of herself.

Their crossing attracted two young boys, who came down to the stone embankment on the opposite shore. The boat nosed in among fishing craft, and Miles accepted the help of the boys in landing. It was more difficult here to climb from small boat to embankment, but Tracy managed it with a minimum of scrambling and the help of Miles's strong grasp.

They stood on the edge of a road down which motor traffic traveled in a fairly steady stream. Across the road an open-air space filled with small tables and chairs climbed the hill beneath tall plane trees, newly in bud. Though the sun had sent a veneer of warmth across the area, most of the tables stood empty.

"It's mild enough for tea outdoors," Miles said. "Let's go up there away from the road."

He found a table toward the rear of the terraced hillside, and they sat in wooden chairs that teetered a little on uneven ground. A waiter came for their order and Miles gave it in Turkish.

At a table nearby a man sat lost in contemplation as he smoked his narghile, and Tracy watched him draw smoke through bubbling water and long coils.

"Like the Caterpillar," she said dreamily.

"That's better," Miles approved. "You're cheering up. What is worrying you? What does it matter if Sylvana scolds? You're involved in nothing but the job you're doing for me. And that's not a life or death matter. For you, at any rate. I'll give Hornwright a good report, if that's what concerns you. Even if Sylvana wants you gone, it's not terribly important."

This was the least of what was worrying her, but she could not say so. The time for decision was upon her, yet she could make no decision. She could only bask in the sun and watch the hypnotic bubbling of the narghile, and listen to Miles's voice.

In the summertime, he told her, particularly on weekends, this place would be filled most of the time. There were many of these tea spots along the Bosporus to which Istanbul people liked to drive. This was one of the most popular. But now they were here ahead of the season and could have it almost to themselves.

Before long the waiter brought a small samovar to their table and a plate of *simit*—round, braided rolls, sprinkled with sesame seed. Tracy filled the teapot from the spout and placed it on the rack to steep, as she had seen Sylvana do. She broke a piece of roll and the breeze blew sesame seed about. Out on the water a tug-drawn string of barges moved upstream in leisurely fashion, leaving a creamy wake behind. Across the strait, some distance below the yali, rose the towers and walls of Anadolu Hisar, the opposite fortress. The scene was disarmingly peaceful and without any sense of tension.

As she bit into her roll Tracy thought again of the fact that today was her birthday.

"My birthday cake," she said, holding up the bit of simit. "Today I'm twenty-three."

Miles bowed his head gravely. "Congratulations. I'm glad we came out to celebrate."

There might be a way to make him understand, she thought, crumbling the roll in her fingers. There might be a way to tell him. She began almost as if she were talking to herself.

"There's something I remember that occurred on my twelfth birthday. A new one always reminds me. I've never forgotten because it was an unhappy day, with the sort of things happening that can never be erased."

Miles had relaxed since coming across the water, as if he had left strain behind him at the yali.

"Tell me about it," he said.

She hesitated, seeking the right words. If she told her story well, this might be the way to reveal that she was Anabel's sister.

# 11

TRACY BEGAN in a light, uncertain voice that grew stronger as she went on and was caught up by the thread of her own memories.

"My parents seldom let me have a party. My father was a doctor, and he did a lot of writing as well. Medical articles. He was a very serious, busy man. He had his office in our house and he didn't like noisy children around. But this time my older sister prevailed on my mother, so the occasion was special. It was to be my day, with everyone coming to see me, bringing me presents. I suppose it went to my head a little. I had a new dress. Mother said I looked very nice, and the other mothers who came said so too. The spotlight was all mine, and I felt practically giddy with conceit and excitement.

"Then my seventeen-year-old sister came home from her dancing school lesson—and everything changed. She didn't intend what happened. She was only being herself. But from the minute she came into the room the party started to be hers. She could charm people of any age and she loved to do it. She loved to be loved and to amuse and please. So she sang for us a bit and she danced. And in a little while no one remembered about me, because how could anyone remember with her in the same room?"

Miles was listening more attentively than she would have expected.

"So your nose was out of joint?" he said.

Tracy nodded. "I was terribly jealous. I loved my sister and admired her and looked up to her. But I couldn't be like her and sometimes I was green with envy. When I turned green enough that day, I slipped away from the party and went to my father's office. I knew nobody would miss me, and that made everything worse."

As she told him what happened next, it was almost as if she lived the scene again. She forgot the Bosporus and the man with the narghile. She nearly forgot Miles himself. Only one part of her remained vigilant, watchful, lest she mention Anabel's name before it was time.

It had been after visiting hours when she left the party and went into her father's office. He was working in deep concentration over papers on his desk. In his preoccupation he hardly noticed as she came into the room. She curled up in a corner armchair where he sometimes let her sit and read, if she didn't disturb him by talking. She had done no reading that day. She began to cry very softly to herself, wallowing in self-pity and disappointment because she was of no consequence at her own birthday party, and people always forgot about her when her sister was there. Through the walls of the room and down the hall, party sounds filtered and the sound of her sister's singing.

Tracy had not thought consciously at the time of why she had come to her father's office, but the reason was there, as she understood later. Dad was her sister's stepfather. Her sister's real father was dead. Dad was the only person who never succumbed to her sister's charms and her coaxing ways. Perhaps there was envy in him too—envy of another man's child. Especially since Tracy's mother always melted with love for her first daughter and was reluctant to heed his criticism. As Tracy very well knew, she compared her younger daughter with the older a dozen times or more a day, and always to Tracy's disadvantage. Now, by coming into her father's presence, Tracy left the magic circle and reached a haven where her sister's charm exerted no effect.

Unfortunately, she had been a little whimpery in her weeping and after a while her father noticed. He glanced around at her impatiently and told her to blow her nose. If she was to stay, she'd have to stop sniveling. He did not ask why she was crying, or show any interest in the cause. He was busy and her presence annoyed him.

She had managed to be silent after that, not even blowing her nose very loudly. A strange thought had come into her mind. A mature and rather bitter thought for a girl of twelve. She had realized quite clearly in that moment that the only reason she liked her father at all was because he did not like her sister. It was a strange sort of thing to hold in common with him, and she did not feel very proud of herself because of it.

After a time even her silence irritated him, and he flung down his papers and turned around. "Out with it!" he said. "What's the matter that you aren't back at your own party where all that uproar is going on?"

She gulped once or twice before answering. Then she blurted out the truth. "My sister's there. It's turned into her party. They don't want me any more."

"I should think not," he said, "if you behave like this—creeping away like a little coward. Come along and I'll get rid of your sister for you. Then you can be belle of the ball again. And I can have peace in this room at least."

As he left his desk, Tracy scrambled to her feet in alarm. For some reason this was the last thing she wanted. She knew perfectly well that her father would not pat her cheek, or cuddle her, or tell her he liked her best. But he would prove again in another way that he did not approve of her sister. Though his intention was to reinstate Tracy, he would wreck the party completely. It would not be hers or anybody else's when he was through with what he might say to the older girl. So she told him hurriedly that she was fine now. That she had recovered and didn't mind any more. He did not push the matter, though he clearly thought her change of heart further evidence of weakness.

She flew out of the room and went back to where her sister was singing her own croony version of a popular tune. Anabel sat cross-legged on the floor with her cornflower-blue skirt fluffed over her knees, and the children crowding in about her. Always they wanted to touch Anabel, to cling to her when she was near, and always it overjoyed her to make them happy. Now they swayed to the beat of the tune she was singing—a song with nonsense words that was current for the season.

Tracy sought her mother and slipped into the warm curve of her arm. An arm that moved automatically, as a mother's arm does, to hold any child that comes within its circle. Yet Tracy knew that all her mother's loving pride was focused upon her older daughter. In that moment twelve-year-old Tracy had faced the truth once and for all. A truth she had been trying all her short life not to face. She had known consciously and without any doubt that she could never be loved by her mother as the older daughter was loved.

A certain pride had possessed her then and made her hold her head high. She watched her sister with that love she had always given her, however laced with envy and hurt it might be. It was at least to her credit that she had let no one know how she felt. And she had not cried again.

The narghile bubbled softly at the nearby table, and fragrant smoke drifted toward the grownup Tracy where she sat with the man who had been Anabel's husband. There was more to the story, but she sought a diversion to postpone the most painful part of this telling.

"Our tea will be dreadfully strong," she said. "I forgot about it."

"I like it that way," said Miles.

She put small spoons in the glasses so they would not break and poured the hot, strong tea. Hot water from the samovar spout diluted her own. When the brew was sweetened and lemon slices added, Tracy subsided into silence, still under the spell of the story she had not yet told fully.

Miles raised his tea glass. "Here's to Tracy

when she was twelve! A young lady of honesty and courage. You learned rather young to accept an unpleasant truth and live with it bravely."

She sipped the tea. "No—I didn't. That's the trouble. The story isn't done. If it was only what I've told you, I don't think I'd have remembered every detail after all these years."

"Then you might as well tell me the rest," he said.

It was strange that she should find him so willing a listener. She sensed an understanding that she had not expected. He did not belittle, or discredit, or sympathize falsely, and she felt drawn to him and unexpectedly trusting.

What had happened later had left a wound that had not healed for a long time. She began to relate the rest, keeping her voice carefully even and bare of emotion. Birthday cake and ice cream, candy and self-realization had not mixed too well in Tracy's interior and she had gone to bed early that night, feeling queasy. Going to sleep early, she had awakened later in the night and begun to think despairingly of her disappointing day. Her sister was asleep in the next room and the house was quiet. The illuminated dial of the clock on the dresser told her that her parents must be in bed and asleep now too. In the lonely darkness in which only she was awake, she could hug to herself all the misery of her resentment against her sister and let it grow and swell almost to the bursting point, like a grotesque balloon.

In the next room she heard the older girl get up and move around softly. Tracy stayed very still listening. She heard her sister go to the window, heard the unlikely bird chirp from the driveway below. This was not the first time such a thing had happened, and she knew what Anabel would do. It was always frightening and inevitably it threw Tracy into an anguish of indecision. If she went to her parents in their room at the front of the house, she would get her sister into dreadful trouble. Yet if she did not it seemed that terrible trouble would come to the other girl.

She listened intently while her sister dressed. She heard her slip out of the room and down the stairs, heard the faint squeak that was the kitchen door opening. Followed by silence. She told herself virtuously that what her sister was doing was wrong, that her parents must be told. She got out of bed, shaking a little, and went into the room where they slept. She wakened them and made it clear what had happened. She could remember her father swearing as he dressed, her mother weeping. Dad had gone searching up and down the streets without success. Tracy, watching from an upstairs window, and no longer pleased with her betrayal, was the first to see her sister come home. She leaned out the window whistling a quavery and out-of-tune *London*

*Bridge* to let her know that everything was indeed "falling down." Anabel, forewarned, was still undaunted. She looked up at Tracy with a smile and waved her hand in a thumb-up gesture that signified courage—or perhaps only recklessness.

When she came in there had been a dreadful scene downstairs, with the older daughter weeping at last, and Tracy's father shouting ugly accusations. It was all quite horrible and Tracy had been thoroughly sick at her stomach.

Her sister, for once shaken and frightened herself, came upstairs and found her in the bathroom. She bathed Tracy's green little face and soothed her and helped her back to bed. She put aside her own grave troubles for the sick younger one, giving her the love and care and consideration Tracy had longed for all day. How bittersweet that comfort had been.

"So that's the way it was," she finished. "That's why I've never forgotten."

"Because you betrayed her?" Miles said. "Yes, I can see that. Yet you were doing the right thing. Your parents had to be told about this."

Tracy shook her head. "The right thing, but for the wrong reason. I didn't do it to save my sister from harm. I did it because I wanted to punish her for being beautiful and popular. And most of all because my mother loved her best."

She picked up the tea glass with a hand that

reached blindly because of the mist before her eyes.

"A few weeks later my sister ran away," she went on. "She couldn't endure the way my father treated her, and for a long time I blamed myself for driving her out."

"But you grew up," Miles said. "And probably she did too."

Tracy sipped her cooling tea. "Yes, I grew up and I learned enough to know that she would have run away anyhow, no matter what I did. It would be foolish of me to go on blaming myself for something that happened when I was twelve years old."

"But you do a little, don't you?" Miles took her glass and set it down and held her hand in his own. His fingers were firm about hers, and there was strength and reassurance in his grasp. She wanted to cling to the comfort his hand offered. At that moment she liked him enormously and did not question the warmth she felt toward him.

"It was all so long ago," she said. "I know it's foolish to remember. But I suppose I'll always wonder if I could have helped her more than I did. Perhaps I could have tried harder to understand whatever it was she wanted. Not just then, but later on when I was old enough. She was a wonderful person, really. There was so much about her that was good. I think she could have made something fine of her life."

"Was?" Miles asked.

"My sister is dead," said Tracy. She drew her hand from Miles's and touched the feather pin beneath her open coat. This was the moment. This was the time to tell Anabel's husband the truth. Yet she was helplessly mute.

Out on the strait a ship moved toward Istanbul. As it glided by, white and shining in the sunlight, Tracy could see beyond it the silver-gray shape of the yali showing among trees on the opposite shore. The whole reason for her being here swept back on a wave of pain.

"I'm sorry," Miles said, his tone surprisingly kind. "But of course it's futile to reproach yourself, or to ask questions that can't be answered. Perhaps there are those who can never be helped."

"We have to try," Tracy said fervently. "Someone has to try! There are too many who give up easily with the ones like my sister." She was aware of his long, perceptive look and knew that his thoughts had turned to Anabel. Had he done all he could for the woman who had been his wife? she wondered.

"I knew a girl very much like your sister," Miles said, startling Tracy by coming close to her thoughts. "My wife Anabel was charming and gay as your sister must have been. And as thoroughly bent on self-destruction."

Tracy waited, knowing that this might be the

brink of the very answer she was seeking.

"Of course the story is that I drove her to her death. You've heard that, I expect. But she had only one interest in me by that time. The fact that I was angry and walked out on her wouldn't have meant a thing. Something happened while I was gone. Perhaps I can even guess what it was. But I'm not sure who was responsible. I don't know who could have wanted her dead as desperately as that."

"Nursel says you did," Tracy told him. "She says you wear a hair shirt by keeping your wife's portrait on the wall of your room. In order to punish yourself for her death."

The words did not seem to anger him. "A plausible enough explanation, I suppose. If I were that sort of man. I'm not. There was nothing I wouldn't have done for Anabel."

He had given her an answer. His answer, at least.

"Why do you stay here?" she asked him. "Why don't you work on your book somewhere else and get away from this place?"

It was almost a relief to have him regard her with more normal impatience. "Do you think it's this book that matters most to me now? I believe in its worth and I'll get it done sometime, of course. But for me it's painting that matters. How do you think it feels to be a sort of cripple—because I want to paint and can't?"

"But why here?" Tracy persisted. "Perhaps you'd paint again if you went away."

He was silent for a long moment. "I've tried it," he said at last. "I'm pulled back every time. It's here the thing left me and it's here I must recover it."

She had the curious feeling that he had turned some corner in his thoughts and had abruptly ceased to speak the truth. The feeling that this was a story he had told often—with the truth well hidden behind it.

"What of your portrait of Mrs. Erim?" she asked. "Isn't this a step toward painting again?"

"I'd like to keep Sylvana content for the moment," he admitted. "But I haven't the slightest desire to immortalize her on canvas. Nothing went right this afternoon until you called my attention to an odd trick of reflection in the samovar. I've decided to experiment with it and find out where it leads. It's a change in my approach, at least. Perhaps not a happy one."

She listened uneasily, still sensing concealment in his words. "It is only because of your painting that you want to stay on at the yali?"

He glanced at her and then quickly away. "Call it a matter of unfinished business, if you like. But don't poke about trying to satisfy your curiosity." His face had darkened and there was a sudden warning in his eyes. "Do your work. Get it done and go home. Play in the shallows, if you like, but stay out of the deeps."

She gave him look for angry look, yet in the very instant of her indignation she sensed it was a pretense. She must pretend anger so that he would not guess that she remembered his brief kindness and the touch of his hand holding hers in reassurance. There was a sense of loss in knowing that moment would not come again.

He pushed his chair from the table. "Shall we return?"

Tracy rose without a word and they went down to the landing. She got into the boat quickly, and when Miles had tipped the waiting boys he pushed away from shore.

On the return trip he paid no attention to her, but kept his eyes upon the far shore. Tracy faced him on the crossboard seat, intensely aware of him—of the rough-hewed look of his face, of dark hair growing thickly back from his forehead, of eyes that had no knowledge of her now, but which she had learned could be warm as well as chill. How far away he seemed there in the stern of the boat with his hand upon the rudder. Eons removed from Tracy Hubbard, who could never be as Anabel had been at her fascinating best. "I would have done anything for Anabel," he had said—and her portrait hung upon his wall, reminding him always of what he had lost.

As they neared the shore, she realized that in returning he had headed the boat farther up the Bosporus. They were approaching the broken palace with its overgrown gardens, where Tracy had wandered that day when she had come upon a tryst in the ruins. When they came opposite cracked marble steps, Miles cut the motor and let the boat drift idly.

"Do you know what this place is?" he asked.

"Only that it's where I fell and scraped my leg the first day I was here," Tracy told him.

"As a matter of fact it's a spot with considerable history behind it. It was a palace in the old days—belonging to the Sultan's mother. The Sultan Valide as she was called. Neither a sultan's wife nor mother was ever called a sultana—that's a word the English created."

Tracy's attention was fully arrested. "A Sultan Valide lived here?"

"This particular one died here—stabbed to death by an enemy among her own ladies."

"In the presence of the Anatolian Samovar," said Tracy softly. She was thinking in sudden excitement of Anabel's confused reference to the Sultan Valide who knew a secret. A secret hidden perhaps in the old palace ruins?

"The samovar again!" Miles said with some impatience. "Did you know that it's one my wife wanted to own—before Sylvana apparently purchased it behind her back?"

"Yes," Tracy said. "Nursel told me."

"Sylvana did me a favor, as a matter of fact. Anabel had a taste for tales of wickedness and evil. The opposite facet to the side of her that looked toward the light, I suppose. She made this old ruin and its gardens her own place. She was always running away to hide here and put on her little amusements."

Tracy watched him, not wanting to stop this reminiscing, or to miss a word, yet touched by an old pain. He did not notice, his attention wholly upon the crumbling building on the shore. Its arched windows and broken veranda were close to them now. The boat seemed to drift in a pocket of quiet made by a jutting point of land that held them away from the main current.

"Once when I looked for her here," Miles said, "I found her putting on one of her performances. For an audience of nightingales and lizards." There was momentary tenderness in his voice. "Like your sister, she could dance and sing a little. She was tripping around over broken floors, making up little steps and singing to herself as though she occupied a stage. She could be an entrancing person. When I applauded she came running to me like a child."

Listening, Tracy could see Anabel there among the ruins, moving as though she were the very spirit of this haunted place, delighting and entrancing in her own special way.

"I might have thought of Ophelia when I found her here," Miles said, "except that Anabel was not mad. Or if she was, it was a sort of madness that often made her more appealing than any woman I've ever known."

The old hurt that was now a new hurt deepened in Tracy. She studied the ruins above the boat, understanding better than he knew. This was what Anabel had been like, possessed of her own special magic, or madness, holding those who loved her with a bond that only strengthened with her perversity and need for protection from herself.

"Well, it's done now!" The change in Miles's tone made her look at him quickly, and she saw in his eyes an anger that startled her.

The quiet of the tiny cove was shattered by the sudden sound of the motor. Their little boat cut through the water as though the very speed of its movement gave vent to Miles's need for turbulent action.

Tracy clung to her seat, wondering that she had ever thought him a man in whom all emotion had died. She had glimpsed just now a degree of anger that she shrank from in alarm. Never would she understand the complexities of his nature. With such a man anything was possible—love and hate, perhaps vengeance. But vengeance against whom? Was his anger against someone who existed in the present, or was there some violence that Miles Radburn had brought down upon one who had incurred his anger in the past? Anabel, perhaps, with her ability to subjugate and repel almost in the same breath? His mood had changed so swiftly from tenderness to rage.

They reached the yali quickly and as quickly his emotion subsided, outwardly at least. He seemed cold again and far removed from all feeling.

Ahmet was waiting as they came ashore. The old man stood back until they were out of the boat, and then slipped silently away through the passage. Was he off to the kiosk to report to Sylvana, as he had perhaps been instructed to do? For the first time Tracy thought of the fact that Mrs. Erim would not approve of this excursion Miles had made across the Bosporus, taking Tracy with him.

But she could waste no concern upon Mrs. Erim. Or even upon Miles and his hidden angers. Not now. Since the moment when he had spoken of the Sultan Valide, she had known what she must do. This was the time, if she could slip away without being seen.

Unexpectedly, Miles was studying her as though she puzzled him for some reason.

"Thank you for tea," she said, stiffly polite, and glanced at her watch. It was nearly five.

He said nothing. It was as if he had become acutely aware of her, as if he searched for an answer to some troublesome problem that had its source in Tracy Hubbard. She had the feeling that he might be asking himself why he had spoken out so frankly to a stranger who meant nothing to him. Perhaps wondering why she had confided in him. She understood, but he could not. He had no idea of the invisible bond that drew them together.

The moment lasted briefly. "I believe I'll walk over to the village," he said, turning curtly from her. His gesture rejected whatever had held his attention, rejected perhaps, the possibility of friendship between them.

The boatman was busy getting the small craft into its place in the boathouse under the yali and Tracy stood watching for a moment until she was sure Miles was out of sight. Then she slipped through the marble corridor of the ground floor and went through the far door to the driveway. No one was there. There was no one at the windows of the kiosk on the hill above. She slipped quickly away up the same winding path she had followed on her first exploration. Winter shrubbery offered little shield for her going, but as far as she knew no one saw her.

She found her way to the side gate. Again it was unlocked. Probably because Miles had gone through. But the village lay in the other direction and she would not meet him now. She hurried along the road, knowing her way.

As she walked, she thought again of Anabel's words. Miles himself had given her a possible answer to them in the fact that Anabel had often gone to the old ruins where the Sultan Valide had once reigned. Perhaps she had hidden something there that she was trying to tell her sister of in that last hysterical effort.

Rounding the turn in the road, Tracy saw the iron gate askew upon its great hinges and she began to run, lest some car come suddenly along the road so that she would be seen entering the old garden.

She went through the gate quietly and trod softly across flagstones, where grass and weeds had sprung up in rebirth. Heavy brown brush cut off the view of the front door and she welcomed it, since it would hide her from the road. She hurried past spiderwebs spun across bushes and ran lightly over the pebbled mosaic below the marble steps.

Even as she moved there was a sound within the house, and before she could halt her headlong pace a man came through the door and stood awaiting her. It was Murat Erim.

## 12

TRACY STUMBLED to a halt, staring at the man in the doorway. He did not seem nearly so surprised to see her as she was to see him. Indeed, he smiled at her easily and came down the few steps to her level. She did not like a smile which touched his lips but did not reach black, unfathomable eyes.

"I have startled you," he said. "I am sorry for that. I did not hear you until you were through the gate. You enjoyed your boat trip across the Bosporus?"

"Why—yes," Tracy said. "We—we had tea on the opposite shore."

He nodded. "I supposed as much. There is a fine view of the water from this place. I could see your boat drifting close to the walls on your way back. I was just in there, you see—at the embrasure of the windows." He gestured toward the house behind him. "You will forgive me—I could not help but hear you speaking together of Mrs. Radburn. It seems he still does not know that you are her sister?"

"No," Tracy said. "I haven't told him yet." She wanted only to get away, to keep to herself the secret of why she had come here.

"As Mr. Radburn mentioned, this was a place your sister loved," Dr. Erim went on. "A place she visited often. Sometimes I used to wonder why. But when I asked, she only laughed and would not tell me. It is possible that you know the reason?"

Tracy shook her head. It was ridiculous to be afraid. This man meant her no harm. Indeed, he had been kind to her in the beginning. But now he probed dangerously near the truth, and she tried to find an explanation that would put him off.

"It's because Mr. Radburn said my sister loved this place that I've come here. It interested me the first time I saw it, and knowing she was fond of it made me want to see it again."

"And I have disturbed your solitude," Dr. Erim said regretfully. "But perhaps you will bear with my presence a little longer. Come—let me show you about. Having hurt yourself the other time, you had no opportunity to appreciate this place where a Sultan Valide once lived."

He held out his hand and she felt compelled to go up the steps and into the house with him. His manner remained formal and stiffly proper, but she knew he was watching her in an oddly intent way—as if he waited for some revelation on her part.

He showed her the safest passage as though he knew the ruins well, and led her from room to room. Here, where plaster crumbled from a wall, there were exquisite mosaics to be seen. Beyond was a door that had been ornately carved, and in another room portions of the elaborate ceiling with its diamond-shaped sections could still be seen. All the while Dr. Erim spoke in his low, cultured voice, as though he were a curator of art conducting a visitor upon the rounds of a museum. Tracy went with him, trying to respond with suitable sounds, but finding little to say.

When she had seen all of the musty, crumbling first floor of the place, they returned to the main salon and stood where the floor was least damaged, watching the Bosporus flow by outside arched windows.

"They say it was in this very room that the Sultan Valide was stabbed," Dr. Erim said gently.

There had been enough of this hinting, Tracy decided, this queer creeping about through an old ruin, as if something dramatic were about to happen at any moment. Or as if they waited for a ghost to appear. She did not like it. She'd had enough.

"I'm not a bit like Anabel," she told him, forcing a light tone. "I'm not romantically enchanted just because this was once a palace. Nor am I frightened because a murder was committed here."

"You do not believe that the past, when it has been bloody, may lay a hand upon the present?"

"Only so far as the present grows out of the past," said Tracy.

"Ah—but that is the important thing, of course.

There is still a present in this place, even though it belongs to the past."

"I don't know what you mean," Tracy said.

He discarded his gentle manner and turned so that his back was toward the light that fell through arched and empty windows. She could no longer see his dark, sensitive face, but there was something faintly menacing about the vigilance of his poised body, as though his very stillness was a threat.

"Where do you think she hid whatever it was she had to hide?" he demanded. "In this very place, perhaps? I have often thought so, but, though I have searched many times, the house does not give up its secret."

Tracy stared at him and the skin crept a little at the back of her neck. "I don't know what you're talking about," she repeated.

"I think you know," he said. "You know or you would not have been so interested in the black amber tespih. There is significance in your interest—of that I am sure. But the beads would do you no good—is that not so? Because they are not the same ones your sister Anabel took. A few things were recovered, but neither that nor any of the other things she stole were found among her possessions afterward. Although we searched for them carefully."

"Anabel—stole?" The words came out in a whisper.

"I am sorry to say this is true. We would have given her what she liked—but no, she must slip about the house at night and take first this small thing, then that. Several articles from among those Sylvana was shipping abroad were taken. Nothing of great value, but important to Sylvana since she meant to sell them abroad and get money for her villagers. It was a sad thing to behold, this sickness of your sister's—this taking of that which did not belong to her. I myself remonstrated with her, but to no effect. Indeed, she laughed at me, as she sometimes laughed at all of us." His face darkened at the memory. Murat Erim did not care to be laughed at.

Tracy wanted to say that she did not believe a word of this. That Anabel was no thief. That she would never have been guilty of pilfering. But the truth was that she did not know her sister well enough to champion her blindly. Behind heavy white lids that green gaze had peered out at the world, never telling all, preserving Anabel's secrets. It was even possible that Murat Erim was telling the truth.

"I don't know anything about this," Tracy managed. "It's hard to believe that Anabel—"

"She was very beautiful." Murat's tone was sorrowing. "But she was also, I think, dedicated to evil. Perhaps without being wholly aware of the fact. Perhaps that is why she had an affinity for this place, with its tragic, evil history. It is perhaps why she wanted to possess the samovar for herself."

This time Tracy responded with angry indignation. "I've never heard anything so silly in my life! I knew Anabel. She did foolish things sometimes, but she was a warm, loving, generous person. There was nothing evil about her."

Murat moved toward the window and light touched his face, glinted in his eyes.

"You do not believe then, that just as a person may be, without knowing it, a carrier of some certain disease, another may be a carrier of evil? Not being evil in themselves, perhaps, but bringing evil to others?"

His voice, so quietly persuasive, held her arrested, frozen, as though in this place, in the crumbling ruins of this palace on the Bosporus, such things might be true and believed in. But the good sense that was so strongly a part of her nature rejected the fancy.

"I don't believe anything of the sort," she said with conviction. "What did Miles do about—about what you claim was stealing? I suppose he knew?"

Murat Erim made a gesture that was wholly of the East, fatalistic—a movement of his head and hands and shoulders that said many things: *Who knows? What is one to believe? What can one do?*

"But didn't he do anything?" Tracy persisted. "Didn't he try to stop her?"

"She would deny everything," Murat said. "And Sylvana did not wish to worry him. She felt she could handle this matter herself."

Tracy stood in stricken silence, staring out across the Bosporus, where the sun dipped toward the hills of Thrace. Along the broken floor at her feet, the arched shadows were many and long. Because she was so still, the small sound came to her clearly—a skittering in the rubble of the next room.

Murat turned at once toward the sound—so faint, so slight. Perhaps only a mouse in rotting woodwork, or a small garden snake wriggling away. Then there was a faint mew and through a shadowy doorway stepped Anabel's white cat. Yasemin paused on the sill and regarded them without surprise, her green gaze unblinking. Murat Erim moved first. He picked up a bit of broken masonry from the floor and flung it with violence at the cat. So quickly did he move that Tracy could only watch in shocked silence. She fully expected the animal to be injured with the force of the blow, but the cat was quicker than the man. Yasemin sprang away and hid herself in a broken place in the floor, looking out at them with only her nose showing and her great green eyes, her ears laid back warily.

"Don't hurt her!" Tracy cried. "Why did you do that?"

She ran toward the cat to lift it from the cavity

in the floor and keep it safe, as she had done the time Miles had tried to cuff it. But Yasemin spat at her and leaped away, this time vanishing through the door to lose herself in the weed-grown garden.

Tracy turned indignantly, to find that the man was smiling at her in his enigmatic way.

"Often Anabel used to bring the cat with her when she visited this place," he said. "Since she is gone, the animal has made the ruin its lair. There is good hunting here. But how strange, since you are Anabel's sister, that the cat does not like you, does not trust you."

"I don't suppose she knows who I am," said Tracy, tartly amused. "Sometimes she likes me. She's been frightened by too many people. She doesn't trust anyone now."

"Perhaps she thinks you will betray her." He spoke softly, almost as if he did not want the white cat to hear, yet as if he mocked at himself the while. "You know the legend of this cat, do you not?"

"I know Anabel made a pet of it," Tracy said. "And I don't understand how grown men like you and Miles can be so cruel."

"Then you do not know. Come—we will start home, and I will tell you on the way."

The place held nothing for her now. It would reveal nothing until she came here alone. She let him lead her from the house and out of the garden.

When they were on the road, he told her the

story and she listened to him with an increasing disquiet that she could not stem.

"Anabel made much of this small cat. Again and again she told us mockingly that if anything ever happened to her she would return and inhabit that small white body. She would look at us out of those green cat's eyes. And then we would be sorry for whatever we had done to her. We would be afraid—and with justification. She could be extremely annoying with this game of hers, this foreboding of trouble to come."

"She didn't want to die," Tracy said out of the chill that held her.

"She did not need to die," said Murat, his tone suddenly harsh. "If she had listened to reason . . ." He broke off and when he spoke again there was sarcasm in his words. "You do not believe in this story of the cat?"

"Of course I don't believe it. And surely you don't either?"

"Sometimes I do not know exactly what I believe. But I think it is not this. I dislike the animal and I would like to see it gone."

"Why did my sister have this foreboding that something might happen to her?" Tracy asked.

The man beside her stiffened. "It is to be remembered that she died by her own will."

"So I understand," Tracy said. "But if that's true, what drove her to it? You've just said she did not need to die."

He walked beside her with his head averted. "Perhaps it is Mr. Radburn who can tell you why she died. Why do you not go to him with your questions?"

"I mean to," Tracy said. "That's why I've come to Istanbul—to find the truth behind my sister's death."

"So? It is as I thought. But let me tell you this one thing, Miss Hubbard. Whatever you find, there will be no scandal, no smirching of the good reputation of my family. If you understand this, there will be little trouble for the remainder of your stay. If you do not—" He flicked a finger in the air and left the words unspoken.

They had reached the gate and he opened it and allowed her to go through. "I will leave you now," he said, and went off through the grounds in an opposite direction from the house.

Tracy hurried to the yali and went inside. Downstairs there seemed no one about to notice her return. When she reached the third floor she saw that Miles was at his desk. He looked up and called to her without questioning her absence.

"Will you do an errand for me?" He held out the strip of paper on which he had done the decorative calligraphy. "I've finished this. Will you give it to Mrs. Erim, please?"

She took the paper and stood for a moment studying it, wondering if she should tell him about her encounter with Murat in the ruined

257

palace. But to tell him would be to betray her own special interest in the place, and this she was not willing to do.

She left him and went by means of the second-floor passage to the kiosk. On the way she stopped again to admire the handsome piece Miles had done. Though the curves and arabesques had no meaning for her, the strip fascinated her and she could imagine how well it would look framed and hung upon a wall. No wonder the Turks had used their script as a form of art, since the painting of men and animals was forbidden them.

In the other house she found the same state of lively confusion she had encountered on her first meeting with Sylvana. Villagers were here again, presenting their craftwork to Mrs. Erim's critical eye. Apparently a different group came every week, bringing her their wares.

Once more Ahmet hovered in the background, quietly watchful and in control of the visitors. Nursel was there too, her eyes bright with interest, her hands respectful as she handled the lovely things. The great samovar had been removed from Sylvana's elbow and stood regally in its place of honor on a carved table, reflecting the whole colorful, excited scene in its coppery tones.

Nursel dangled a pair of silver filigree bracelets at Tracy. "Are they not lovely? This is some of the best work I have seen. Sylvana has done well to encourage these people, scold them a little, and insist upon the best. She will not allow them to fold their hands and wait for Kismet."

Mrs. Erim paid no attention to Nursel's words as she discussed business matters in Turkish with a headman from the village. When Tracy gave her the strip of calligraphy, she broke off to study it.

"Ah, but this is excellent! The finest work Mr. Radburn has done." She held it up for the men to see, and they exclaimed in admiration of an ancient art, though undoubtedly few could read the script.

She set it beside her on the divan and spoke to Tracy. "Perhaps tomorrow Mr. Radburn will lend you to us. We will need every hand possible to assist us in the packing and wrapping of these articles. Now I have enough for shipment to America. Everything will be carried over to the second-floor salon in the yali and if the day is not too cold we will work there. I do not like clutter about me here."

"I'll be glad to help, if it's all right with Mr. Radburn," Tracy promised.

She stayed long enough to look at a few of the articles and listened to the arguing and declaiming. All Turks loved to talk, it appeared, and part of their pleasure in this event lay in the discussions that went on between the men and Sylvana.

When Tracy left she returned to her room. The

door stood ajar and when she went in she found Yasemin asleep on the bed. Lying beside the cat was one of the Turkish books Tracy had been reading.

The circumstance was mildly puzzling. She always closed her door when she went out, though she did not lock it. And she was sure she had left the book on the table with a marker in it. Since Yasemin, for all the whimsical faculties Murat Erim might attribute to her, could not open doors or read books, it was clear that someone had been in the room. Perhaps only Halide.

As she reached for the book, she saw that something bulky lay between the pages. When she flipped it open she found that a black amber tespih marked the place. The sight was utterly chilling, bringing with it the memory of Anabel's words on the telephone: "It's the black amber again! It turned up yesterday."

Tracy stared at the place the beads had marked and saw that someone had underlined a passage in ink. Since it was a passage she had read before, the marking was new. Meaning sprang out at her from the page and she began to read the flowery paragraph again, word by word.

The Bosporus has always been a receptacle for ugly secrets. A head floating downstream in a basket, or bodies of those whom a sultan might fear tumbling in its waters. Perhaps a

260

harem beauty neatly tied in her sack and flung into the shallows off Seraglio Point, to stare with sightless eyes at the wickedness men have for so long hidden beneath the innocent blue surface. Beautiful and treacherous, this is a watercourse to give one pause. Is it to be trusted today any more than it was in the past? To which of us does it still promise an evil retribution?

That was all. The single gruesome paragraph had been marked and left for her to read. Marked by the string of black amber beads. She examined the strand briefly, but it told her no more than the black tespih in Murat's collection had done. She did not expect it to. An inkling of the use made of the beads with Anabel was dawning in her mind. This was the "poltergeist" again, intending to tease and torment and frighten. Black amber, it appeared, was being used as a warning.

She took the cat into her lap and sat in a chair. Yasemin yawned with wide pink mouth, rubbed her head against Tracy's arm, and went to sleep again, purring softly.

Who in this household would do such a thing as this? Was Anabel's sister indeed too close to the brink of discovery for comfort? Perhaps Tracy Hubbard was more feared than she had suspected.

She whispered into one white ear of the cat, "I won't go home!" If she was as close as this, she would stay and find out what it was that someone wanted so terribly to conceal.

But though her words sounded brave enough, the sense of an evil that was all too imminent had settled upon the room. This was more than mischief. She found herself recalling Murat Erim's words. Was it possible, as he claimed, that the past could lay a continuing hand upon one's physical surroundings? That past tragedy could mark the present with an extra dimension, sensed if not seen? There must have been times when Anabel sat in this very room, frightened and tormented by such tricks. So tormented, perhaps, that she was driven at last to her death in Bosporus waters.

"They won't do that to me!" Tracy whispered fiercely to Yasemin. She would stand up to them. She would beat them at their own game! Whatever had been done to Anabel would not succeed with Anabel's sister.

# 13

THAT NIGHT Nursel and Tracy dined alone in the yali. Dr. Erim had received a sudden call from Istanbul and had gone there to spend the night. Miles was dining in the kiosk at Sylvana's invitation.

Tracy considered bringing the Turkish book to the table to show the underlined passage to Nursel, but it was better to trust no one, to be suspicious of everyone. The trickster might be more concerned if she carried this off by saying nothing. She would not even tell Miles Radburn what had happened.

She did, however, tell Nursel about having tea with Miles across the Bosporus—something Nursel already knew from the well-informed Sylvana. And about what Miles had said concerning Anabel and the ruins of the old palace.

"Did she really like to go there?" Tracy asked.

"This is true," Nursel agreed. "It is of course a conveniently lonely place. Always Anabel loved to be alone, except for the white cat which was often in her company. In the last months she did not enjoy being with her husband. This I understood later when we learned the terrible thing he was doing to her."

"What terrible thing?" Tracy asked, once more baffled and annoyed by Nursel's hinting.

The other girl shook her head gently. "Please— it is better to allow all this to be forgotten. I do not wish to speak of it. If you wish to know, ask him."

Tracy let it go for the moment. "I went to that place this afternoon, after Miles told me about Anabel," she said. "Your brother was there."

Nursel glanced at her quickly. "You did not tell him of the time when I met Hasan there—when Ahmet Effendi saw us?"

"No, of course not. I've never mentioned that to him."

"I am afraid he is suspicious." Nursel sighed. "If he wished, he could make much trouble for Hasan."

"I don't think he was there looking for you," Tracy said. "He told me he thought Anabel might have hidden something in those ruins. He said there was a time before her death when she began taking things that did not belong to her. Do you know if this is true?"

Nursel did not look at her. She toyed with the food on her plate, studying it with grave concentration before she answered.

"You must not concern yourself," she said finally. "Anabel was not well. There was much to disturb and frighten her. The small articles she took perhaps made her briefly happy. She could be like a child in her wish to possess what was pretty and shiny and bright."

"Like black amber beads," said Tracy, half to herself. "What is there to know about black amber?"

"It is only that such beads were a part of Anabel's derangement toward the end. She behaved as though she believed in magic and spells. Black was the color of magic, she said, and the black amber was a stone for the working of black magic. For a little while in this house it was the way it must have been in the old days in Turkey, when everyone was governed by superstitious beliefs."

"I suppose it was more of the same thing with the cat?" Tracy said. "Your brother told me Anabel said that if harm came to her she would return and watch this house through Yasemin's eyes."

Nursel's faint smile was rueful. "Yes—but she did not use the name you have given the cat. She said she would come back and watch us all through Bunny's eyes. That foolish name by which she called the animal. She would hold the small white thing up to her cheek and stroke it and threaten any who might injure her with this promise of what would happen after her death."

*Through Bunny's eyes.*

Tracy found herself no longer hungry. She could swallow nothing past the tightness in her throat. Now she understood the secret little game Anabel had been playing with the cat. Anabel had been saying in effect, "If anything happens to me, my sister will come and she will watch you. She will find out what drove me to my death and she will punish you for it." How like Anabel to comfort herself with such a fantasy.

Nursel saw her face and reached out to touch Tracy's hand across the table. "Please—you must not be frightened. There is no harm in this cat. I have no fear of it. The men drive it away to show they are brave and not superstitious, though you can see that they are remembering and are disturbed. Even my brother, who is an intelligent man, dedicated to his work and with nothing to fear, becomes uneasy when the white cat is present. Women are not so foolish."

Tracy was glad when she could leave the table and slip away to her room. She took with her scraps of uneaten food on a plate for Yasemin, and the cat awaited her with confidence as though she knew she would be fed.

In her room Tracy watched Yasemin eat with her delicate, tidy manners. She sat in the chair by the veranda doors and thought about Anabel, who had at the end trusted only one person in the world—her faraway younger sister. Yet even in her cry for help, she had thought of possible danger for Tracy. If her warning had only been more coherent, if only she had named a name. Now someone in this house recognized Tracy as an enemy and was embarked on an effort to frighten her away. With mischief and with the warning sign of black amber. Perhaps with nothing more if it stopped there. Yet Anabel had said, "It is the end of everything." Would it mean the end of everything, the tumbling of the last bridge for Anabel's sister as well?

No—that wouldn't work with Tracy Hubbard.

It must not be allowed to work. The pattern of following Anabel must not continue.

During the evening she did not venture from her room. Yasemin at length tired of her company and went to the balcony doors. When Tracy let her out she ran along the veranda with a flick of her plumy tail, past the empty room next door that had once been Miles's, and on around the corner, on her own nocturnal pursuits. Tracy closed the door against the cold and got into bed. For a time she sat up, trying to absorb herself in Turkish history—though not from the book with the marked passage. It was impossible to concentrate, however. Her thoughts went round their endless circling, and somehow always returned to Miles.

How foolish if Sylvana Erim thought she could win this man for herself. Or for any other woman to think she might win him, for that matter. Foolish indeed the woman who came to love him.

Unbidden, the memory of Miles's hand, strong and firm about her own, returned, and with it a sense of painful loss. Again Anabel had gone ahead of her. The pattern still held.

She put out the lamp beside her bed and turned her head against the pillow. The patch beneath her cheek was quickly damp and she did not know why she cried, except that welling up in her were old defeats and old longings and old loneliness. Always where Anabel had been, nothing could ever be right for Tracy. Yet this had been neither Anabel's fault, nor Tracy's.

She slept fitfully for a time, and then could not sleep. After that she lay wakeful, listening to the creakings of the old wooden house, astir on a windy night. Massive doors and shutters rattled, and loose panes of window glass set up a clatter, until Tracy's every nerve was alert. It seemed that footsteps moved everywhere, that all the house was on the prowl. At last restlessness drove her from her bed. She flung her coat around her and opened the doors to the veranda.

It was the dark of the moon and scudding clouds hid the stars. Across the Bosporus most of the lights had gone out and there was little radiance anywhere, except for lamps on fishing boats out in the strait. She stood at the rail with a shoulder to the wind and watched the black water flowing below the jutting balcony. Its surface caught a wavering ladder of light cast from the dim lamp that burned all night at the house landing. There were no ships passing, and the lapping of water over stone steps seemed the only nearby sound in the night. It must be well past midnight, and yali and kiosk were soundly asleep. Everyone was asleep except Tracy, who had been drawn to this dark, pointless vigil.

She was about to return to her warm bed when she heard a slight sound behind her, and whirled.

The veranda lay still and empty. No white cat emerged from the shadows. Her bedroom was dark, and she knew the door to the salon beyond was locked. Yet there had been a sound somewhere near. The closed shutters of the room next to hers were the old-fashioned shutters of a Turkish house, left perhaps from the days of the haremlik, with their latticework and lozenge-shaped openings—meant for someone to see through without being seen.

An eerie conviction was upon her that eyes indeed watched behind the shutters. That someone in the room beyond had moved, making the slight sound she had heard. She wondered what would happen if she pulled the doors suddenly open to reveal whoever stood hidden there. It took all the courage she possessed to make the quick move. But the shutters resisted her. They were latched from within the room.

Her very gesture terrified her. She stood in full view of a watcher who knew she suspected his presence. She began to edge toward her room, afraid to make another sudden move lest he unlatch his door and be upon her. But there was no further sound, no pursuit. She was opposite her door when a faint splash from the water reached her. She looked over the rail and saw one of the fishing boats gliding past not far from shore. She had a single glimpse of its light before something blocked it from view. There was no sound of a motor, no sound of oars, just that faint dip and splash that she had heard. Strange that such a boat seemed to be coming so silently in toward shore. She wondered if it was approaching this house, and looked down at the landing again. Something seemed to move in deepest shadow, as though another watcher observed the boat.

Again there was a sound from the room next to hers—like a door being opened and softly closed. The sense of watching eyes was gone. Tracy ran through her own room and unlocked the door. In the dim light from the chandelier above the stairs, she saw a man running lightly down. It was Miles Radburn, and she knew that he had gone to meet that boat coming so quietly in to shore over the dark Bosporus.

She did not hesitate. She dared not wait, lest timid fears hold her back. She dared not count the risk. This was an opportunity to find out what stirred in this house, what midnight excursions might have roots in a past that had once involved Anabel.

Her bedroom slippers were soft upon her feet and they made less noise upon the stairs than the old house voiced of its own accord. She stole to the second floor, where all was empty and quiet. Both Murat's bedroom door and Nursel's were closed. Murat, of course, was away in Istanbul. The door of their shared salon stood open, and

270

she saw that it and the main hall were heaped with the merchandise Sylvana Erim must have sent over from her house. Evidently preparations had already begun for the work to be done tomorrow.

Tracy wasted no second glance on heaped tables and piled-up chairs. Moving more cautiously now as she rounded the lower bend of the stairs, she went toward the lower corridor that ran from front to back of the house. There were no lights on below. Only the faint light from high over the stairs kept the marble corridor from being utterly black. She could see no one, hear nothing. Step by step she ventured down the lower stairs and stood upon cold marble.

At first she thought the corridor empty. Then she realized that a darker massing at the end near the boat landing was the figure of a man. His back was toward her as he faced the water, and she did not think she had been seen or heard. She could not go that way. But there seemed to be no one near the door at the other end that opened on the driveway, and she ran toward it soundlessly, thankful that marble did not creak. The door was locked with a huge, old-fashioned key and there was a more modern lock as well. She hoped the turning of the key, the click of the lock would not be heard. In a moment she had the massive wooden door partly open. It would creak if she opened it wide, so she slipped through the crack

271

and was outside where the wind was rising, hiding all other sounds.

The area between the two houses lay quiet. In the garage the car Murat Erim should have taken to Istanbul stood in its place, but she did not pause then to question its presence. Wind swept between the two houses and whipped at her coat, stung her bare ankles, tossed her hair. She fled from the lighted area around the corner and found herself in the dark garden. Here grass deadened the sound of her steps, and there were the black forms of bushes and trees guarding her all about. She picked her way carefully, able to see but little, moving in the direction of the water. At the corner of the house she blended into the thick darkness of a hydrangea bush and started toward the landing.

There was nothing there and no one. No small fishing boat with oars muffled had come in to shore. All stood empty and without life. Only wind ruffled the dark waters of the Bosporus. Yet she had been sure the boat was approaching the shore. There would have been no time for it to dock and get away again. She had been sure, too, that a figure had stood not far from where she stood now, watching. And she had seen Miles come downstairs.

The very emptiness of the place was somehow alarming. She had gone far enough. She turned and hurried back through the garden by the path along which she had come, knowing her way now and able to distinguish objects in her path. She reached the front door and found that the wind had blown it shut. It had latched itself behind her, and she could not get in. Whether she liked it or not, there was nothing for it but to return through the garden and go around to the water side.

She approached the landing warily, but it stood empty as before. There was no tide in these waters that opened eventually to the Mediterranean, but the wind was pushing the Bosporus into a squally pattern, sending dashes of spray against the landing, so that she felt the wetness upon her bare ankles as she ran toward the corridor.

Here she did not hesitate, lest she be silhouetted to watching eyes against water and sky as Miles had been. She darted into the gloom, relieved to find the corridor empty. There was something almost eerie about the way everyone had vanished, and she wanted only to regain the safety of her own room and lock the door behind her. There had been no time to be frightened, but now cold tremors seized her and she found that she was terrified without knowing what there was to be terrified about.

She ran upstairs as quietly as she could, and shut herself into her room. But she did not go to bed. She did not take off her coat. She stood for a time on the balcony again, watching the water and the landing below. Nothing stirred. There was clearly no one there. Once it seemed that she heard not too distant sounds from the water, but nothing was visible close in, and such noises were usual all night long. Out on the water the lights of fishing boats moved like fireflies.

When she tired of watching the landing, she closed the balcony doors and set the inner door ajar, listening now for Miles's return upstairs. Again there was only the usual creaking of stairs and house. More than a half hour had passed since her excursion and it began to seem probable that he had returned to his room earlier. There was no purpose to be gained by listening all night for footsteps that never came any closer. Then, just as she was about to close her door and go back to bed, a sudden clamor arose from the floor below. She heard Miles shouting, "No, you don't! Drop that stuff! Drop it!"

Tracy ran toward the stairs and down them. In the big second-floor salon two figures struggled together. Something crashed with the sound of breaking glass and a strong scent of heliotrope flooded the air. The larger figure that was Miles won its struggle with the smaller more wiry one—Ahmet. Miles held the captive by the loose cloth at the back of his jacket, shaking him roughly. The odor of heliotrope bathed them both, bathed the very air about them.

As he shook the fellow, Miles ran his hands over Ahmet's pockets, divesting them of assorted contents. He flung objects away from him across the floor. A comb and coins and other small articles skittered toward Tracy. She bent to pick up two strings of beads. One was the somewhat greasy brown tespih she had seen often in Ahmet's fingers. The other was of black jet.

"Were you stealing for yourself?" Miles demanded. "Or is this something you do for your master?"

It was a strange question, and by way of reply Ahmet turned upon Miles a look which indicated that he understood the words and was angered by them.

Miles went on and Tracy wondered if he deliberately baited the man. "Perhaps this is a matter for the police. Perhaps it is now time to show everyone the source of our thefts."

Before Ahmet could manage an answer, Nursel's door opened and she came from her room wearing a flowing green gown, her black hair long upon her shoulders, her dark eyes wide with alarm.

"What is it?" she cried. "What has happened? Miles, what has Ahmet Effendi done?"

The houseman ceased to struggle and turned limp. Cautiously Miles released his hold. "I'm not sure. He seems to have been taking stuff from this merchandise of Sylvana's." He gestured to the floor about him, where Ahmet had dropped an armload of goods. "A queer assortment. Pillows and embroidered bags and table linens. Suppose you ask him to explain."

Nursel questioned the man in Turkish while Miles listened. Ahmet shook his head in sullen refusal and would not answer. Abruptly a new voice spoke from the head of the stairs, and Tracy turned to see Dr. Erim standing there. He regarded the tableau for only a moment and then strode to Ahmet, addressing him without excitement, coolly, quietly. Ahmet hung his head as if in shame, as if admitting his iniquity. When Murat had listened for a moment or two to what appeared to be mumbled confession, he turned to the three who waited.

"If you please—the occurrence is over. I will deal with Ahmet Effendi myself. I see that a perfume bottle has been broken—let us open windows to air the room."

He followed his own suggestion with the veranda doors, and Ahmet, after another dark look at Miles, began to gather his scattered possessions from the floor. Tracy held out the two strands of beads and he took them from her sullenly.

Nursel came to Tracy. "Can you tell me, please, what has happened? Why does Ahmet Effendi touch such things for which he has no use? I have asked him, but he does not tell me the answer. Nor does he tell my brother."

"Perhaps he meant to sell them," Tracy suggested.

Nursel looked indignant. "He has been trusted for many years in this house—almost like one of our family. I cannot believe he would do such a thing." She lowered her voice for Tracy's ears only. "Hasan, his son, will be most upset. I do not know—perhaps it is better if we do not tell Hasan."

She threw a concerned look at Ahmet, still pocketing his belongings, and saw the broken scent bottle on the floor.

"But what a sad thing! It is Sylvana's perfume bottle that has been shattered, the perfume wasted. Sylvana will be annoyed. She ordered this container herself from a village glass blower. I cannot understand what Ahmet Effendi can be doing with that or with any of these things."

Neither could Tracy. And there were other things she did not understand. Miles had said nothing of the boat, if he had seen it, or of being in the corridor below—if his had been the figure she had seen. But he was not through with his notion about summoning the police, and he said as much to Murat.

The other man answered coldly. "We do not take such action with one who has served us as long and faithfully as Ahmet Effendi has done. There will be no reporting of this to the police. You understand? If you are so foolish as to take

277

some action, my sister and I will protect Ahmet Effendi. We will deny that anything has happened."

Tracy glanced at Nursel and saw that her eyes were downcast. It was clear that she would do exactly as her brother wished.

Miles turned his back on Murat and spoke to Tracy. "I don't know how you got into this, but it seems to be over. You'd better go back to bed."

Tracy started up the stairs. As she looked down over the rail she saw Murat gesture Nursel away and take Ahmet into his bedroom. Tracy continued upstairs and Miles followed.

As they reached the upper floor Miles sniffed at himself ruefully. "I need an airing too. He spilled most of that stuff over the two of us. Deliberately, I think. If the bottle had merely slipped out of his hands, it would have broken on the floor. But he got the stopper out first, so it went all over him and over me."

"But why?" Tracy asked. "Why would he do that?"

"Who knows? Perhaps to cover up some other smell? Don't ask foolish questions. It's too late at night."

His tone was snappish and she snapped back. "I have plenty of questions to ask, and I don't believe they are foolish!"

He took her firmly by the arm and marched her to her door. "There's just one question I'm

278

interested in now. How did you get down there so fast?"

"I was out on the veranda," she said. "I think you know that. I saw a boat coming in toward the landing. The same one you were watching."

"By the dark of the moon," he said. "This was a good night for it. Go on. What else did you see?"

"Nothing," she admitted. "I ran downstairs after you to find out what was going on. But by the time I got to the landing there was no one there."

"Exactly my deduction," Miles said. "The boat comes in elsewhere, I suppose. Have you ever considered that it might be wiser for you to stay out of an affair like this?"

"As you are staying out of it?" Tracy asked.

"It's my business, not yours. I'll thank you to keep still about having seen me go down there."

Her feeling toward him was one of greater irritation than ever before. "Why should I keep still? What are you trying to hide?"

He looked at her with such exasperation that she feared he might shake her, as he had shaken Ahmet. She backed away from him hurriedly.

"You do smell quite dreadful," she said.

He neither shook her nor swore at her, though he might well have done both. "From the moment you arrived in this house I haven't known what to do about you. That sister you told

279

me of would have had her hands full trying to keep up with you. Now—will you go to bed and stay out of this from now on?"

His look told her that she was pushing him too far, but she had to stand her ground. "No," she said, "I won't keep out of it."

He put his hands on her shoulders, but he did not shake her. Quite astonishingly he pulled her to him and kissed her on the mouth—with great impatience and a sort of rough tenderness. Then he shoved her away.

"Now will you go home? Slap my face, if you like, and go home. Get out of this! You're way beyond your depth in dangerous waters and you don't belong here. You can't remain any longer."

She felt a little sick with shock because two totally opposing currents were charging through her in almost the same instant. To her distress, she liked being kissed by Miles Radburn. She liked it that he had wanted to kiss her. And then he had told her why he'd kissed her and the current had flashed distressingly the other way. Her eyes were bright with outrage and her cheeks flaming, but again she stood her ground.

"I *do* belong here. I *am* involved. Nothing you can do will change that. Anabel was my sister and I belong here as much as you do."

He stared at her while color drained slowly from his face, leaving it pale and cold. Abruptly he turned on his heel and walked away from her across the salon. She watched him go. Watched him disappear into his own room, where the portrait of Anabel would look down upon him with its secret green gaze.

Feeling thoroughly shaken, she went into her room. She had left the veranda doors open and the air was cold. She closed them with hands that shook and caught the sweetish odor of heliotrope upon her own person. It was a dreadful, sickly smell. She knew she would detest it for the rest of her life. It was on her coat and she flung it off to escape the scent and shivered in her thin nightgown. Quickly she got into bed and lay beneath cold sheets thinking. But not of Ahmet; or of the larger events of the night. She could remember only that Miles had kissed her in order to anger her and be rid of her. He would never forgive her for being Anabel's sister, or for the hoax she had played on him. While she, after all her resolution, her determination never to follow in Anabel's footsteps again, was moving helplessly down a road that could lead only to pain and frustration she had brought upon herself. No matter how hard she tried, she could not put out of her mind and her heart the man Anabel had loved. The man others claimed was responsible for Anabel's death.

# 14

IN THE MORNING Miles was up and out early and Tracy did not see him at the breakfast table. She went downstairs, to find Murat and Nursel breakfasting alone. Ahmet was nowhere in evidence.

Dr. Erim greeted her cheerfully enough and rose to pull out her chair. "Good morning, Miss Hubbard. We are sorry you had to lose your sleep because of the disturbance last night."

She undoubtedly looked as though she had lost sleep, Tracy thought. She murmured a "good morning," and waited for Halide to bring her coffee. She needed it strong and thick today.

Nursel smiled at her sadly. "Murat and I have been discussing this foolish act of Ahmet Effendi's. He has been all his life with us. For servants to take small items of food—this is not unknown in Turkey, as in other countries, but to do such a thing as this! How will you deal with him, Murat?"

"Unfortunately, it is not in my hands," Murat said stiffly.

Tracy knew he was thinking of Sylvana.

"Does Mrs. Erim know what has happened?" she asked.

Nursel rolled her eyes heavenward. "She does not know. I am afraid of what will result when

282

she learns. But my brother and I are also discussing another matter. I have suggested to him that if Ahmet Effendi has done such a thing before, it is possible that your sister was judged falsely and blamed for taking what she did not take."

Murat shook his head in disagreement. "This I do not believe. Certain articles were found in Mrs. Radburn's possession. There is no question about what she was doing."

Tracy looked at her plate and did not speak. Her head ached and her eyes felt heavy. At the moment it was impossible to concern herself with Anabel's behavior or Ahmet's guilt.

"Last night I told Mr. Radburn that I am his wife's sister," she said. "Have you seen him this morning? Has he mentioned the fact?"

"We have not seen him," said Nursel. "But do not be concerned—we will protect you, even if he is angry. When you wish to go home we will arrange it—at any time you wish!"

She wasn't concerned, Tracy thought. She was simply numb and shocked and sickened. Because of the discovery she had made about herself last night and which she could not manage to live with this morning.

As they were about to leave the table, Sylvana appeared. For all her bright, calm air of efficiency, Tracy sensed again her single-minded determination to bend persons and events to her own use and eventual profit. Yet it was not entirely clear what lay behind this desire to rule, to manage, to manipulate. Tracy remembered the odd distortion that had appeared in the samovar reflection and the interest Miles had shown in it. Had that accidental glimpse revealed a disturbing truth about Sylvana that Miles had recognized?

Glancing at Murat, however, she knew that he was not fooled by the woman. Dr. Erim, at least, saw her with a contemptuous clarity he scarcely tried to conceal as he told her curtly what had happened last night.

Sylvana took the account with a tranquil acceptance that seemed faintly exaggerated.

"We cannot do without Ahmet Effendi," she decided at once. "I cannot imagine how this household could be run without him. Every servant has faults and makes mistakes at times. If nothing has been taken, and if you have reprimanded him, I think we must give him another chance."

"I have spoken to him," said Murat. "I believe there will be no more trouble."

"Good. I shall add a few words of my own and then we shall go on as before—yes?"

Murat shrugged and left them, to retire to his laboratory in the other house. Within Tracy's hearing no one had asked why he had come home unexpectedly last night, and he had offered no explanation.

"Where is Ahmet Effendi now?" Sylvana inquired briskly.

"He has remained in his room downstairs, waiting to be kept or dismissed," Nursel said. "He is very gloomy. Would you like me to bring him here?"

"Not now. Let him commune with Allah for a time. Perhaps he will chasten himself sufficiently. Undoubtedly he took these things to give to his son Hasan to sell in that poor little store. Come, let us begin sorting the articles which must be shipped. Then we will start the packing. Is everything ready?"

As Sylvana spoke she had moved into the main salon where the disturbance had occurred last night. Behind her back Nursel looked at Tracy and shook her head vehemently, denying the implication that would have involved Hasan. She did not argue openly with Sylvana, however. Tracy might have admired her more if she had. Always Nursel gave before the slightest pressure, no matter what her inner feelings might be.

The tall green porcelain stove in the salon had been lighted earlier, and the room, for all its vast reaches, was not uncomfortable in the springlike weather. Halide came to help and later one of the girls from the kitchen joined them. Wrapping paper and twine had been set out and there were shears and cardboard and large boxes. Sylvana gave crisp instructions and insisted upon wrapping each breakable object herself. When she discovered that the bottle of heliotrope scent had been smashed, she seemed more annoyed than she had been over the actual thieving.

"Such carelessness! It is difficult to forgive Ahmet Effendi for this. But of course one of my special scents would have been a fine thing for his son to sell in the bazaar and he would try to take this."

Nursel went so far as to make a clicking sound of disagreement with her tongue, but Sylvana seemed not to hear, or ignored it if she did.

Tracy sat at a table, wrapping various articles— a shepherd's bag, handwoven and embroidered in brightly colored wool, a shallow bowl of beaten copper, silver jewelry, and innumerable tespihler.

After a time Tracy's hands moved automatically and she paid little attention to the talk around her. The problem of Miles must be faced. She must see him and talk to him, perhaps tell him of Anabel's phone call, show him the strand of black amber left between the pages of the book with a passage marked. She must tell him why she had come here, try to make him understand her need for secrecy. He had sounded last night as though he knew something of what went on in this house. He had accused Ahmet of working for a master—meaning Murat? How much of a thorn of trouble between Miles and Murat had Anabel herself been? It was possible that Tracy and Miles might help each other if they pooled their mutual knowledge.

Yet even as her thoughts turned along a practical course, there was an aching in her that would not be quiet. Ever since she had come here, she had been moving surely and inevitably toward Miles Radburn. Even in moments of antagonism the chemistry of attraction had been drawing her to him. When Nursel had warned, she would not listen. Had she been more honest with herself, she might have felt the strength of the current before she was helplessly caught up in it.

But no—she would not accept that! She was not helpless even now. Anabel had drifted with whatever current had caught her up. But this was not for Tracy Hubbard. It was nonsense to believe that she could fall in love so suddenly that she was unaware of what was happening until it was too late. Or—the pendulum swung again—was this the fundamental and irreversible truth that she must now face—that in spite of herself she was in love? Because of Anabel this would be a particularly difficult thing to accept, and she winced away from it in her own thoughts.

Sylvana's voice broke in upon this unhappy circling. "Are you dreaming, Miss Hubbard? If you please—we cannot waste good twine like that."

Tracy apologized and unwound a few wasted lengths of twine. She was well aware that Sylvana regarded her with cold distaste today. Beneath all that mock calm, the woman was still angry because Tracy had defied her and remained at the yali. But at least it would not be for long. Now that Miles too wanted her to go, Tracy's days in this house were numbered. With that thought came further realization of the cause behind her hurt and confusion and self-blame. Miles had loved Anabel first. He still kept her picture on his wall. Last night he had rejected Tracy Hubbard unequivocably. It was this that hurt so much and would not release her from pain.

Again Sylvana's voice cut into her thoughts, drawing her back to petty reality, whether she liked it or not.

"Where is the strip of calligraphy Miles has made for me?" Sylvana was asking. "I have a cardboard roll in which to place it so that it will not be damaged in mailing. I thought it was here among these things, but I do not find it."

At once a search began for the Turkish script. It was not among the articles in the big room where they worked. Nor could Nursel or Sylvana find it in the living quarters Nursel shared with Murat, where other articles had been piled.

Halide was sent to the kiosk to search for it there, but returned empty-handed.

Sylvana shed her air of tranquillity and began to look seriously disturbed. "I have several regular buyers for these pieces in New York. Miles has contributed his time for this work and the money goes with the rest to the villagers' fund. This must be found."

Tracy remembered Ahmet's odd interest in the piece when she had surprised him in Miles's study.

"There's still Ahmet," she suggested.

"He would not take such a thing," Sylvana said. "Still—we must be sure."

"Let me speak to him," Nursel offered. Her concern about Hasan's father was evident to Tracy, but Sylvana lacked the key to an understanding of Nursel's feelings.

"Yes—it is time," Sylvana said. "Bring him here, whether he has the script or not."

Nursel hurried away. During her absence Miles came indoors from his walk. He would not have stopped on his way upstairs if Sylvana had not spoken to him.

"I am sorry that I will not have time to give you a sitting for a day or so," she said. "As you can see, we are well occupied. This will take up all of today and perhaps some of tomorrow. After that, we will continue with the portrait."

"The painting can wait," Miles said.

He did not look at Tracy and she could sense his displeasure with her, his continued rejection. She gave her attention to tying a secure knot in carefully apportioned twine and pretended not to know that he was there.

When he had gone upstairs, Sylvana spoke again to Tracy. "I think we shall not tell Mr. Radburn about this small matter of the calligraphy. Assuredly it will be found. He would be disturbed if he thought his contribution had been carelessly treated."

Tracy said nothing. Perhaps she would tell Miles, perhaps not, but she wondered at this small effort at deception on Sylvana's part.

A few moments later Nursel returned with Ahmet. Last night the man had seemed murderously angry with Miles, then apologetic with Murat. Now he had returned to his usual sullen, uncommunicative self.

Nursel produced the rolled-up script and placed it before Sylvana. "What has happened is nothing for us to be excited about, I think. Ahmet Effendi tells me he has only borrowed this. He took it to his room yesterday, thinking you would not mail it at once. Then, after what happened last night, he was upset and forgot to return it."

Sylvana unrolled the strip of paper and spread it out upon a table. Then she spoke to Ahmet in Turkish.

He answered her readily enough, repeating the

names of Allah and the Koran several times. As they talked, Tracy stepped close to the table to study Miles's careful, precise work, once more fascinated by it. The ancient calligraphy had been truly beautiful with its vertical lines, its dashes and loops and convolutions. There were bows like small crescent moons, and lines that wriggled up and down like the moving body of a snake. All meaningless to eyes that could not read, but endlessly intriguing as a pattern. Miles must have reproduced the script meticulously.

In one corner was a sort of hatchwork design with small ripples around it like falling leaves. This Tracy had not noticed before and she studied it, puzzled. Before she had come to a conclusion, Sylvana picked up the script, rolled it into a cylinder, and slipped it inside the mailing tube. She spoke a few more words from the table to Ahmet and he bowed to her and went away, looking not at all repentant.

"I suppose it is reasonable that this piece should interest him," Sylvana said. "Ahmet Effendi can read the old characters as young Turks cannot, thanks to Mustapha Kemal. I do not believe Atatürk did only good for Turkey. So much of the old and picturesque is gone."

"This is true," said Nursel dryly. "Before I was born my mother wore a veil and my father a fez. Murat and I are no longer able to be so picturesque."

Sylvana sat down at a table to address the tube, paying no attention.

Nursel whispered to Tracy, "We will not tell Hasan. I do not know why Ahmet Effendi is so foolish, but he will continue to work here and I do not think this will happen again. Hasan would be worried about his father."

Tracy scarcely listened. A clear picture of the calligraphy as she remembered it lingered in her mind. A picture that was without the cross-hatching and falling-leaf design in one corner. Had Miles added some further touch after the script had been delivered to Sylvana? Or might Ahmet have been so whimsical as to have put in something of his own—perhaps out of his knowledge of what was correct in Turkish writing? Both seemed unlikely. Apparently Sylvana had noticed nothing. Or wished to notice nothing.

Uneasiness began to grow in Tracy's mind. This was something Miles should know about. And he must be told before Sylvana sent the tube off in the mail and it could not be examined.

She worked for a little while longer and then told Sylvana she would go upstairs to see if there was anything Miles wanted of her.

Sylvana objected as though she could not bear to agree with any suggestion Tracy might make. "He has promised me we could have your help today. We have only today and tomorrow to finish this work. The shipment must be ready to be sent at the proper time. I myself will deliver it to the airport—where it will go by air freight."

"Perhaps I'll come back," Tracy said.

She went upstairs to Miles's study. The door was closed and she stood before it a moment, waiting for the thumping of her heart to quiet. She detested this excitement in herself at the mere prospect of seeing him. She would have none of it. Where Anabel had gone, she would not follow. But when she rapped on the door the sound had a hollow and hesitant ring to her ears.

Miles called, "Come in."

She stepped into the room and closed the door behind her. "There's something I want to tell you," she said.

He sat at his desk with a sheaf of manuscript fanned out before him. There was no welcome in his eyes as he looked up. Not even in the beginning had she seen his expression so remote, so coldly forbidding.

"I have nothing to say to you," he told her. "I have only one thing to ask—that you go home at once. There's nothing else I want of you."

It was difficult to stand her ground, when he looked like that, but she fought back an inclination to retreat.

"I won't leave until I have a chance to talk to you. I want to tell you why I came. About what brought me here."

"Why you came or what brought you here has no interest for me. I've no taste for hoax players. You had only to say who you were the moment you arrived."

"And what would you have done if I had?" Tracy demanded.

"I'd have refused to let you stay, naturally. If you came as far as this house, I would have sent you home before you took off your hat."

"That's exactly what I thought!" Indignation restored her courage. "That's why I didn't tell you. I intended to stay."

He returned his attention to the papers before him, waiting for her to go. But there was still something she must report, whether he liked it or not.

She spoke quickly. "Ahmet took your strip of calligraphy to his room yesterday without telling anyone. I think it's possible that he added some characters of his own to the script. Sylvana is going to mail it and I thought you ought to know."

He left his desk before she had stopped speaking and went past her on his way downstairs. She followed him to the stair bend to watch the scene below.

Sylvana and Nursel turned from their work in surprise as he broke in upon them.

"I'd like to have another look at that calligraphy piece before you send it off," he told Sylvana.

She waved the cardboard tube at him. "But I have already packed it to mail. I am about to seal it."

"Let me see it before you do." He held out his hand.

For a moment it seemed that Sylvana might not oblige. Then she gave Miles a brittle smile and handed him the tube.

He drew out the rolled sheet of heavy paper, uncurling it so that he could study it carefully. Tracy leaned upon the rail and watched.

After a moment he nodded. "Something has been added. Something I didn't put there. Halide"—he turned to the little maid—"find Ahmet Effendi. Bring him here."

Sylvana objected quickly. "I have already spoken with the man. He has been reprimanded for what happened last night. I do not wish to disturb him further."

Miles repeated his words in Turkish and Halide flew toward the stairs, with only a backward glance of apology for Sylvana.

"I'm sorry to interfere," Miles said quietly, "but when I turn out a piece of work I don't want it tampered with by amateurs. Did neither you nor Nursel notice anything different about it?"

Sylvana's usual manner of calm affection toward Miles had begun to show signs of cracking. "It looks exactly as before to me," she insisted. "As for Nursel—she would not know. She is not familiar with this work as I am."

At that moment Sylvana glanced toward the stairs and saw Tracy leaning on the rail. The flat blue surface of her eyes took on a baleful expression. She had an outlet now for mounting tension.

"You are a maker of trouble!" she accused. "Whatever this is, it is a small matter and we do not need such a disturbance about it."

"Miss Hubbard is going home," Miles said. "She's going back to New York as soon as I can send her there. She will cause no further disturbance of any kind."

Nursel stared at the star sapphire on her finger, aloof from the discussion, while Sylvana looked pleased. "It is time you agreed," she said.

When Ahmet appeared, Miles showed him the script, pointing to the hatchwork in the corner, to the curving lines that had been added. "What is this? What do you mean by tampering with my work?"

Ahmet understood English well enough when he pleased, but he answered with the Turkish gesture of the negative, throwing his head back abruptly. He had seen nothing, done nothing, added nothing. *Allah ashkina*—for the sake of God, would they not believe in his innocence?

Miles shrugged and let him go. "He doesn't mean to talk. Nevertheless, someone has put in several additional characters and I'm not at all pleased."

As Ahmet turned away, Tracy saw again the look of dark resentment he gave Miles. A look to which Miles seemed indifferent.

Sylvana was increasingly displeased. "Is this of consequence? I am sure my purchaser in New York will not know the difference. I cannot believe these small scratches have so much significance."

Miles studied the script for a moment longer. "Perhaps you're right. If it's important for you to mail this at once, then I won't object."

Sylvana's smile rewarded him, though it seemed a bit frayed around the edges and the flat blue gaze was without warmth. "Thank you, my good friend. It is important to me only because I do not like to disappoint the buyer who has ordered this calligraphy and has someone waiting to purchase it from his store."

"Very well," said Miles. "But after this, let's have no fancy additions to what I've done."

Sylvana seemed about to answer sharply, but when he had rolled the script and put it carefully into the tube, taking his time, she accepted it without a word. Miles went upstairs past Tracy. She had to hurry to catch him before he shut himself into his study again. She reached the door just in time.

"You'd better watch Ahmet," she said breathlessly. "He dislikes you intensely. I wouldn't feel comfortable if someone looked at me like that."

"Thank you, Miss Hubbard." Miles was elaborately polite. "I must take lessons from Ahmet Effendi. I'd like to learn his method of frightening at a glance. Then perhaps I could persuade you to go home without further delay."

He went into his study and she found the door closed in her face. She stood looking at it stupidly for a moment. Then she went back to her room and lay down on the bed, feeling more frightened than she had at any other time in this house. Her fear was not for herself, but for this man who openly detested her and would not recognize his own possible danger.

# 15

FOR THE REST of that day Tracy was of little help to Sylvana. She did not need to placate the woman now, or to keep to any commitment Miles might have made in offering her services. Nor did she mean to accept the order from him to go home at once. She would stay until they sent her home forcibly. Now there was something she must still do this very day.

In the afternoon she picked up Yasemin for company, and she and the white cat went again to the ruins of the Sultan Valide's palace. Today it seemed a melancholy place, for all that the sun was shining. At least it was empty. There seemed to be no one here ahead of her and she had no sense of a hidden watcher. She set Yasemin down and the cat ran off on a hunting expedition, while Tracy began her own search. There were only two places she did not attempt to investigate. She avoided the veranda with its rotting wooden arches and broken roof, since it looked to be an exposed and unlikely hiding place. Its floor overhung the water, and she had no wish to trust its boards beneath her feet. The stairs and second story looked even more treacherous, and she doubted that even Anabel would go up there. Room by room, however, she went through the lower floor of the house.

She suspected that her search would be useless since Murat had apparently done a good deal of looking himself, without result. Still, there was the chance that some inspiration would come to her, that she might find some answer, simply because she had once known Anabel.

The main difficulty, of course, was that she did not know what she searched for. Had Anabel hidden something in this place, or perhaps discovered something hidden here? What other "secret" was possible?

If it was a hiding place she looked for, a thousand crannies offered concealment. Rotted floors presented pockets by the score. Stone crumbled and could be moved to form apertures.

Plaster had fallen away, leaving bare lath exposed, offering possible compartments in the very walls. Only marble stood solid, and even that was cracked in places.

When she had wandered outdoors in the garden, she found that vines and weeds and newly budding shrubbery grew in a vast tangle, with secret concealment likely almost anywhere. What particular place among all these would have suggested itself to Anabel—if, indeed, this was the answer?

Tracy poked here and there in a desultory fashion, with no inspiration coming to her. Her efforts were as useless as Murat's had apparently been. She wondered again what his interest in such a search could be. What did he know? How deeply had he been involved with Anabel?

Once more she stepped through the marble doorway and was in time to see Yasemin vanish into the same large hole in the floor of the main room that she had hidden in when Murat had threatened her. A place, perhaps, with which she was familiar. With quickening interest, Tracy called to her and Yasemin mewed in plaintive alarm from within the hole. Today going in had apparently been easier than coming out.

Tracy knelt on a board she thought least likely to crack beneath her weight, and reached gingerly into the splintery hollow beneath. Something blocked the way. It seemed to be something loose that must have moved when Yasemin crept in, wedging itself against her exit as she turned around inside.

Tracy scolded gently as she worked the object free. "You could get caught in there and starve to death, you foolish little cat. No one would ever know where you were. You must be more careful in your hunting."

The object felt like an oblong box with a slippery plastic wrapping around it. Excitement grew in her and she worked earnestly until it came free in her hands. She lifted out the closed wooden box and laid it upon the floor beside her. At once Yasemin sprang free, her white fur streaked with grime and splinters of wood. She went off a little way and set herself busily to work, washing and tidying.

How fitting that Anabel's cat should be the one to lead her sister to whatever had been hidden in this place. Tracy stared at her find. The package was the size of several cartons of cigarettes. She pulled off the plastic wrapping and found that the wooden lid had already been pried loose and came off easily. Inside were a number of lumps of some substance she could not identify. The stuff looked rather like thick pats of porous, yellow-brown dough. Or even like dried manure. When she crumbled a bit of the substance it came away in her fingers. She pressed together a small wad the size of her thumb and wrapped it in a

301

handkerchief. Then she sniffed her fingers and turned her head away. The odor was sickeningly sweet.

What this box and its contents meant, Tracy could not be sure. Someone had hidden it here. Ahmet, perhaps? Had the fishing boat that had veered in toward shore last night come, not to land at the yali, but farther upstream at the marble steps of a ruined palace?

It was time to go—and quickly. She had discovered something she had not been meant to find. Perhaps not Anabel's secret, but someone else's. Perhaps something far more dangerous and illicit than anything Anabel could have been involved in. A faint illumination, a suspicion was beginning to form at the back of her mind. She shivered as she replaced the wooden lid and plastic covering, slid the parcel into its hollow in the floor. She hoped she could approximate its original position so that no one would guess it had been moved. The small lump of yellowish-brown stuff was in her pocket, and she wondered if her whole person was permeated with the smell. She had better go home at once and get rid of it.

She was suddenly aware of her exposed position and she glanced around hastily. Overhead the sun shone through a break where roof and upper floor had crumbled into ruin. The empty palace rustled faintly with its own sounds of deterioration. Birds sang undisturbed and the Bosporus lapped gently nearby. Otherwise stillness lay upon the ruins and their surrounding vegetation. Yasemin sat unconcernedly washing her fur with an energetic pink tongue. The cat, being a nervous creature, would have told her if any watcher was about.

Nevertheless, she felt increasingly uneasy. All too well she remembered other encounters in this place. The very first time she had come here, Ahmet had appeared suddenly from the veranda. That was one place she had not looked into. She glanced toward it hastily now, but all seemed quiet and at peace. The wide arch of a doorway opened upon the overhanging gallery above the water. Through splintered wooden balustrades the Bosporus was visible. Examining the expanse for the first time at floor level, Tracy saw something that brought a catch to her breath.

The toe portion of a man's shoe, sole upward, protruded its tip past the place where the arch met the floor. It lay motionless as though the shoe had been tossed there carelessly. Moving as quietly as she could, Tracy went toward it.

As she peered around the arch she saw the man who lay there face down upon the broken floor. One leg was fully extended, the other drawn up to his body. His head lay cradled in the crook of an arm and he was fast asleep.

Tracy fled the house, picking Yasemin up on

her way. Out upon the road she met no one, but she hurried as though pursued. She had recognized the man who lay sleeping on the veranda. He was Hasan, the son of Ahmet.

The side gate to the Erim grounds stood open when she reached it, and Miles Radburn leaned against a gatepost, smoking his pipe and staring expressionlessly at the sky.

She went toward him and at once the white cat sprang out of her arms, streaking through the trees toward home. Tracy came to a quick decision. From her pocket she took the wadded handkerchief and held it out to him.

"Will you tell me what this is, please?" she asked, sounding stiff and unfriendly as she remembered their last encounter.

He caught the odor at once. "Good Lord! What have you been into?"

He opened the handkerchief and looked at the contents with an expression that told her nothing. "You'd better tell me where you found this."

She told him exactly and he listened without comment. From his pocket he drew a tobacco pouch and put the lump, handkerchief and all, into it. Then he rubbed his fingers with tobacco until he had satisfied himself that the odor was sufficiently disguised.

"You probably smell of it thoroughly," he said. "You'd better go back to the house and take a bath."

"Or douse myself with perfume the way Ahmet did last night?" Tracy said.

Miles made no reply. He was staring at the sky again as though he had not heard her.

She spoke impatiently. "Just tell me what this stuff is. You owe me that, at least."

He grimaced. "You don't know how to stay out of trouble, do you? All right—it's opium. Crude opium, my innocent. Now that you know, what use do you mean to make of the information?"

This was the inkling that had stirred at the back of her mind. Turkey, she knew, grew a good portion of the opium poppies of the world as a legitimate business intended for medical use only.

"Then this means that Ahmet is mixed up in a smuggling operation?" she asked.

"I have no idea," said Miles remotely.

"His son Hasan is there now. I found him sleeping on the veranda."

"And I suppose you wakened him to announce your find?" Miles asked.

"Of course not! I got out of there as fast as I could."

"May I congratulate you on such excellent judgment," said Miles.

She had no time to be angry with him now. She went on, half to herself. "I've read about Turkey's exporting of opium. But the poppies are grown under government control, aren't they?"

"At a place called Afyon Karahisar," Miles informed her. "Afyon means poppy. It's a long way from here. Three hundred miles, at least."

"And this isn't the season for poppies," Tracy mused.

"All the better time for moving the stuff after it's been secretly stored for a few months. Farmers have been known to withhold a portion of their production for greater profit. Inspectors have been known to take bribes. The stuff is easily hidden and could be moved gradually toward Istanbul and the outer world. The undercover drug traffic is always a worry to Turkey. In the last few years everything has tightened up and all precautions increased. But still a quantity slips through."

"What are you going to do?" Tracy asked. "Will you call the police and turn this information over to them?"

"I shall do nothing," Miles said, his tone coolly remote. "I advise you to do the same."

She could only gape at him in dismay. "But I should think—"

"Don't think about things you're ignorant of," he said, suddenly angry. "Go wash off that smell and forget what you've stumbled on. Can you understand that much in simple language and get out of here? Go home, American. Go home to the Hilton at least!"

Again he had made her furious, but she could

306

think of nothing to say in the face of his determination to be rid of her. She wheeled abruptly and walked through the gate, following the path that led to the house. She walked with angry resolution. Not until she reached the point where the path turned, and the gate would be lost to sight, did she stop and look back. Miles had closed the gate and was strolling leisurely off in the direction of the ruined palace. To inspect the cache? To retrieve it? Uneasily she hoped that he would not linger there and be caught by Hasan, alone and away from the house. What that young man's part in this affair might be was as much a question as everything else. She had half a mind to turn back, but she knew very well what he would say to her if she did.

When she reached the yali, she obeyed one set of instructions at least. She drenched a handkerchief in Anabel's perfume that Murat had given her, and thrust it into the pocket of her coat where the opium smell was strong. Then she went into the bathroom and by luck found water still hot in the tank so that she was able to have a thorough scrubbing at once.

She got into the huge tub and worked with a brush upon her skin until she glowed and the sickly sweet odor was gone from her person. While she was scrubbing she remembered Yasemin. She had handled the cat and she wondered if the odor might have rubbed off on white fur. Perhaps she had better go in search of the animal when she was bathed and dressed.

In the meantime she lay back in the tub and tried to think about her discovery and its significance. Into her wondering slipped the persistent ghost of Anabel. Was this matter, after all, apart from Anabel? Her sister must have been involved in some desperate and dangerous affair to sound as frightened as she had on the telephone. Was it this? Had she learned something of a boat that came along the Bosporus by the dark of the moon?

A second question came to mind as well. Was Ahmet working with Hasan, if it was he who had hidden the box? Were they working together for someone else in this matter—someone in this house? Which of the three—Nursel, Murat, Sylvana? Or perhaps for two of them, or all working together?

She did not want to think of Nursel, but she must. It was difficult to know whether the girl was for or against Ahmet. Nursel worried about him because of Hasan. Yet Ahmet apparently opposed her marriage to his son as strongly as Murat would have done. Why had Hasan been idly asleep there in the ruins?

Or was Sylvana back of this? She would have no moral scruples, Tracy felt sure, and she had deliberately protected Ahmet. She would not have him discharged and she had dismissed as unimportant his tampering with Miles's calligraphy piece. Perhaps this was because she valued Ahmet as a servant, as she claimed, or perhaps it was because she already knew very well what had happened during the night and was concerned lest he be unmasked. Of what significance was the change Ahmet might have made in Miles's script? This question seemed especially baffling.

The third person who might be involved was Dr. Erim, and here Tracy drew a blank. The man was an enigma. There were contradictions in him that left her always undecided. He might well be involved in some sort of intrigue, and he too had been tolerant with Ahmet. Murat had claimed an overnight trip to Istanbul last night. But if he had gone at all, he had returned early; when Tracy had gone outside she had seen his car in its place in the garage. And later he had come in from outdoors.

Anything was possible—anything.

When she left the tub and toweled herself dry, she felt no wiser than before. She wrapped herself in a woolly bathrobe and went into the hall just as Miles came up the stairs. They met at Tracy's door and he regarded her grimly.

"You smell a bit more wholesome, at least," he said. When she would have opened her door, he put a hand on her arm, his voice low. "I had a look for myself and found the stuff. But this is only a fraction of the picture. The rest may be a good deal more frightful. And more dangerous. I meant it when I asked you to go home at once. Your work for me is over. There's no point in your staying."

Stubbornly, she would not answer. She drew her arm from his touch and went into her room. There was nothing more she could say to Miles Radburn.

When she was dressed she searched for Yasemin. The white cat was in none of her usual haunts, and Tracy could find her nowhere.

The remainder of that day and all of the next passed slowly. The work on the shipment was completed, and with Ahmet's help Sylvana took it to the airport. Afterward there was little for Tracy to do. Miles would not let her work on his files, or remain in his study. No further mention was made of her going home, but she was left so completely to her own devices that she began to wonder if staying could serve any useful purpose. If she were away from Miles, perhaps she could begin to forget him. Futile and foolish though her feeling for him might be, she could no longer hide it from herself. She had indeed followed Anabel. Yet she was no mooning schoolgirl to enjoy the pangs of unrequited love. It would be wiser to take a decisive step that would remove her from his too immediate presence.

But even as she thought about this in sensible terms she knew with another part of her mind that leaving Turkey at this time was impossible. Her discovery of the hidden cache of opium had pointed to an involvement with far larger elements of danger than any she had hitherto suspected. Those who trafficked in drugs did not play nursery games. Miles was in possession of knowledge that made him vulnerable, and she knew that he waited only for the right moment to use it. *If* they gave him time. Feeling as she did, she could not turn her back and go home knowing the danger of his position. As long as she stayed she might be useful in some unexpected way. At least she would be one other person on his side, whether he welcomed the fact or not.

On the third day after her discovery in the ruined palace, Tracy sat alone in her room. It was late afternoon and the day had been a lonely one. She wished for the white cat's presence, but she was beginning to fear that it had run away.

The wind had begun to rise, whining through window cracks and about the eaves, while gray clouds scudded overhead. A storm seemed to be blowing up.

As she sat there idly, Nursel came tapping upon her door and looked in with an apologetic smile.

"I may enter, please? We have neglected you. You are unhappy, that is clear. And Miles does not permit you to work for him. We have all seen this. But now I bring you something to make everything better for you."

Tracy put no trust in the girl's apparent friendliness. Nursel bent with whatever wind was blowing and she was thoroughly under her brother's thumb. Now she came into the room and laid something upon the table beside Tracy. The airline insignia on the folder was plainly in sight. Tracy stiffened in resistance.

"Sylvana sends this," Nursel said before she could speak. "Everything is arranged. Your flight to New York leaves tomorrow morning. If you like, I myself will drive you to the airport."

"I'm not going until Mr. Radburn sends me away," Tracy said.

Nursel moved graceful shoulders in one of her delicate shrugs. "Then let us not speak of it. I have done as Sylvana wishes. There is another matter that brings me to speak with you. I have kept silent because you have great love for your sister and I have respected this. But now you must know the truth—not only of Anabel, but also of her husband."

Tracy watched the other girl warily. She would listen, but she would not necessarily believe.

Nursel seated herself on the edge of a chair and went on, speaking softly, as the story she told took shape. There had been a party in the kiosk on the day before Anabel died. One of

312

Sylvana's famous parties, with many important personages from government and diplomatic circles present. Always Sylvana cultivated friends in important positions. Miles had come alone to the affair. His wife was ill, he said, and was not able to appear.

"Nevertheless, Anabel came," Nursel said. "We were standing about talking before dinner. I was not far from the stairs and I saw her first. But I could not reach her, I could not stop her. No one could have stopped her, I think."

In her telling Nursel omitted no detail. Anabel had worn a misty, gray-green gown that night, softly draped. Her arms were bare, her golden head rising on its slender, fragile neck, her green eyes huge and intense. Across the room Miles saw her and started toward her. Before anyone could reach her, she deliberately called the attention of the guests to herself. She flung out both slender arms in a gesture of entreaty, the soft inner flesh exposed.

"Look!" she cried. "Look at what my husband has done to me!"

A dreadful silence had fallen upon the room. Laughter and talk died, heads turned and eyes stared. Sylvana herself stood frozen and helpless, and for an instant not even Miles could move. The accusation was tragically clear. Where veins neared the surface of the skin were the betraying bruises left by a needle.

Anabel had laughed then, mockingly, laughed in Miles's face as he came toward her.

"You know I will die of this!" she cried. "In the end I will die of it. Then you will be rid of me and free to do as you please."

There had been hysteria in her voice and she would have said more, but Miles reached her and picked her up bodily. She did not fight him, but lay limply in his arms, as if the effort she had made had exhausted her. He carried her down the stairs and back to their rooms in the yali.

Nursel broke off and covered her face with her hands. Tracy could only stare at her in horror.

"The next morning Miles went away," Nursel said. "He abandoned his wife in her time of greatest need and disappeared. She could not face what had happened, what she herself had done to condemn him in public. Yet she was the victim, not the one who had committed this wickedness. Afterward she must have known there was no hope for her anywhere and she dissembled that day. She fooled us all. We knew she was ill, suffering from a withholding of the heroin he had been giving her, but we did not think she would take such action. She slipped away in the early evening and managed to get the small boat out on the water with no one knowing. She did not want to live."

"But why?" Tracy said. "Why would he do a thing like that? I don't understand—"

"Nor I," said Nursel bitterly. "He is a man I have never understood. I have not wanted to tell you this thing which can bring you only grief. But he has drawn you also under his spell. You must know the truth and escape him."

"What if you aren't telling me the truth?" Tracy asked bitterly. "What if I say I don't believe you? You aren't your own woman, you know."

Nursel regarded her curiously. "What is this—I am not my own woman? What do you mean?"

Tracy found herself speaking out of her own pain and despair, seeking to discount anything Nursel might say.

"You talk about independence for Turkish women!" she cried. "But you act like those women who hid behind veils and scampered for the haremlik at the sight of a man. You never stand up for yourself. You never stiffen your spine and go your own way. Because you don't know how to be yourself, I can't believe anything you say."

Nursel rose and went quietly to the door. "I am sorry for you," she said. "If he blinds you in this way, the end is foreseen. But you may ask him, if you like. Tell him what I have told you and ask him for the true answer."

She slipped out of the room and went softly away. Her steps were light upon the stairs and left behind a ringing silence.

# 16

TRACY DID NOT know how long she stayed where she was, unable to think clearly. She felt ill to the point of nausea. The room about her seemed tight and close, the air stifling.

Hardly knowing what she did, she put on her coat and went into the hall. Miles's doors stood closed across the salon. She could not bear to face him now. What had Nursel told her—the truth or a fabrication of lies?

There was no one in sight as she went downstairs and through the lower corridor to the garden. She wanted to be outside in fresh air where she could walk vigorously and be alone. Physical action might stop the whirling confusion of her thoughts. Wind from the Black Sea blew sharply cold as she followed the path through graying light. The treetops were whipping now with the threat of the coming storm. She did not care. She would welcome a storm. She would stand in it and let it quiet her, let it quench the rising of an anguish she could not bear to face.

The side gate was unlocked and she went through. It was not likely that she would meet anyone in the ruins today. Not with a storm coming up. She could not walk slowly and she began to run along the road. Once a car went past

316

and she glimpsed astonished faces staring. She ran headlong, stumbling more than once, nearly falling, picking herself up to run on. The first drops of rain struck across her face with stinging force and she put her head down as she ran.

It was because she scarcely looked where she was going that she ran full tilt into him there on the road. He had heard her coming and turned so that she ran straight into his arms. He held her, steadied her for a moment, then set her on her feet and she raised startled eyes to the face of the man she wanted least of all to see—Miles Radburn.

She wrenched herself away from him. "Let me go! I don't want to talk to you. Leave me alone!"

He took his hands from her arms. "Where are you going? There's a storm coming up."

"I don't care!" she cried and ran from him down the road.

She did not look back or stop running until she reached the gate of what had once been the palace of the Sultan Valide—that place of ill-omen to which Anabel had come so often. Perhaps she could find something of her sister here that would help her. Something that would restore her to belief in both Anabel and Miles, help her to refute Nursel's terrible words.

She scarcely heard the rumble of thunder and did not mind wet slashes of rain as she stumbled through the garden and up marble steps. Within the house faded flowers bloomed dimly, tranquilly, barely discernible upon the wall in the stormy light. Toward the rear of the big salon a portion of the upstairs floor and the roof above were intact. There the rain could not reach her. She took care at least to walk carefully across the broken floor. As she passed the hiding place near the door, she bent to look in, but there was no obstruction visible. The parcel of opium was gone. When she reached the sheltered corner of the room, she stood against the wall and listened to the storm crash about her. The wind made a dreadful sound, howling through the broken house. Its intent was surely to flatten the whole structure into final kindling wood and tumble the very blocks of marble. A corner of the remaining roof, two stories above, lifted and flapped as though it would ride off upon the wind at any moment. Perhaps this was the time when the whole haunted building would topple and crash into the waiting black waters of the Bosporus.

Yet so great was Tracy's inner anguish that she could not be physically afraid. Even when lightning flashed and she saw its forked tongue strike downward toward the water, she was not afraid of the storm.

At least its fury prevented her own feelings from rising and engulfing her. The very uproar numbed her, kept her from thinking. With all the trembling and creaking, the thrashing of tree branches against paneless windows, she could only endure mindlessly, without ability to reason and think.

Then, through the storm clamor, a sound close by reached her—a faint creaking nearer at hand. It was like the squeaking of a rope that held a boat to dock or shore. The sound focused her attention, and she began to search idly for its source. It came from inside the house apparently, and across the vast room. Her eyes searched the far side where rain pelted in and found the cause of the faint, rhythmic squeaking. Something lay upon the floor, just inside what had once been a balcony door. Something she had never seen there before. It was a large rock, and about it had been tied a length of rope that stretched tautly from rock to balcony, disappearing over the rail. It was this rope, moving slightly against the rail, that caused the sound. As though a small boat might lie in the water beyond, tossed by the waves, its swaying weight bringing about a slight movement of the rope that held it.

She left her dry corner and stepped into the roaring wetness. Lightning flashed brilliantly and the thunder that followed marked it as very near. She reached the rope and felt the wet tautness of it in her hands, felt the weight beyond. Something fairly heavy had been tied here in this curious place. Rain drenched her hair and ran in rivulets down her face and into her collar. Her hands were slippery wet. She followed the rope to the rail and looked over. In the dim light she could see no small boat in the roiling water below. A wave splashed her as she leaned upon the rail, and she saw that something hung there over the balcony, something heavy that did not pull up easily when she began to haul on the rope.

She leaned closer, bending toward the water, trying to make out the thing that moved toward her up the side of the balcony. Suddenly she saw the wet white head, the ears that were no longer pricked in wary listening, the drowned eyes with the green no longer showing. A cry of horror choked in her throat and she pulled fiercely on the rope until the bundle came over the rail and fell onto the floor with a heavy clatter.

In that instant lightning brought everything vividly sharp for a fraction of time and the terror that lay at her feet was fully revealed. It was not only that poor Yasemin was dead—it was the terrifying, heart-shaking way in which the little cat had died. What had been done was more cruel, more horrible than anything Tracy could have imagined.

In the full revelation of the lightning flash she had seen the face of ultimate evil. Vicious evil that could place a small white cat in a sack weighted with rock, a sack tied beneath the chin in the old, dreadful way, leaving it to hang over a balcony rail till Yasemin had drowned in surging black Bosporus waters.

Tracy put both hands to her mouth to keep from screaming. Terror engulfed her—as it was meant to do—and she fought against the sickening waves of it.

Then Miles's arm was about her shoulders, drawing her back from what lay upon the floor, forcing her gently toward shelter at the rear of the room. When rain no longer washed over them in a torrent, he held her quietly and she dissolved into tears and trembling in his arms.

She did not scream now. She clung to him and wept. He held her close and let her cry.

Against his shoulder she wept out her terror and anguish. He soothed her and dried her wet face with his handkerchief. When at length he kissed her, she clung to him, returning the touch of his lips with something like fury. Around them the tumult died a little. The voice of the wind dropped a decibel and the house ceased its wild complaining. Lightning flashed more dimly and thunder rumbled farther away.

"It's stopping," Miles said against her cheek. "We'd better go back to where it's dry and warm. Then you can tell me all about this."

She flung out a hand in the direction of the water. "Yasemin!" she choked. "Anabel's little cat."

"I know," Miles said. "I saw."

Reason was returning a bit at a time. "I was meant to find it. Someone knew that I come here—as Anabel used to. It's another warning. The first one was the disturbance of my work. Then a paragraph was marked in a book." She blurted out the story of the underlining she had found in one of the volumes he had loaned her. That marking of a story about drowned harem ladies. If someone had wanted to frighten her, this was a way to manage it. If he had not been here—she broke off, and Miles held her tightly to still a new onslaught of shivering.

Outdoors a trace of late sunshine touched the water to blue and brightened the wet garden.

"We can go now," he said.

"Let's bury her first," Tracy pleaded.

The earth of the garden was soft. Miles found a stick and a broken piece of tile and dug a grave beneath the rhododendron bushes. With gentle hands he freed the white cat from the ignoble sack and laid it into the hollow. Tracy helped him scrape earth over the small sodden body. She had recovered herself now, recovered the power to be angry.

"They can't frighten me like this!" she cried. "Such wickedness has to be exposed. Not just for Anabel's sake. It's a bigger thing than that."

She remembered then. Nursel's words, the story of Sylvana's party. As they stood there in the dripping garden beside the white cat's grave, she told him all that Nursel had said. His mouth was tight as he listened, his eyes cold again and on guard. The look of his face began to frighten her and she ended piteously.

"It's not true, is it? It can't be true? Nursel didn't understand. Or else she was making it all up."

He shook his head. "She wasn't making it up. It happened just as she says. It's true. All of it."

"But—*heroin?* Then it must have been Anabel who was lying. You couldn't have—" she choked again. "I don't believe it!"

For a moment he stood looking at her, his face haunted by memory. Then he spoke in the old, curt way.

"It's true. All of it. Come, we'll go back now."

She went with him in silence while a new fear possessed her. The face of evil was one thing. It could even be accepted and confronted—if only there was someone nearby to be trusted. Someone who was good and sound and not given to the wicked harming of others. If there was not . . .

He did not speak until they reached the gate to Erim property. "Now will you go home to New York?" he said. "Use the plane ticket. Sylvana consulted me, and I told her to go ahead with the arrangements."

She shook her head numbly. She could not answer him with words. There was no one to

323

whom she could turn. Yet she must stay and see it through. She owed this to Anabel, to herself. And even to a small white cat. She was no longer certain of what she owed to Miles.

Inside the gate he paused. "You'll get back to the house all right by yourself? I'm not going in yet."

She nodded and went away from him, following the path to the yali. As she passed the kiosk she saw lighted windows on the laboratory floor. Above there were no lights in Sylvana's windows. Tracy stole past silently and slipped into the house. Not even Ahmet watched her from the shadows. She reached her room without meeting anyone.

The room awaited her undisturbed. There was no black amber warning, no marked pages in a book, no white cat lying asleep on the bed. Her throat tightened, but she would not give in again to useless tears. The terror was there and it must be dealt with. First, however, she must find the way to unmask its face.

The room was a haunted place. There were two ghosts to inhabit it now. One a girl and one a little white cat. Tracy could see them both at every turn. She could see Anabel sitting before the dressing table with the mirrors that had once returned her image. Anabel sleeping in the huge bed where Tracy had slept. And Yasemin everywhere. They had not known what the

Bosporus held for them—those two. Was a third ghost now intended to join their company? Another for whom Bosporus waters could mean cold, smothering death? This was the threat promised to Anabel's sister if she did not leave Istanbul.

She paced the big room from wall to wall and tried to shut such thoughts from her mind. She must think only of finding the answer. An answer that lay in what had happened to Anabel. Perhaps in the very marking of her arms with a needle that had brought her narcotic oblivion. By his own admission administered by Miles.

But she could not accept this as a fact. Even though Miles himself had admitted the truth of Nursel's words, she could not believe it to be the whole truth. There was more here—something that went deeper than seeming evidence indicated.

She could endure the room no longer. She knew, as she had known before, that she must somehow recapture Anabel—find again the very essence of her sister's spirit. Not the sad spirit that haunted this room, but the joy-giving girl she had once been. Perhaps the portrait would bring her back. If Miles had not yet returned to the house, this was her chance.

She crossed the salon to the door of his study and knocked lightly. There was no answer and she went in, closing it softly behind her. The last light was fading beyond the hills of Thrace, and here on the land side of the house the room was dim with shadows. She fled them and slipped through the door to the bedroom. In the moment before she flicked on the light to face her sister, she tried to erase from her mind the picture Nursel had put there, the image of a desperate, hysterical girl displaying ugly marks on her arms, denouncing Miles. It was the Anabel of Tracy's childhood who must help her now. The Anabel Miles had painted in the early years of their marriage.

She touched her finger to the switch and faced the wall where the picture hung. The shock of surprise made her stand blinking for a moment. The portrait of Anabel was gone. In its place above his bed Miles had hung the unfinished portrait he was painting of Sylvana Erim. The substitution was in itself a disturbing thing, but Tracy had no interest in Sylvana's picture and she would have turned from it if the samovar had not gleamed so brightly in the painting that it drew her attention.

Instead of turning away, she went close to the canvas to study it in some astonishment. The portrait of Sylvana had progressed little since she had last seen it. Perhaps a bit more work had been done upon the dress, but the face was still an empty blur. Miles had given his time to the reflection in the samovar and he had portrayed it in full. The bulging copper sides had distorted Sylvana's image and made a mocking caricature of it—this Tracy remembered. But a mocking caricature was not what Miles had painted. With deliberate intent he had created a miniature of something far worse. Line by line Sylvana's face had been cunningly altered to reveal avarice, cruelty, deceit.

The thing had been subtly accomplished— there was no flagrant distortion. At first glance the intent might have been missed. But it was there—an implication of all the evil of which the human soul might be capable, all reflected in a face that was still Sylvana's.

Once she had looked, Tracy could not withdraw her fascinated gaze. She stood shocked and wondering, not a little frightened. The miniature was a revelation, not only of Sylvana, but also of Miles Radburn himself.

When she heard the outer door of the study open, she did not move from her place before the picture. She was beyond caring if he found her here. There was nothing she could say to him at this moment, but perhaps it was best that he know what she had discovered.

She heard steps approach the bedroom door she had left ajar. There was a light tap upon it, and Sylvana's voice called out sharply, "Miles? I may see you, please? There is an urgent matter—"

She did not finish, because Tracy went swiftly

to face her in the doorway. Sylvana was the one person who must not be put on guard by seeing the picture before Miles intended her to see it. Tracy tried to block the opening, but Sylvana pushed past her into the room. At once she saw the portrait on the wall. Its presence did not seem to delight her, as might have been expected.

"But this is amusing!" she exclaimed tartly. "He has taken down the picture of his wife and set mine in its place."

"You're not supposed to see it until it's finished," Tracy warned. She could only hope that Sylvana would miss the reflection in the samovar.

"Then we will not tell him I have seen it," said Sylvana. "You do not expect me to turn away when I have this opportunity to discover exactly what your sister's husband has painted."

There was left only the possibility of distraction. "I found the cat," said Tracy abruptly, her gaze fixed upon Sylvana's face.

The woman gave no sign that she understood. Much of the time she had absolute control over her own reactions. Now, if she knew about the cat, she was well prepared to conceal the fact.

"The animal was missing?" she asked carelessly, and stepped closer to the wall, the better to examine the portrait.

"Someone put Anabel's cat into a sack weighted with stones and hung it by a rope over the balcony of the Sultan Valide's palace. Yasemin was drowned. And her body was left there for me to find. Do you know why?"

Sylvana had stiffened, and there was a glitter to the blue surface of her eyes. But it was the portrait upon which her attention was fixed. She had seen what Miles had painted there and now she saw nothing else.

Watching her, Tracy half expected the woman's face to change before her eyes, to take on the ugly revelation of Miles's portrait. Sylvana stared coldly at the picture, her eyes hard and bright, yet still without emotion. If she had ever known an infatuation for Miles Radburn, it was over. Perhaps it had ended long before, when she had found him a dangerous enemy within her household.

Sylvana stared for a long moment without speaking. Then she turned and went out of the room. The sound of her high heels upon the floor of the salon had a sharply purposeful ring. There was no telling what the woman now intended. Tracy knew she must find Miles at once, warn him, let him know all that had happened.

But when she ran downstairs she found that the garage where he kept his car stood empty. Both car and man were gone, and she had no idea where. The thought that he might have left the yali for good came uneasily to her mind. But surely he would not go away and leave her here alone. Not after the way he had held and soothed her after Yasemin's death. Not after the gentle way he had kissed her. As Anabel had said, he was *accountable*. Yet later Anabel believed she had been wrong, and he was a man whom Tracy, after all, did not really know. It would be better for him if he forgot everything except his own safety and left Istanbul for good. In which case she ought to do the same.

Her heart had no interest in listening to reason. It told her that he would return, and she knew that she could not leave the yali herself and have him walk unwarned into some trap of Sylvana's making.

Since the only safe haven seemed to be that of her room, Tracy went back to it. There she locked herself in, drawing the draperies across the balcony doors, shutting out the last daylight. When she had packed her suitcase and was ready to leave, she sat down to wait. If Miles returned to this floor, she would hear him.

Time had never passed more slowly.

During the evening a tap on her door startled her. She called through the panel before she drew the bolt. Nursel answered, and after a moment's hesitation Tracy let her in.

"I have brought you something to eat," the girl said, setting down the tray. "My brother is most disturbed. It is best if you avoid him. Please—I may stay a little?"

Tracy wanted no company, least of all Nursel's, but to reveal the fact might make her seem afraid.

"Of course," she said. "Thank you for remembering me."

She sat down to onion soup and forced herself to eat, deliberately silent, while Nursel watched in concern.

"It is a terrible thing about the small cat," the other girl said at last. "Sylvana has told us."

So—in spite of the portrait—Sylvana had heard Tracy's words very well.

Nursel stirred uneasily in her chair in the face of Tracy's silence. "What does this terrible happening with the small cat mean to you?"

From beneath the table, Tracy drew the book Miles had loaned her and opened it to the passage where a black amber tespih still marked the place.

"This was left in my room," said Tracy, holding up the beads. "And a passage in this book has been underlined."

Nursel shivered at sight of the tespih and would not touch it. The beads seemed to mean more to her than the words in the book.

"It is as before," she murmured. "This is what your sister called the 'black warning.' It has come again. Someone wishes you ill. Someone wishes you to go away."

"I've begun to suspect as much," said Tracy. "In fact, I can even guess the connection between the marking in the book and what was done to Yasemin. I suppose the next logical step will be me."

Nursel stared at her. "You do not mean—"

"Of course I mean. Me—in a sack weighted with rocks and tied about the throat. Isn't that what is being threatened? Only it would be harder to manage in my case. Because I would fight."

Nursel bent her head and covered her face with her hands. "You must leave this place at once. You must leave Istanbul."

"Who do you think is behind this?" Tracy persisted. "Is it your brother who has behaved in such a monstrous fashion? Or perhaps Ahmet? Or Sylvana perhaps? Or was it you?"

Nursel did not raise her head. "It is better if you do not risk any more anger against you in this house."

"Don't worry," Tracy said. "I've already packed my suitcase. I'm ready to leave. I'll lock myself in tonight, and tomorrow Miles will come to take me to the airport."

"This is the best way," Nursel murmured faintly. She sat up, drawing her hands from before her face.

Tracy studied her curiously. "Don't you ever blame yourself, Nursel?" she asked. "Don't you ever suffer qualms because of what happened to Anabel, or what might happen to me?"

"I—I do not understand," Nursel faltered.

Tracy went on without pity. "I've said it before. I'll make it stronger now. You let your brother dominate you. You lower your eyes if Sylvana scolds. You run their errands. You probably do exactly as Hasan tells you to do, except when you're sure he won't find you out. You don't like Miles, yet you never stand up to him. You don't even stand up to me!"

There was shock in Nursel's face.

"You do not appreciate!" she cried. "I have been your friend—as I was Anabel's friend, and you do not—"

"But never a good enough friend. Never a good enough friend to either of us. Perhaps if you'd been a little braver, Anabel would not have died. Perhaps if you were just a little braver now, nothing dreadful would happen to me."

Nursel left her chair in agitation and ran to the door. "You do not understand! I cannot speak—I cannot! All would be destroyed. But soon, *soon* the matter will be ended. This I know. Perhaps by tomorrow. But it is best if you do not stay for the ending. You are not involved. It is not your affair."

"You forget," said Tracy. "Because of Anabel, it has always been my affair."

Nursel pulled open the door with a despairing gesture and rushed through it. Tracy locked it after her and sat again in her chair.

333

The encounter left her drained and limp, as reaction set in. She was a fine one to taunt Nursel, to criticize her for not acting, when blame lay so heavily on Tracy Hubbard for that very fault.

Oh, *where* was Miles? Why didn't he come?

Once she tried to read to pass the time, but found it impossible. Always the underlining of words about drowning and weighted sacks interposed themselves upon the page, and she saw again the stiff, sodden body of a white cat. Now and then she paced the floor of Anabel's room and looked into Anabel's mirror at her own pale face. And she waited for Miles.

She did not undress to go to bed, but at one o'clock she lay down and, at some time or other, with her clothes on and covered by a quilt, she fell asleep. She heard nothing until the soft tapping on her door began. Her light was still on and her watch said three-thirty. She flew up from the bed and ran to the door.

"It's Miles," his voice said softly.

As she opened the door a wave of relief that had nothing to do with reason flooded through her. It did not matter that he had marked Anabel's arms with a needle, painted that hideous picture of Sylvana. Nothing mattered except that he was here and she loved and trusted him with all her heart. But when she would have clung to him, he smiled wearily and held her away.

"I waited till now so they'd give up expecting me. If anyone is watching, it will be for me to come by car on the land side. But I've left the car on the opposite shore. I've hired a small boat. Come quickly—I'm taking you across."

"I'm ready," she said. "I've been waiting for you."

He picked up her suitcase. The house was still except for its usual creakings. They stepped lightly on the stairs and there was no Ahmet waiting for them in the marble corridor below. Miles hurried her toward the boat landing, where a man sat waiting in a hired boat. Miles helped Tracy into it and followed her. Their boatman used the oars at first, rowing strongly out upon the black current. It was not wholly dark. Above the fortress of Rumeli Hisar hung a widening crescent of moon, brightening the towers and spreading a ladder of light across the water. They headed toward the fortress and did not start the motor until they were well out upon the strait. Among fishing boats and other night traffic, the sound of the motor was lost in the voices of the Bosporus.

They ran in a diagonal toward the opposite shore.

# 17

ON THE FAR SIDE Miles's car awaited them near the wide stone landing. While he paid the boatman, Tracy stood looking across the water toward the yali. There were lights on that had not burned when they left. Near the house landing a light bobbed as if from a boat pushing out upon the water. She touched Miles's arm.

He stared across the water. "Someone's up after all. Let's move along. At least we've got a head start."

They got into the car and he backed onto the road and turned in the direction of the inland highway. The road was almost free of traffic and Miles knew it well. They picked up speed, leaving the Bosporus behind as they reached the crosscut into the city.

"Where are we going?" Tracy asked.

Miles was curt. "To the airport."

"But what about your book? All your papers?"

"I'm not leaving," he said. "I'm going to put you aboard the first plane possible—a plane to almost anywhere. Then I'm coming back."

"I won't go," Tracy said. "I won't get aboard a plane alone."

His face was grim as he watched the car's headlights pick out the road ahead. "You'll go. You have no choice. Do you think I want you to wind up in a sack the way Yasemin did? You know too much for your own safety."

"But not enough!" she wailed. "I won't go away and leave you. Do you think you're not vulnerable too?"

He reached out his hand and covered her own. "Hush. Be quiet. Listen to me. I want to tell you about your sister."

She slid down in the seat and closed her eyes. She did not know what was coming, or whether she wanted to hear it or not. But the time for the truth had come. She could turn from facing it no longer. He began without emotion, and as he spoke she could conjure up her sister's secretive green eyes watching the world with their sidelong glance.

"I first knew Anabel when she began to work for me as a model," Miles said. "Her contrasts, the elusive quality of her fascinated me and I kept trying to capture it on paper. While I painted, she used to talk to me about her friends and about her life in New York."

"Did she tell you about her family?" Tracy asked.

"Never about her family. Never about anything that had happened to her at home in Iowa. I found that she was running with a worthless crowd in New York and I tried to get her away from them. I didn't know for a while that she had been taking narcotics. When I found out—I married her."

337

Tracy sat up and stared at him in the dim light from the dashboard.

He nodded. "Fairly insane, I'll agree. Against the best of advice, I had to play the rescuer of a lady so obviously in distress. I was in love with her then—though in my own way, not in hers. Partly, I suppose, I was in love with the way I had painted her on canvas. After we were married, I took her out of New York to be cured. She was loving and grateful and, for a time, devoted to me. I suppose we were happy in an uneasy sort of way. I painted her as I saw her that first year and put more into the portrait than I knew."

"She came to see me before you were married," Tracy mused. "She believed that everything was going to be wonderful from then on. She thought she was going to be happy—and safe."

"I remember too." His tone was dry. "I believed in all this and I thought I could keep her safe."

"Yet she went back to drugs. Why?"

"Who knows? Who can say whether it is childhood environment, or the accident of circumstance, or something in the genes that drives a person like Anabel? In spite of all I tried to do, she took up the habit again whenever she found an opportunity. I saw her through two more so-called cures. That's when I came to abhor the creatures who are behind this vicious traffic."

Sylvana, Tracy thought—that miniature of evil he had painted.

"When Sylvana's invitation came to visit her here in Turkey, I seized on it," he went on. "Anabel was pulling out of her last bout, and I thought we'd be safe for a time in that quiet place on the Bosporus. For more than a year I hadn't been able to give myself to painting. I'd been going downhill for a long while anyway. I didn't care enough any more. I had always been interested in Turkish mosaics, and I decided to do a study of them for my own satisfaction. Sylvana was generous and made us welcome. Or so I thought. And I believed the trip would offer a haven for Anabel. But at the yali someone began giving her heroin again. Someone who wanted to destroy her."

There was silence in the car. Tracy hugged her arms tightly about herself, waiting.

Miles's eyes were on the rear-view mirror. "There's been a car on the road behind us for some time. Up in this rolling country, I can see for a couple of hills back. It means nothing, perhaps. But that was a boat leaving the yali."

Tracy turned and saw the distant headlights. Miles stepped up the car's speed and the other lights fell away.

"Was it Sylvana who gave her the heroin, do you think?" Tracy asked. "Because she wanted you herself? Because it was an easy way to be rid of Anabel? I saw that picture you painted—the reflection in the samovar."

"I'm not sure about Sylvana's infatuation. Sometimes I think she has used me mainly to torment Murat and let him know he lacks the money to be master in his own house. Once you'd called that reflection to my attention, I could see the portrait in no other way. I found something I wanted to paint—my hatred for the predators.

"But there was more than possible infatuation to furnish a motive. I believe that Anabel stumbled on some dangerous knowledge. It's even possible that she was actively involved. By playing on her need for the drug, she could have been made a useful tool in this beastly undercover affair that was going on. In any case, she must have known where the heroin was coming from. The source, that is, behind those needle marks on her arms. Once she brought me some beads. A black amber tespih. Nothing unusual. But she sounded strange when she asked me to consider it. I didn't pay much attention at the time, and she changed her mind and took them away. When I asked her about the tespih later, she wouldn't explain."

"The beads were a warning," Tracy said.

"Perhaps. But I think they were more than that. I think they must have been used as a signal. Though I'm not sure exactly how."

By now they had reached the sleeping suburbs of Istanbul, though Miles hardly lessened his speed. The tiered white balconies of new apartment buildings came into view, and the road dipped at length toward the water. They passed the great white cake ornament that was Dolmabache Palace and followed a narrowing road.

Tracy, lost in her own thoughts, hardly noticed the increasing traffic that was slowing them down at last. There was still so much that she wanted to know.

"Why have you kept Anabel's picture on your wall ever since her death?" she asked.

His voice was cool again. There seemed no emotion left in him but fury, and he kept that hidden from view a good part of the time.

"Because I wanted to stay angry," he told her. "I didn't want to lower my guard, or to forget what had been done to her. But when I started that portrait of Sylvana, I had a far stronger reminder and I could let Anabel rest."

It was hard to imagine Anabel resting, or at peace. In life she had always been moving, seeking. Even her joyous moments were never quiet.

"Tell me what really happened that night when Anabel came to Sylvana's party," she begged him. "You've told me you were giving her drugs, but you haven't told me why."

He hesitated so long that she began to think he would not reply. Then he lifted a hand from the wheel as if in relinquishment.

"It's not something I like to talk about to Anabel's sister, but perhaps you had better know. I don't suppose you've ever seen a heroin addict in the throes of what they call the withdrawal syndrome? It's pretty ghastly. Sweats and chills. Running nose, running eyes. Pains in the back and the abdomen. Twitching and shaking and repeated vomiting. In England addicts are treated a bit differently than they are in America, you know. They are permitted doses of drugs to keep them going as they taper off. Sometimes they're able to lead almost normal lives. I'd got myself a hypodermic syringe and a medicinal supply in case I had to deal with an emergency. With a serious addict the drug must go directly into the bloodstream. I tried to relieve her suffering until I could put her in professional hands. I went to Ankara that last day to consult a man I knew there about her."

So he hadn't simply abandoned her, after all. "But if someone in the house was giving her heroin—"

"The supply was suddenly stopped. To make her suffer, I suppose. Perhaps to keep her under control. She came to me in desperation. But she wouldn't tell me her source. My endurance was nearly at an end. I said I would help her this time,

342

and then there would have to be an end to it. I'd see her through once more—but after that I wouldn't try again. Or at least I told her that. I thought I might shock her into taking hold of herself. So I gave her one more shot. I hadn't marked the veins in her arms as she tried to make everyone believe that night. That had taken years to accomplish, and I'd given her only occasional shots. She took care to wear long sleeves most of the time. When the drug began to wear off, she remembered what I said and she chose that way to punish me, to put me in the wrong with all those who were present. Indeed, if it hadn't been for Sylvana's discreet intervention, I might have found myself criminally liable, while the real culprit went free."

"How could Anabel do such a thing if she loved you?" Tracy felt sickened, revolted.

"Love is not an emotion the narcotics addict is capable of. Except love for the drug he's taking. Nothing else matters. Eventually he becomes incapable of loving or responding to love. Everything of that sort had been dead between us for years. I owed her the best I could give her because she was desperately in need, and she was my responsibility. But I couldn't love her as a man loves a woman. When a heroin addict is sober, he's full of terrible guilt and rage and self-pity. After a shot he becomes lethargic and sleepy. All he wants is to indulge his dreaming.

343

In either state she had no feeling left for me, unless it was occasional anger."

A bitterness she had never felt before surged up in Tracy. An unfamiliar bitterness against her sister. "My father was right about her! When I remember how I envied Anabel and how I believed in her and tried to help her in all the small ways I could—"

"You did help," Miles said.

"I shouldn't have! It would have been better for me if I'd let her go. Better for you if you'd never tried to save her!"

He was silent for a little while. When he spoke again his tone had changed, as though all anger, all the old bitterness had drained from him. "Have you forgotten what you said to me a few days ago when we went across the Bosporus for tea? You were the one who said somebody had to try. You said most people were too ready to give up with the ones like your sister."

"But I didn't know the truth then," Tracy said miserably. "If I'd known, I couldn't have—"

He touched her hand lightly, quieting her. "If you'd known, you'd have tried even harder. You aren't the giving-up sort. Anabel was worth trying to help, you know. In spite of everything."

Tears were wet upon her cheeks. What he said was true. Even though the goodness and worth had been somehow lost and all effort hopeless in the end, it had been necessary to keep on trying, to keep on loving. Miles had given her sister back to her.

"I think she tried to free herself at the end," she told him. "She telephoned me in desperation the very day she died. She tried to tell me about some dangerous secret." She did not add that Anabel had spoken out against her husband as well. Now Tracy understood why that had been. "I think she wanted to break away and save herself. That's why she wanted me to come. Because I'd always given her support, even though I didn't know how much was going wrong. I want to believe that she tried at the end. What do you think happened that day when she went out in the boat?"

"I don't know," Miles said. "That's one of the reasons why I've stayed in Istanbul."

"Just as it's the reason that brought me here," Tracy said. "I don't want to go home yet. I can't go home without knowing."

"What good will it do you to know? This part is my job, not yours."

There was no use in arguing with him. Time enough for that when they reached the airport. She couldn't change his mind while they were in the car. Her eyes were dry now, her determination strong.

The traffic on the streets had increased as the sky brightened with early light. They were hardly moving now. Behind them cars were crowding in, slowing everything to a crawl.

Suddenly aware of what was happening, Miles looked about in dismay. "Good Lord! I'd forgotten the bridges. They were opened at 4:00 A.M. to let boats get in and out of the Golden Horn. Now they won't close to permit traffic across until six o'clock. We've got to get out of this."

He searched for a turnoff into a side street, but it was already too late. Gradually all movement had come to a halt. The traffic leading to Galata Bridge penned them in. Unless they got out of the car and walked away, they would be here until the bridge swung shut again. Down near the water men with small boats were offering to ferry pedestrians across, but that would do them no good.

Miles glanced at his watch. "Another half hour at least. What a stupid thing to do. I've been concerned with other matters." Tracy turned anxiously to see what lay behind in the brightening light of dawn.

"At least, if there's someone following us, he'll be caught too," she said.

Miles nodded grimly. "We'll make up time on the road to the airport."

Over the Bosporus behind them the sun was rising out of Asia, and a soft rosy light touched the city that lay ahead across the Golden Horn. Rounded domes and the spires of minarets were turning to glinting rose and gold. The towers of

346

the Seraglio glowed in the rising sun. All about, napping car drivers stirred, restless now and eager for traffic to move again. But still the bridge had not closed the gap.

"At least this gives me a chance to show you something," Miles said.

He opened a compartment in the dashboard and took out a brown paper parcel.

"Look inside," he said and handed it to her.

She unwrapped the paper and saw that it held one of the large shepherd bags, wool-embroidered and fringed, that Sylvana liked to ship abroad. She looked at it, puzzled.

"I got curious the other night as to what Ahmet was up to," Miles continued, "and I began to put two and two together. Before Anabel's death there was an accusation made that she had been stealing articles from Sylvana's shipments, though she denied everything when anyone asked her. After her death nothing was found among her possessions to indicate that the claim was true. Perhaps because someone else got there first and cleared everything out. I can guess now what she was about. She must have been collecting evidence. Like this bag."

Again Tracy looked at the bag in her lap, but it told her nothing.

"When things quieted the other night I went back and stirred around in the stuff Sylvana was planning to wrap for mailing the following day. I was curious enough to look pretty carefully, but perhaps, because of my earlier interruption, the job wasn't finished. This was all I found. Look inside."

Tracy opened the bag and saw that instead of the rough self-material that usually made up the interior of such bags, this one had been given a plain cotton lining. When she reached into the bag she found that a bit of the lining had been ripped up to reveal a sheet of plastic underneath. She looked at Miles.

"That inner plastic bag is filled with white powder spread out carefully over the whole," he said. "It's a hundred per cent pure heroin. I checked with a laboratory friend, who tested it for me. These shipments are not likely to be too carefully examined by Turkish customs, since they go out under Sylvana Erim's philanthropic protection. Nor have the U.S. customs caught on as yet. The concealment has been clever, and the shipments always seem above reproach. Probably most of the things shipped are innocent. Whoever manages this at the yali must take the stuff to his room, where he can work on it at night before a shipment is made."

"So that's what Ahmet meant to do?" Tracy folded the package, feeling a certain repugnance about handling it. "For Sylvana, or for Murat?"

"I can guess, but I'm not positive. You already know what I think."

Tracy remembered the portrait and nodded. "Then there must be an accomplice in New York?"

"Undoubtedly several. This is no small operation. It could be that the buyers who accept these things to sell in their stores aren't necessarily involved in what is happening. Seemingly casual purchasers in the stores could have the stuff spotted and pick it up."

"But—how would they know what to choose if most of the shipment is untouched?"

"I think we'll have evidence of that shortly," Miles said. "I've made a phone call to New York. There will be someone on watch for whoever buys that strip of calligraphy Sylvana sent by airmail to a Third Avenue dealer. I noticed the address on the mailing tube. Remember those marks you spotted on the script? I think there's a code involved. Whoever receives that strip will know exactly which goods to buy to get the smuggled heroin."

"And Anabel knew," Tracy said.

"Maybe she even helped for a time," said Miles. "She couldn't bring herself to blow up the whole thing and cut off her own supply of heroin."

"She must have known that opium was brought by water and hidden in the ruined palace, since she spoke of the Sultan Valide when she telephoned me."

"Exactly. The way she haunted the place, she could easily have happened on the truth."

"Even Yasemin knew about that hole in the floor," Tracy said. "She led me to it. But there's still a long step from the raw opium we saw in that box to pure heroin."

"Not so long as you might imagine. There's no need for fancy stills and elaborate equipment, you know. The process can be managed with ordinary kitchen utensils and a few chemicals bought from a drugstore. Ethyl alcohol, ammonium chloride, sulphuric acid, and a few other cozy little items. From the crude opium you get morphine, and from morphine comes diamorphine. Heroin is the trade name for diamorphine, the final step. The whole operation takes only a little knowledge and some hours of time. It could be done anywhere."

"Perhaps in one of the laboratories in the kiosk?" Tracy said softly.

"Of course. I've often wondered how much of Sylvana's perfume operations were a blind. And if Anabel's interest in perfume-making grew out of something she happened on down there. Now I have the proof, and all I need is to know which of them stands behind the operation. I have to be sure, no matter what I suspect."

Tracy was thinking of something else. "If Anabel was involved in all this, how could anyone withhold heroin from her as seems to have happened at the end? Wouldn't she have made sure of a supply from the articles she took—like this bag?"

"She was no beginner to get relief through sniffing heroin. And she had no needle. I kept watch for that. Besides, this is the pure stuff and as much as a tenth of a gram will kill. It would need to be cut back."

On ahead the windows and towers of old Istanbul were beginning to catch the full rays of the rising sun. The rounded mound of buildings shimmered in golden haze, like a splendid Arabian Nights vision floating above the Golden Horn. But Tracy could see only the evil at its heart. An evil that had threatened Anabel's very life. And now would threaten Miles if he returned to the yali. "It's all so dreadful, so horrible," she murmured. "I never imagined!"

"Now you're imagining too much," he said. "It's time to think of something else." He reached into his pocket and drew out a small packet and handed it to her. "I picked these up for you in a shop off Taksim Square. See what you think of them."

He was trying to distract her and she did not want him to succeed. Without interest she removed the cover of the small box. On a bed of cotton lay a pair of earrings delicately carved in ivory. They were neat button clips, etched in minute fretwork. Modest earrings that would not dangle. Quite suitable for a girl who could never be like the Anabel of Miles's portrait.

He was watching her. "I can see that you don't like them. What's wrong?"

The last twenty-four hours had been too much. She was beyond being rational and sensible. These earrings were a verdict that she would not accept.

"Murat said I ought to dress in a more fashionable and frilly way," she told him. "He thought dangling earrings suited me and made me more feminine."

Miles's snort disposed of Murat Erim. "You're quite feminine enough as you are. Besides, he's not the one to listen to. The man was half in love with Anabel himself. He probably thinks you ought to pattern yourself in your sister's image. Even though he turned against her at the end."

So Miles had known about Murat. Of course there would have been no need for jealousy under the circumstances that had existed.

"Forget about Murat," Miles went on. "And forget Anabel for the moment. While you're often a thoroughly exasperating young woman, you are at least, as I've told you before, all of one piece. You fit yourself. You wear yourself well. Simplicity is your style. And so is your long shining hair that you wear so neatly. Earrings that dangle are not for you."

"You've never approved of me!" Tracy cried,

still lost to reason. "All you want is to send me home and—"

"Stop being an idiot!" he said roughly. "That doesn't suit you either. What I shall do without you once you've gone back to New York, I can't think. The prospect looks fairly dull and bleak."

"But you said—"

Cold fury was upon him again. It was in his eyes, in the set of his mouth, and she shrank from the sight of it.

"I said I wanted you out of this. I've been trying to keep you out of it all along. There's a demon to be unmasked and I don't want you around when it happens. I've been using delaying tactics on my book for months while I tried to get to the bottom of what's going on. And then you come out and disrupt everything. Cause for Anabel's actions can be traced clear back to her childhood. But the immediate and terrible blame isn't yours, my prickly darling, or mine either. It belongs to the creature who drove Anabel to her death. Even if I'd stayed at the yali the day she died, a way would have been found. If only she had come to me—but she didn't."

Tracy stared at the city across the Golden Horn. She found to her surprise that her spirits had lifted enormously, in spite of everything. The spires and domes looked unbelievably beautiful in the morning light and she wasn't angry any more. Miles had called her his darling. He was

353

concerned about her. He didn't want her to be like Anabel. Surreptitiously she clipped on the button earrings.

"Traffic's beginning to move," Miles said, and started the car.

Tugboats in the water had pushed the floating section of the bridge into place. All about them cars, motorbikes, bicycles, handcarts—with pedestrians on the far edges—were coming to life, beginning to move.

Neither Miles nor Tracy saw the man who slipped through the traffic behind them until he suddenly opened the back door of their car and got in. There was nothing of friendliness in the look Murat Erim turned upon Miles as he spoke.

"When you cross the bridge," he said, "you will take the turn I indicate."

Miles glanced at him in the rear-view mirror. "I will if it's the way to the airport," he said, inching the car into the narrowing stream that approached the bridge.

Murat Erim lifted his right hand briefly and Tracy saw the automatic in his fingers. "It is better if you do as I say. Since we have come this far, there is something I wish to attend to."

Tracy sank down in the front seat. Miles gave no sign except for the tightening of his hands on the wheel. It was easy to guess what had happened. Murat had been in the boat that set out in pursuit across the Bosporus. It was the car he drove whose headlights they had seen behind them on the hills. He could not catch them on the road to Istanbul, but he had counted on the bridge to hold them for him. Somewhere back on the road he must have left the car and come forward on foot, searching through waiting traffic. By their bad luck he had reached them in time.

"How did you happen to spot us when we left the yali?" Miles asked casually.

"Unfortunately, we expected you on the land side," said Murat. "Ahmet Effendi did not realize a boat had come and gone until you were out on the water. Then he came to summon me. Our start was late. After we crossed the Bosporus I borrowed a car from a friend. Ahmet Effendi is now at the wheel. For the time being, your car will be more convenient for me and he will return the borrowed one."

"Would you mind telling me what you're up to?" Miles asked.

"Did you think I would let you leave the country if it was possible for me to stop you?"

"I meant to return, never fear," Miles said. "It's Miss Hubbard who will get aboard a plane."

"She will not," said Murat flatly. "If she had gone home to New York in the beginning, she might have remained uninvolved. But now you have committed her by your own actions. As you committed Anabel. We will end this thing today. And we will end it in my way."

Tracy remembered Nursel's words, ". . . soon, *soon* the matter will be ended." Nursel must have known very well what was in the air.

Miles said nothing more, but gave his attention to driving. Solidly packed cars were moving slowly over ancient Galata Bridge. On the sidewalks masses of people streamed across the Golden Horn, coming from and going toward old Istanbul. In the water on either side of the bridge, a curious pattern was evident. A good many ships and boats anchored in the Horn had drawn aside to let other craft flow through the opening. Now, on their right, a mass of seacraft of every size flowed out toward the Bosporus, while on the left all that were willing to be shut in for another twenty-four hours had entered the upper reaches of the Golden Horn.

At the far end of the bridge a traffic policeman directed the cars, and Tracy saw Miles glance at him speculatively. But the man was interested only in keeping the way open, the cars moving. In the back seat Murat was alert, his hand hidden, but ready.

On the far side he indicated the course and the car followed a cobblestoned street up the hill. Tracy lost count of the turns they took, the labyrinth of narrow streets they followed, until Murat at length gestured Miles to the curb.

"This is good," he said. "You will get out, please, both of you, and go upstairs ahead of me."

Miles hesitated for a moment before he left the car, and Tracy knew he considered opposition. But there was little chance of summoning help in this remote Turkish street. When Murat jerked open the car door and gestured, Miles got out, turning back to extend a hand to Tracy. She felt the warm, reassuring pressure of his fingers, and tried to take heart.

# 18

THE HOUSE WAS very old—one of the now forbidden wooden houses of an older Istanbul. Weathered to a smoky brown, it rose flush with a sidewalk too narrow for more than one person to pass at a time. There were three tall, narrow stories above a basement, and from the second floor two old-fashioned Turkish balconies overhung the sidewalk, rather like suspended sentry boxes.

When Miles hesitated at the doorway, Murat prodded him and motioned Tracy to go ahead. The entryway was darksome, unlit, and there was a smell of long-stale cooking. The wooden stairs turned crazily upward, and sagging treads moved and creaked beneath their feet as they climbed to the third floor. Here Murat called out and a door opened upon the darkness, blinding them with morning light.

Ahmet's son, Hasan, stood silhouetted in the

doorway. He was already up at this early hour and indeed looked as if he had slept little during the night. He greeted Murat respectfully and, if he felt surprise at this early visit, he did not show it, but stepped back to allow his visitors to enter the single room he occupied. After the dark stairway, Tracy stood blinking and uncertain in the small bright room.

A rumpled bed occupied the greater part of the space. There was a table with books upon it near a window where sun poured through. A porcelain stove stood against one wall, cold and unlighted.

Murat spoke to the young man, regarding him with a disapproving eye. He spoke in English, as though he wished to make sure the foreigners understood.

"You have served me badly, Hasan Effendi. You were set to watch at a time when watching was important, and you failed by falling asleep. It has been necessary to repair your mistake."

Hasan ceased to smile "I do not fall asleep, *efendim*," he denied. "I stay in the house of the Sultan Valide and I remain awake and watchful."

There was nothing like setting one thief against another, Tracy thought, and interrupted abruptly.

"I saw you there asleep on the veranda of the mined house, Hasan Effendi," she said. "You were very sound asleep. You did not hear me at all."

"Thank you, Miss Hubbard." Murat bent a

mocking look upon her and went on sternly to Hasan. "It is better if you do not lie to me. We will now return to the yali and you will accompany us there. Your father wishes this. It is possible that we may give you an opportunity to make up for your negligence."

Hasan bowed his head submissively, offering no objection, and when Murat turned to Miles, Ahmet's son flung Tracy an oddly enigmatic look. Where she might have expected resentment, he seemed almost pleased.

"It is necessary for you to understand, Mr. Radburn," Murat continued, "that the end has come for you. This matter will now move as I wish. Any resistance on your part may result in an unfortunate accident. You understand what I say to you?"

"I think I'm beginning to," Miles said.

Murat gestured to Hasan to go downstairs first, and then to Miles and Tracy to follow. When they reached the car, Miles was put in the driver's seat, with Murat beside him, while Tracy got into the back with Hasan.

Though the blockage around the bridge had been broken, morning traffic was still heavy and moved at a crawl in this congested area.

Under cover of noisy city sounds, Hasan spoke softly to Tracy. "Thank you, *efendim*, for informing the Doktor of my negligence in falling asleep."

Tracy stared at him, trying to read the brown eyes and the face she had seen wear dark scowls directed at Nursel. Former anger seemed to have given way to a surprising mood of cheer.

"But you told Murat you were not sleeping," she said. "So why are you pleased when I told him you were?"

"I knew he would not believe me," Hasan said. "You confirmed what I wished him to know."

This oblique approach was too much for Tracy, and she attempted no comment. When they were across the bridge and moving toward the car ferry, Hasan spoke to her again.

"I wish to thank you for befriending Nursel. It is well. I, personally, will see that no harm befalls you in whatever may come."

Such an offer of friendship from this young man, who had not in the beginning approved of her, was astonishing, but Tracy did not stop to question it now.

"It's not myself I'm afraid for," she said quickly. "What does Murat intend to do about Miles?"

Hasan's face darkened. "It will be as this man deserves."

"But why—why?" Tracy pressed. "Why does Murat—"

"You speak my name?" asked Murat from the front seat.

"Why shouldn't I?" Tracy asked. "I want to

360

know what is happening. Why are we being taken back to the yali as if we were prisoners?"

"This you will know soon," Murat said. "Let there be no talking now. If you must choose your friends unwisely, then there are consequences you must suffer. As it was necessary for your sister to suffer the consequences of her acts."

From then on there was silence. During the brief crossing of the Bosporus no one left the car. There were people all around going to work, but there seemed no one to whom an appeal by foreigners in trouble could be made. Miles remained alert and watchful, but he took no step toward freedom. On the Anatolian side early morning traffic had quickened and he drove with concentrated assurance. Whatever faced them at the yali, Miles's courage had not been shaken and Tracy tried to take comfort from the knowledge.

When they reached the house Nursel was waiting for them. She smiled briefly at Hasan, but scarcely glanced at Miles or Tracy.

"Ahmet Effendi has returned," she said. "All is ready."

"Where is Sylvana?" Murat asked.

Nursel moved her eyes in the direction of the kiosk across the drive. "She has breakfast in her rooms. We will find her there."

"Good," said Murat. "We will go there now. The moment is here. It is time for the truth to be known."

On their way upstairs in the kiosk Ahmet slipped out of the shadows of the upper salon, where he had apparently been watching, and joined them.

In Sylvana's room, Nursel drew uneasily apart, as though she wished to leave all that might happen here to others. Not once had she met Tracy's eyes. Ahmet had a quick, almost scornful look for his son, and Tracy saw the young man lower his eyes.

Mrs. Erim seemed surprised and not a little annoyed with this invasion of visitors before she had finished her coffee and rolls. When she saw Miles, her eyes sparked with anger and she would have spoken to him indignantly if Murat had not stopped her.

"Let us waste no time. I have brought your accomplice back when he would have escaped from the country and left you to suffer all consequences alone."

Sylvana made an effort to recover an illusion of serenity. "What nonsense are you speaking? What do you mean—accomplice? Accomplice for what?"

"It is not necessary to dissemble," Murat told her. "We know all that you have done. Where is the samovar?"

For the first time Tracy glanced about the room, missing the now familiar gleam of burnished copper.

362

"Why do you wish the samovar?" Sylvana asked. "This morning I shall dispose of it. I shall have it thrown into the Bosporus from the boat landing. It is an evil thing which has brought great trouble upon me. All—all the misfortune that has come upon this house is the fault of that evil object." She looked at Miles. "That one could see me as you have painted me is the blame of the samovar!"

Murat ignored this outburst. "What have you done with it? Tell me at once where it is!"

"I do not like this tone in which you speak," Sylvana said. "But it is there—in the corner, hidden from view so that I will not see the wicked pictures it makes."

Ahmet went to the indicated corner, where scarves and cushions from the divans had been flung to hide the samovar. He pushed them aside and pulled the samovar into view.

"Open it," Murat ordered. "Remove the lids, Ahmet Effendi."

The old man worked quickly, taking off the copper chimney, removing the other parts until the charcoal tube and hot water chamber stood open. Murat himself went to the samovar and reached through the narrow neck into bulging depths. A moment later he drew out a plump plastic bag, packed like a sack of salt. But the white powder it held was not salt. Balancing it on his palm, Murat extended it toward Sylvana.

"This contains perhaps a kilo. A little over two pounds of pure heroin. You see—we know all. We have the final evidence. We know the crime you have been committing under cover of the Turkish goods you send abroad. We know how you have operated with this Englishman's help. You managed to use his wife Anabel also, until she became difficult to control because of her own addiction. Now you have brought in the young sister as well. This is a terrible thing."

Sylvana gaped at him in horror. She seemed to have lost the power to speak, even the power to stand, and she might have fallen if there had not been a divan for her to sink upon.

"We know all that is to be known," Murat continued ruthlessly. "We know that you have ceased to trust your accomplice and that he has tried to escape today, lest you betray him entirely."

Miles broke in. "This is a pack of lies!" he cried, and took a step toward Murat. At once Hasan stood warningly at his elbow.

Tracy glanced at Nursel and saw that the girl had shrunk back in her chair as though she wanted to take no part in what was happening.

Murat ignored Miles's outburst. "You can see that we have enough evidence to put you in prison for many years," he told Sylvana.

"Perhaps I shall go for the police now, Doktor?" Hasan inquired, his tone false. In spite of Murat's threats about prison, Tracy suspected that the police would not be informed. This was a further ruse to control Sylvana.

Dr. Erim shook his head. "Not yet. Perhaps I will offer this woman an alternative. I do not wish to have the reputation of my house disgraced, or my work discredited with the government. I wish only to have Sylvana abdicate her claim to my brother's property and wealth. If she will sign over all that belongs rightfully to me and my sister, I am willing to let her go free."

Miles's outrage was evident. "You mean that even if she were guilty of narcotics smuggling, you'd release her, allow her to leave the country without punishment so she could commence her operations elsewhere?"

"A strange question," Murat said, "coming from you. I do not care what she does, so long as it is stopped in this house. The punishment will, I think, be enough. I have been waiting for this moment for a long time. The signal of the black amber has appeared recently. On the dark of the moon a boat comes down the Bosporus to the ruins. You think I do not know this, Sylvana? Many times when the moon is right I have watched, but nothing happens. This time I go to the palace ruins and find Ahmet Effendi there also. My good and faithful Ahmet. He too has been watching. He tells me that strange men have brought the box ashore to hide it in the broken floor of the house. When they leave, he opens it and finds crude opium from which Sylvana makes the heroin she sends abroad."

Sylvana cried out, and he silenced her with a gesture.

"On this night when I come upon Ahmet Effendi, there is the open box at his feet. I send him back to the house while I examine everything for myself. At the yali Ahmet Effendi has attempted to pick up some of the articles Sylvana meant to send from the country. He wishes to see if heroin has been hidden in them. He has taken the strip of calligraphy as well, to study it for the code we know is being so cleverly used. Of course Mr. Radburn is angry when he finds what Ahmet Effendi is trying to do. Perhaps it is you, Miss Hubbard, who are helping these two—you who are being used, as your sister was used?"

"That's ridiculous!" Tracy cried.

Murat went smoothly on. "You can see that I know everything. Ahmet, Hasan, Nursel—all have worked together with me to expose this woman and her accomplices. Now there will be an end to such things in this house."

Sylvana started to rise from the divan, and Hasan stepped forward to thrust her back with a none-too-gentle hand, apparently eager to reinstate himself in Murat's favor. At once

366

Ahmet spoke to his son in Turkish, clearly reproving him. Then, paying no attention to Murat, the old man went to Sylvana and addressed her gently in his own language, as if he were reassuring her, as if he still remembered that she was the cherished wife of a master to whom he had been devoted.

Murat watched in displeasure, but he did not reproach the old man.

"There's a point you seem to have missed, Dr. Erim," Miles said, speaking more quietly than before. "You and I appear to be working on the same side without recognizing the fact. Why else do you suppose I've remained here since my wife's death, except to learn the truth?"

Murat threw him a look in which there was a certain triumph. He was paying Miles off, Tracy thought. Paying him off with malice because of Anabel, with whom Murat had for a time been in love. She realized with growing dismay that Murat might not even care whether the words he spoke about Miles's complicity were true or not, providing he could injure the other man.

"Be quiet!" he told Miles. "I do not care for more of your lying words. When I am done with Sylvana, your turn will come, my friend. For the moment you will go to one of the empty rooms on this floor and remain there. Hasan Effendi— you will guard him well?"

To Tracy's dismay, Murat took the revolver

from the pocket of his jacket and handed it to Hasan. That young man looked enormously pleased as he gestured Miles from the room.

Murat did not wait to see them go, but turned at once to his sister. "You have the documents ready for Sylvana?"

Nursel brought forward a folder of papers she had held in her lap. Sylvana's eyes had a blank, glazed look as if she did not wholly comprehend what was happening. Her fingers would not grasp the pen Murat tried to thrust into her hand. Ahmet and Nursel stood watching. For the moment, no one was thinking about Tracy Hubbard.

She had remained near the door, and she slipped through it unnoticed in the wake of Miles and Hasan. Across the salon Miles had been ushered into a room and Hasan stood in the doorway, the revolver held confidently in one hand, his back to Tracy.

She ran downstairs, pushing past a startled Halide and out into the garden. She had no plan, no purpose—she wanted only to get away before someone remembered her and she too was imprisoned in that house.

The familiar path beckoned and she ran through newly leafing woods toward the side gate. Out on the road, she turned from the direction of the palace ruins and hurried toward the village. Perhaps there would be someone there to whom she could turn for help. Perhaps she could find a telephone and call Istanbul. Or go to the police.

But as she walked, turning these plans over in her mind, their futility grew increasingly clear. The barrier of language was too great for her to hurdle. The red tape of going to any authority would be immense, or of putting a call through from a place where no one spoke English. The time which any sort of action would take defeated her.

She did not know how much Murat might be concealing in his accusation of Sylvana. She did not know how far he might go in order to silence Miles. Certainly there had been a threat in his words. The stake was high for all of these people. Once rid of Sylvana and her hold upon the Erim wealth, they all stood to gain. Even Hasan, whose help with his education had been cut off when the older brother died and there was little money left for Murat and Nursel. Under other circumstances Nursel might have been an ally to whom Tracy could turn for help. As things stood, she would certainly do as her brother and Ahmet and Hasan ordered her to do. Aside from her Turkish heritage of obedience to the male, she too stood to gain. Once Tracy had hoped to sting her into action, but that hope had dimmed completely.

Only Tracy Hubbard was still free to stop what

was happening. Yet she could think of no possible way in which she might take action swiftly.

More and more she distrusted the scene she had witnessed in Sylvana's room. As she followed the road, her mind turned it over again and again, allowing it to spin through her thoughts like a reel of film that could be replayed while she watched and listened to it all over again. The conviction was growing in her that something was vitally wrong with both picture and sound. Sharply, acutely wrong. Not just because of Murat's false accusation that Miles was as guilty as he claimed Sylvana to be. Something was missing. Something that Tracy could not find in Sylvana's shocked and helpless state, in Nursel's downcast eyes and uneasy manner, or even in Murat's triumphant anger. The thing that had not appeared was the face of evil. The face that Miles had painted in the samovar reflection.

She had reached the streets of the little village that ran uphill from the water. This was apparently the day for an open market, and she saw that stalls had been set up, displaying fruits and vegetables, articles of clothing, all sorts of oddments. Her attention was solicited by eager sellers as she went by, and on any other day she would have stopped to look. Today she passed the stalls without pause. Once she nearly stepped on one of the numerous cats that abound in every

Turkish city and village. The animal spat at her and leaped away.

When she had escaped the bustle of the market, she found a stone wall where she could sit undisturbed in the sun. She knew that she could not linger idly. Somehow she must act. After what she had just witnessed, she could not believe in Sylvana's guilt. And from the gentle way Ahmet had treated her, she did not think he believed in it either. Miles had painted the evil he saw in the crime, but he had not painted Sylvana.

Whose, then, was the face she must identify? Whose was the wickedness that had returned Anabel to the taking of drugs, played tricks to frighten and threaten and eventually destroy by driving her to her death? Tracy had not seen that face as yet. The mask was still in place, the identity hidden. Yet there must be some way in which to snatch the mask away and expose the truth. But how—how?

A small, plaintive mewing sounded nearby. Tracy turned, startled, as a white cat sprang onto the wall to sit inquiringly behind her. A cat not unlike poor Yasemin, though perhaps a little larger and not as well groomed. It was the same breed, however, and its eyes were as green as the eyes of Anabel's cat.

Tracy put out a coaxing hand and the cat did not leap away. It seemed more friendly than Yasemin and was willing to come close and rub

371

its head against her hand. She stroked it gently and talked to it for a moment or two. Once it looked up at her as though the sounds she made were puzzling and unfamiliar. Still, it was a friendly cat and after a moment it stepped into her lap and settled down to a pleasant purring.

The beginning of a plan stirred in Tracy's mind. What if there was a way, after all, to get behind the mask? Here was a chance—wild and fantastic, perhaps, but still a chance. And nothing else had offered itself. She bent above the purring white creature in her lap.

The cat offered no resistance, but hung limply willing when she picked it up. It cradled itself against her shoulder with none of Yasemin's suspicion and allowed itself to be carried as Tracy started back toward the yali.

She had no knowledge of custom when it came to Turkish cats. They swarmed everywhere and were always being chased from restaurants. But if she seemed to be kidnaping somebody's pet, there might be an outcry that she would have no way of answering. However, she met no one as she followed back ways to avoid the busy area of the market. The cat, undoubtedly, would find its own way home from the yali, once she set it free.

When she reached the road, she hurried so fast that once or twice the cat set its claws uncertainly into her shoulder. Tracy soothed it and went on without slackening her pace. When she neared the gate, she put the cat under her coat, where it made no objection to the warm shelter that hid it from view.

She avoided Sylvana's kiosk and went directly to the yali, passing no one on the way. She climbed the stairs to the second-floor salon where, clearly, she had the upper house to herself. Everyone must still be across the way in the hillside house. The test she considered must be made as unobtrusively as possible and with only one person at a time. Perhaps that very fact made the whole idea impossible. How, for instance, was she to see Sylvana alone?

For the moment she could only wait and do nothing. Sooner or later she would be missed, and the likely place to look for her was here. She held the white cat in her lap, shielded by a fold of her coat, whispering to it soothingly, petting it into a continuous purr of contentment.

The big, empty salon stretched in echoing shadows about her, replete with the usual creakings that haunted the old wooden house. The big green porcelain stove stood cheerless and unlighted, and the room seemed damper and colder than the outdoors.

When steps sounded on the marble corridor below and someone started up the stairs, Tracy sat up expectantly, breathing more quickly, her hand tightening without intention upon the warm fluff of the cat. But it was only Nursel coming up the stairs. Of course she was the messenger they would send, once they remembered Tracy Hubbard. She drew the coat more closely about the cat and waited.

As Nursel came around the bend of the stairs, she saw Tracy sitting there, and paused. Her eyes moved evasively from Tracy's own, and it was easy to guess that the girl was torn by feelings that warred within her and left her not without a sense of guilt. If only it was possible to play upon this guilt.

"My brother wishes to see you," Nursel said in a low voice.

"Then let him come here," Tracy said. "I'm tired of being ordered around. I'm not guilty of any wrongdoing and I'm not a prisoner in this house. Or am I?"

Nursel sighed. "It is better if you do as Murat wishes. He will not like it if I return without you."

"That's your problem," said Tracy boldly. "Are you planning to take me to him by force, perhaps?" She braced herself mockingly in her chair. She did not believe Nursel would attempt any such thing. With all the stubbornness in her Tracy meant to stay where she was and force them to come to her—one at a time, if that was possible. Nursel moved somewhat uncertainly toward her, and at that moment the cat mewed in protest against a hand that had forgotten to be gentle. The Turkish girl stopped in her tracks.

"What was that?" she asked in surprise.

The moment for the first test had come. "Why, it's Yasemin, of course," said Tracy and drew back her coat.

The white cat sat up and stared at Nursel out of sea-green eyes. Then it struggled free of Tracy's restraint and sprang through the air. Nursel froze where she stood, and Tracy saw her face, saw the reaction of shock, the rousing of superstitious terror. Nursel started backward out of the cat's path, crying out in fear. Without warning, the mask was down and the face behind it revealed. The thing that Miles had painted in the samovar reflection was exhibited in all its frightening reality for anyone to read.

Tracy touched her tongue to dry lips. "Did you think you could send Anabel twice to her death? Did you think she would not return to accuse you? You'll never be free in all your life of what you've done!"

Nursel recovered herself and clapped her hands furiously at the cat. There was a wild brightness in her eyes. "This is not Yasemin!" she cried.

"Of course it isn't," said Tracy softly. "How could it be? You drowned Anabel's cat in that dreadful way and left her for me to find. You thought you could frighten me into running away, didn't you? It was you all along who played tricks on Anabel, and then on me. On Anabel because she had discovered what you were doing. She knew it wasn't Sylvana. Or your brother Murat, whom you've duped so wickedly. It was you who gave Anabel drugs to keep her quiet. You could control her for a while that way, couldn't you? And you managed to poison her mind against Miles. But what did you do in the end to send her to her death? You might as well tell me, Nursel, since I know everything else."

The wildness had not died from Nursel's eyes, but she veiled them now with lowered lids and made an effort to control herself. "We cannot speak together here. If you wish to know the answer to such questions, then come to my room."

She circled the cat warily and walked toward her bedroom door. For a moment Tracy hesitated. It would be better to remain here in the open, but she was not particularly afraid of the other girl now that she knew where true danger lay. There was much more she needed to know. As yet she had no proof of Nursel's guilt that anyone else would accept. She bent to pick up the cat and followed Nursel into her bedroom.

She had never been in this room before, and she found it crowded with huge black walnut furniture and heavy draperies that shut out the sun. She blinked for a moment in this murky twilight, trying to orient herself. Nursel went to a cabinet across the room and took from it some object wrapped in a handkerchief. When she turned she made no effort to veil what Tracy had seen in her eyes.

"You are as foolish as your sister!" Nursel said. "How I have despised you! Telling me always that I am meek and too easily managed—that I can be used by anyone. When it is *I* who have used these others. They are not so clever as they think. Murat believes what I wish him to believe. Sylvana walks stupidly into every trap I have set. Hasan kneels at my feet and will do all that I ask for love of me—though I let him have the illusion that he rules. Of course it was I who devised the calligraphy code and made the changes. And now I must deal with you—another silly Anabel!"

She whisked away the handkerchief and Tracy saw the thing in her hands. It was an object that had not only the look of evil, but the look of death. Yet, strangely, she was not afraid. With sudden clarity she knew her own identity. She was Tracy Hubbard and she would not flee across the Bosporus in a boat she could not handle, as Anabel had done in her terror. *This* was why Anabel had gone, of course—the death Nursel held in her hands. Miles's words flashed through Tracy's mind: "A tenth of a gram will kill." Anabel must have known it would come to this. And she had lacked the strength and courage to stand and fight.

Tracy found that she was keyed to a pitch of excitement so heady that it filled her with a queer confidence. Knowing that death was inches away, she did not move. She had only herself to depend on. Herself—all of one piece, as Miles had told her she must be.

The door behind her stood open, but if she tried to escape, the other girl would be upon her at once. If she so much as opened her mouth to scream for help, the plunge of the needle would come. She had only words to fight with. Perhaps with words there was still a chance.

"Anabel told me about the black amber, you know," she said almost conversationally. "That was the signal, wasn't it? Of opium coming down the Bosporus?"

Nursel watched her warily, not altogether certain, in spite of the weapon in her hands.

"I suppose it was Hasan who set the black amber among the other tespihler so you would know the load was expected," Tracy went on. "And it must have been you who retrieved the box from the ruins."

For an instant amusement flashed in Nursel's eyes. "My foolish brother sets Hasan to guard the opium, to watch who comes to take it away. How we have laughed over that! Hasan had only to spend the hours sleeping, so that it would seem to Murat that Sylvana had taken the box while Hasan slept. When of course it was both Hasan and I who took it away when we were ready. Sylvana has made an excellent dupe for fooling Murat. It was a simple thing to make him believe that it was she who hid the heroin in the samovar."

"You've used them all cleverly," Tracy said. "But not cleverly enough, Nursel."

The other girl took a step forward, and Tracy cried out in warning.

"Don't come near me or it will be the worse for you. Don't make the mistake of thinking I'm like Anabel. You haven't the nerve to use that thing on me. You've always had someone to do your work for you—someone you could hide behind. Now you have only yourself. You're the one who must do this, Nursel. Only you. And I don't think you can."

As her eyes grew accustomed to the dim light, Tracy could make out Nursel's face more clearly now. She saw the wide, dilated eyes, the lips that trembled—the uncertainty.

"You're a disgrace to all Turkish women!" Tracy taunted. "It's a good thing others aren't like you. Trafficking in drugs, tricking and cheating and ready to murder!"

The cat in her arms squirmed, but Tracy held the writhing body, heedless of claws.

"Anabel never meant to kill herself!" she cried. "She was foolish enough to run away from you, instead of standing to fight. Anyone who turned on you could beat you down. It's you, Nursel, who are foolish and weak."

Nursel screamed in a queer, hoarse way and lunged toward her. Tracy had been waiting for the moment. She flung the cat directly into Nursel's face and dashed out of the room. Behind her she heard the frenzied squalling of cat and woman.

Miles was coming up the stairs. He rushed past her toward the outcry, and Tracy turned back in time to see him set his foot upon the syringe where it lay on the floor. The white cat sprang frantically away and fled through the salon. Nursel had gone thoroughly to pieces. She sagged against a chair, screaming imprecations that gave her away with every word.

There was a sound of running on the stairs, and Tracy whirled to see Ahmet brandishing a revolver and apparently in pursuit. She cried out a warning to Miles, but he did not move as the old man reached the doorway.

"There is the woman who has betrayed your son," Miles told him. "She will tell you all you want to know."

Ahmet made no gesture toward Miles. He stood in the doorway, listening, comprehending. He looked older than before, more shriveled and wrinkled in his shabby suit.

"You'd best take her to Dr. Erim," Miles said. "He will have to face the truth now and see where the real guilt lies."

Ahmet had pocketed the gun. He went directly to Nursel, and she did not resist as he took her arm.

When they had gone away, Miles drew Tracy out of the dark, crowded room and up the stairs to the empty third floor. She found that she was trembling as reaction set in.

"You're all right?" Miles said. "She didn't touch you?"

"I'm all right," said Tracy. "The cat—if it hadn't been for the cat—!"

He held her tightly. "Don't talk about it. It's over now."

"But Hasan had the gun. How did you get away?"

"Ahmet is no fool. Apparently he's had some doubts about what Murat was cooking up. He knows Sylvana well, and he began to think as I did, that her collapse was due to fright, not guilt. Murat was obviously convinced of Sylvana's guilt, and thus could not be the one himself. That left only Nursel. When Murat sent her to look for you, Ahmet took things into his own hands. He demanded the gun of Hasan, who handed it over, not knowing what his father intended, but he told me to go after Nursel. I had a tussle with Hasan, but he'll be quiet for a while. I came over here as fast as I could."

"I needed you and you came!" said Tracy, weeping against his shoulder, not caring how ridiculous she sounded.

Miles chuckled. "Obviously you didn't need me at all. You had everything very well in hand, my determined young American."

He held her away from him so that he could look at her, held her not very gently, and shook her a little. She stopped shivering and weeping and recovered herself with a single deep, indrawn breath.

"Are you sure who you are now?" he asked.

She nodded. "I'm not Anabel. Not in any way at all. And I don't have any more secret wishes to be like her. You've taught me a better way."

"You've taught yourself," he said. "And now, shall we get that book done between us?"

"Here?" she asked, astonished.

"Certainly not. You're going to help me pack my books and manuscript and then we're going back to New York. You'll not be out of my sight again. I can't get on with my painting until after we're married."

She gulped and did not argue. The matter was clearly settled. She didn't quite believe it yet. She would have to get used to the idea, but she knew she would do so blissfully.

"What will you paint? Is there something you want to paint now?" she asked him.

"A leading question," he said. "You, of course," and he bent to kiss her. "You'll sit for me without benefit of reflections in a samovar— I don't want to be misled again. You'll wear the sun in your hair, that feather pin in your lapel, and ivory earrings for your ears. You'll put up your chin and thrust your thumbs in your belt— and I'll paint you with love and tenderness."

She smiled at him joyfully. Two things, she knew, would never appear in his picture. There would be no hint of Anabel, except for happy memories evoked by a pin. And there would be no tespih of black amber. The warnings were over and done with, the Bosporus ghosts were stilled forever as far as she and Miles were concerned.

She kissed him back without restraint, and with his arm about her they hurried toward his study where the last of their work in Turkey awaited them.

**Center Point Large Print**
600 Brooks Road / PO Box 1
Thorndike ME 04986-0001 USA

**(207) 568-3717**

**US & Canada:**
**1 800 929-9108**
www.centerpointlargeprint.com